AF374378

Published by Truborn Press
Edited by William Sterling
Cover & Interior Design by Truborn Design
Interior Format by Truborn Design

ISBN 979-8-9938468-2-8 (Back-to-Back Paperback)
ISBN 979-8-9938468-1-1 (Paperback)
ISBN 979-8-9938468-0-4 (E-book)

FIRST EDITION

PUNK GOES HORROR

II

HARDCORE FOR THE ENCORE

DEDICATION

This book is dedicated to the outsiders, the punks, the loud ones, and the ones who refuse to stay quiet.

To the people fighting for dignity, safety, and the right to exist without fear.

Punk has always stood against cruelty, against systems that dehumanize, and against the idea that some lives matter less than others.

This anthology stands with immigrant communities and with everyone pushing back against injustice.

STAY LOUD. STAY STRANGE.

HARDCORE FOR THE ENCORE

Edited by
William Sterling

Truborn Press

PUNK
goes
HORROR
II
2026 WORLD TOUR
A-sidE

To lay out the context, plain and simple- each story in this anthology has been inspired by a PUNK or Punk-Adjacent song of the author's choosing.

Here's a list of the songs and musicians who inspired our writers. For legal purposes- we have no official affiliation with these bands or songs. Each story in this anthology represents our author's own artistic interpretations of the moods, themes, or emotions they feel when listening to these songs. Lyrics, tales told, and exact messaging remains distinctly separate from those songs being paid homage to, but we hope that if any of the original artists come across this "album," they'll understand how inspiring they have been to us. And we hope readers discover a banger of a new band thanks to all this.

Circle With Me -- Spiritbox

Better Half -- Jawbreaker

Fem In A Black Leather Jacket -- Pansy Division

London Calling -- The Clash

Veins -- Fea

Loud Bark -- Mannequin Pussy

Cat Like Thief -- Box Car Racer

Shipping Up To Boston -- Dropkick Murphys

Asesinos -- Los Crudos

INTRODUCTION

WILLIAM STERLING | EDITOR

*A*h, *shit.*
We're doing this again?"

The words tumble from your mouth as you sit up and look around, tinnitus a bitch despite the hearing protection you swore you wore.

The venue remains on fire. The stage is decimated. Some rando's shoe sits in a puddle of beer, piss, or blood—it's hard to tell without the house lights on. It feels wrong to be back here again. Jagged. Like the cassette just rewound itself. The vinyl turned itself over. The playlist on a loop.

But you knew this was inevitable, didn't you?

You knew that **PUNK goes HORROR** wasn't gonna be a one-off, right? There's no one-punch knockout to be had here. No quick fix to the machinations of fuckery that propel the modern age.

Off in the distance, you can hear S.A. Bradley's skelepunks still hotwheeling around in their condiment trucks. There's a fire, just beyond the horizon, and pages worth of what could be

Rachel Harrison's love drift around, ashes in the wind.

Something began here. On this stage. In this mixtape.

Something that isn't finished with us yet.

Pillars of corruption still loom, high and proud in the distance. They still need to be torn down. You hear dictators on the radio. Obey, obey, obey. Don't think—don't fucking question it. You see those goose-stepping bastards getting more and more and more brazen. More vocal. More scared.

The horrors persist, and so **PUNK** persists.

The horrors grow louder, and so the **PUNKS** must grow louder as well.

A new band of rebels have selected more songs that empower them. Written more stories inspired by them. Cover songs, scribed with a literary bent. We're using them to construct a second stage. A bigger, more abrasive, **ANGRIER** stage.

More songs this time.

More messages.

More cracked knuckles and larger circle pits.

And as you reset your jaw, and you rise back to your feet, you say it a second time. A little more conviction now.

"Ah, shit. We're doing this again."

And somewhere in the rubble of this capitalist wasteland, an amplifier gets plugged in.

The sound that comes out is sad. A chorus to remind you of your first love. Your first heartache. It takes you back there. Gives you a second chance to run that gauntlet.

The sound that comes out is happy. Joy as an act of defiance. Our smiles, our laughter, our bouncing, moshing souls coalescing into a wave of camaraderie that might drown out their oppression that's been closing in around us.

And, again, that anger. That callout, right before the breakdown. The knowledge that everything can be broken.

The emotions and the energy and the dancing all pull you back to your feet, because fuck going quietly.

It draws you to the stage. To the barrier. Buoys you through the   horrors and knocks you back loose. Gives you the strength to stand among the rest of the faithful, the unafraid. Because you know this trope. This rhythm. This song.

It all coalesces into one, glorious chord.

And you feel your head begin to nod.

And ah shit, we're doing this again.

And our first author grips the microphone.

And our screams shake the walls once again.

CiRCLe
WiTh Me
Safe
Sermon
VAIL
PUNK
goes
HORROR
II
2026 WORLD TOUR

CIRCLE WITH ME

ABBY VAIL

THE THICK BOOM OF THE LOW B NEVER FAILS TO FUEL HER.

Demri screams into the mic, a growl with eyes closed tight. When she looks out at the crowd again, all the faces remain, sweating with passion. A landscape of open mouths spewing her own words back at her. The scenery is the same here in Lancaster as it is in New York, in Germany— heads, bodies, spit, and spirit.

She prods herself to remember the joy of it. The way it felt in the beginning when the music was the most important thing. Demri centers the bass against her middle, hiding her biggest insecurity from the garden of blooming cameras, but damnit, she knows she shouldn't. She doesn't want the bass to be a shield to hide behind. She'd rather it be a weapon. But the unflattering photo circulating online is too in her head. The comments have dug too deep.

Metal fans can be the genre's own worst enemy.

Atrophy for the coroner.

Dig through your body for days.
To find the thing inside only you, only you can remember.

As Demri belts her favorite line of the song, she can't help but think of how often her words get twisted. So many article headlines skewing quotes out of context for clicks. It's par for the course for a woman in metal to face a more critical eye, but Demri longs for the days when those comments prickled her skin and didn't get all the way under. Hell, they live there now, under the skin.

The low B rumble should always go deeper than thoughts like those. Should always be louder.

The eyeballs in the crowd all bulge in her mind. They stick out like a cartoon's before their heads explode. Griff jumps to land at the right time in the song, maybe his most impressive height yet. Demri turns away from the crowd's inflating viscera, closer to Stanley as he throws himself into the drum fill. Her bass strings lap up the maple fretboard with the outro riff. She promised herself she wouldn't let anything rob her of this.

Griff removes his guitar, letting the final note ring out, and he raises an arm to the audience as goodbye. Like tall blades of grass in the breeze, arms of the crowd wave in response. Their eyes are back to normal. Demri folds over the bass, taking a bow.

"We're Birds of Prey. Thank you all for coming out tonight," she says into the mic, then waves, exiting stage left.

The pleading for an encore fades into the background as Griff grips Demri's shoulders. Sweat drips down the bridge of his nose. "Did you enjoy yourself?" he asks through heavy breaths.

"Yeah. It was good. It was… I felt good." No mention of the eyes. No dissection of those recent thoughts.

"Perfect." His arms flop to his sides before running a hand through his soaking wet hair, sighing, and collapsing onto the green room couch. If he wasn't so beat, he might not have let Demri off as easy with her answer. He's been on her like a hawk ever since the Sickly Sweet tour started, checking in to make sure she's holding up. It's nice.

Demri peels her bass off. Tomorrow's a new town. Scranton. The Ritz Theater. Maybe tomorrow she won't have to lie in Griff's (sickly) sweet face.

Stanley pops in.

"You guys down for an encore?"

Griff groans, but it's fake. He's tired but alive, arguably more so than ever. He springs off the couch, then jumps from one foot to the other, side to side, a boxer before his match.

We've already won.

"Let's do it," says Demri, the bass gravitating toward its place on her body.

...

"Are you sure you don't want me to come with you?" Griff asks as Demri steps off the bus.

"I'm sure. Just want to clear my head." She has a handful of hours to herself, sandwiched between now and showtime, and Scranton looks like a cute little city to walk around. Maybe not the cleanest air, but air to breathe, nonetheless. She loves the guys, she really does, but each step on a new square of sidewalk gives her the space she so desperately needs.

As she passes Friendly Alien books and gawks at the

bookshelves through the windows, her phone dings. A text from Moriah.

< Miss you. Happy for you, but… COME HOME. >

Demri smirks and sighs simultaneously before typing back.

< Almost over! Did you see that picture everyone's been sharing? >

She shouldn't have asked. A friend like Moriah would deflect anyway. She's giving it more power, feeding the hungry beast, the critical eye which beats down like an unblinking sun.

< What picture? Dem, you better not be letting it get to you again. You're famous, it's gonna happen Embrace it. Then get home and embrace me. >

She's right, but the eye never sleeps.

"What is wrong with me?" Demri accidentally says out loud, there on the street.

"Oh my God, are you Demri from Birds of Prey?" an excited passerby approaches.

"Y-yeah." Demri's normally better at these interactions, but she's caught in such a strange place. Not in the mood. Still, she won't be rude to a fan.

"Can I get a picture with you?" The young man, looks to be in his twenties, whips his phone from his black jean pocket.

"Of course."

Demri uncomfortably huddles with the fan between his arm and the raised phone. Just has to get this out of the way, then she can find a nice little spot to Zen before showtime.

"Say sacrifice!" The man prompts, but as he does, his eyeballs grow two sizes on the phone screen. The pink veins in the white sclera become creeks of blood, levels rising in torrential rain.

Demri's already fake smile warps into worry, her head hovering inches from his. She ducks beneath his outstretched arm before the photo is taken (*God*, she hopes the photo hasn't been taken) and stumbles backward, staring into the confusion he now wears. His eyes are back to normal size, but she can't shake what she saw.

"What's the matter?" The man asks, hand upturned in *what the hell* fashion.

"I-I don't know." Demri fumbles before taking off in a sloppy jog, looking back to give reality a chance to grip her, to redirect her.

It doesn't.

She doesn't know if she runs for a block, or for two. She doesn't know whether she's blowing off any cute cafes or ice cream parlors. Splashes of color whiz by as murals come and go. That big critical eye in the sky beats down with every step. Judges every move. Every stride is second, third, fourth guessed. She must get out of the sun, the eye, the vision of the—

A bell jingles above a door as Demri barrels into a dim building. Any building. The low, eerie lights are red, almost like a safe light in a dark room for developing film. She stalks her breath carefully as if it's a moth insistent on drifting away to a brighter place. She creeps forward, deeper into the room. Is it a bar? No tables, no chairs, no alcohol in sight. Must not be a bar.

"Hello?" she calls out, but as soon as she does, she regrets the volume. The sound of her lone voice in this place sends a chill down her soft spine. It's like singing to an unresponsive audience, but worse. It's nothing like a stage. The opposite of a show—

—a hide.

For the first time in God knows how long, the stabbing of eyes into the back of her head has ceased, and it feels like the all-seeing judgement has lifted. But Demri's voice shrivels up inside her body. It seeks refuge in tissue, seeks moisture in the dry embarrassment of this... *hide.* She couldn't sing here if she wanted. Couldn't scream if she needed. Something tells her even her bass would refuse to boom in this place.

There is no stare strong enough to penetrate the barrier of this... hide. Silence is thick honey suspended in the air, muffling even Demri's thoughts inside her brain. She's never craved sound this badly, not when standing in the wings before a show, not when waiting for the timer to sound on a frozen pizza after a night out. She'd do anything to hear one note, two notes, a ringtone, the siren of a savior coming to pull her from the magnetism of the room.

With a raisin tongue, Demri licks her lips and turns a corner.

A red, velvet curtain hangs from ceiling to floor.

Scranton is weird as hell, she thinks, but doesn't say, because her voice is still curled up somewhere inside, refusing to emerge. Red lights flicker through the thickness as if finally waving hello.

She should've picked a different door to run through, she thinks. But...would it have mattered? Would any door she opened have led to a hallucination? Another slip into absurdity? The urge to find out what's behind the curtain now is a seduction she can't fight. Real or not, she's reaching for answers. Reaching within herself. Demri slowly grips the soft edge of one side.

Peeling back the velvet reveals a restaurant booth, its table set for one with ornate silverware and a simple paper placemat. On the table's center sits a round box. Not just any round box, but one that's been painted like an eyeball.

Anger rises in Demri's throat with nowhere to go. The anger turns around inside her mouth, knocking against the backs of her teeth, seeking a voice it can't find in her limbs, fingers, or toes. Her voice, lauded by critics for its ferocity, is hiding much deeper than that. The surge of hot energy coursing through her pushes her to touch the eye. To open the box. That's all it is, just a box.

She flings the lid onto a cushion of the booth like a frisbee to reveal a single black feather. How odd a thing to find in a place where flight feels impossible. The air in this place just wouldn't allow it. Picking up the feather, it's heavier than a feather should be, just by a little. Just enough to notice. There is a word written inside the box: ***FEAST***

That's what the eyes do. They feast. Every time she's on stage, they consume her. They don't stop there. Not anymore. They follow, consuming her thoughts, feasting on her confidence and nibbling at the reason she picked up a bass to begin with.

She looks at the setting on the table and again weighs the feather in hand. It must be an omen. It must mean something to be heavier than expected. Demri slides the feather into her bra, right next to her heart, and it ignites something in her. Memories of early days in the band charge forward like lions from a cage, ravenous and vengeful. They chew through the clouds of criticism, clear visions of playing to a handful of drunks in local dive bars, how easy it was to let the music do the talking. Friendship in a basement, cracking open cans of beer as notes rang out. Nods of approval after a cleanly recorded bassline—one take. An eye or two would try to have their way with her, but she'd brushed them off so easily back then.

Her heart drums like the double bass in their first hit single. Her anger stands at attention, and she knows she must get to the show, let the anger slide into her voice like a hand into a puppet. She must give a performance so powerful it puts an end to insecurity. She must silence the static feedback of the ever-present eye in the sky.

To hide is to suffocate.

With each step closer to the door, her voice uncurls. Her stride gains confidence through the sea of red.

Ding

The bell signals her leaving, and there on the sidewalk, hands on knees, she lets out a bloodcurdling scream.

Heads turn as they pass. Let them look. Let them judge. She needs the sound. Needs the passion.

Scranton isn't ready for tonight.

...

"There you are." Griff ties his boot backstage. "Head all clear?"

"Clear as the skies." Demri nods. She purged it, then filled it with rage. Filled it back up with forgotten passion. She puts a hand on her chest to ensure the feather's still there, and it is. She hasn't been this ready for a show since two tours ago, the first time Moriah got to be part of a sold-out stadium crowd. Demri's glad Moriah won't be in the crowd tonight.

Griff looks up from his laces. "Woah. Cool contacts."

"Huh?"

"The red eyes. Nice touch."

Demri swerves in front of the green room mirror. Two raging red eyes stare back, and they're her own.

Stanley sneaks up from behind, leather pants crunching, and he wraps his arms playfully around Demri's neck. "Knock 'em dead." His embrace reminds her again of the basement days, of the music they made, the infantile riffs they raised through demo adolescence and nourished into full-grown songs, and how much it matters. His cheap cologne reminds her how little he's changed amidst the fame.

She smiles. "That's the plan, Stan."

The intro music starts as they make their way to the wings. Demri's bass awaits her on stage. The crowd already rumbles, an earthquake in the theater.

Birds of Prey!
Birds of Prey!
Birds of Prey!
Birds of Prey!

Her stomach rumbles, too, with no lunch or dinner to fill it. Red velvet curtains frame the stage like the ones by the booth earlier. The stage lights flash and Demri walks on. The crowd's chants turn into indistinguishable cries. She picks up her bass and settles the weight of it on her shoulder before giving the loud bodies a first glance. She scans them, the darkened shapes of them as they jump and push at the foot of the stage. The whites of their eyes shine, gorging themselves on her from the shadows.

The feather flutters against her chest.

Demri leans into the mic in the center of the stage. "How we doing tonight, Scranton?" Her voice soars through the speakers as if never having hidden at all. This is where it belongs, showing. It claws at her throat for more time to shine, behaving so differently since being in that red room. Since uniting with the feather.

Stanley's kick drum booms and it kickstarts Demri's heart. The sticks clack together three times and the song begins. Demri slides down the B string, dropping in and letting her body fall into the heaviness of the intro without a single thought about how it will look in a photo. Let it be clickbait for keyboard warriors. The comments that dug so deep dissolve beneath her skin, leaving room for something else to fill the space. Griff is in perfect sync as he loses himself to the rhythm. This is going to be an enjoyable show if it kills her.

She rushes the mic, words of the verse oozing out like liquid gold from her lips, rich with power. Her stance is firm, legs spread shoulder width apart. The fingers on her right hand sprint along the strings like it's a race to the end, but this will be the beginning of something new. With each note closer to the chorus, the feather goes wild against her chest. Instinctively, she grabs it by the shaft and raises it high.

Demri screams the crowd's favorite refrain:

Say sacrifice!

All the mouths scream along as Stanley stomps robust triplets, but all the eyes on Demri shift above her as she opens her arms wide and points her chin to the ceiling, skipping the words to the rest of the chorus.

From the red velvet wings of the stage, a flock of crows spills into the theater.

Little by little, the crowd settles their thrashing and singing in awe. Birds of Prey has never put on a show quite like this before.

Demri stays in her stance, feather in hand as the crows form a neat ring up above. The black birds glide around the theater like vultures circling prey. On the stage, Demri can sense Griff drifting closer.

"What's going on? Did you plan this?" he shouts over the music.

Demri doesn't answer. Instead, she jerks the feather to point at the crowd. A sharp movement. As if obeying a silent command, the crows leave their circle to descend on the audience. First, the chaos is a blur of black fluttering wings. Then, a single scream. Not a metal scream, but a danger scream, and everyone can tell the difference.

A crow in the pit with an eyeball in its beak tears the remaining meat string from a man's eye socket and takes off. The optic nerve dangles. One, after another, after another, birds peck the eyes of every unlucky audience member who chose to see Birds of Prey tonight. Only, they can't see the band anymore, can they?

Trickles of blood fall from above as birds with torn eyes fly away with their prizes. Demri smiles and turns to her bandmates. Griff and Stanley wear matching looks of terror, but they can't stop playing. They drip sweat, battling their own muscles. Their disobedient limbs will not quit strumming or drumming. Demri and her newfound power won't allow it.

The theater doors lock. The panicked voices in the crowd evaporate to silence. The struggling lips can plead all they want. They've had enough time for commentary. The eyes have done enough feasting. It's Demri's turn to feast.

With only ears remaining, the music can be what it was always meant to be—the most important thing.

Say sacrifice.

beTTER HALF
ROSSON
PUNK goes HORROR II
2026 WORLD TOUR

BETTER HALF

KEITH ROSSON

SUNDAY AFTERNOON, the brutally hot, ass-dragging end of August, and Evan and Benji are reading Punch's diary and throwing stuff into the hole in the middle of Benji's living room.

Punch, Benji's older sister, is sixteen. She has fallen in with the goth kids, who dye their hair black and give each other stick and poke tattoos on their fingers, the insides of their wrists. Upside down crosses, pentagrams, crescent moons. Kids who smoke cloves, whose shadows have long stopped darkening the doorways of classrooms.

Evan is twelve and he's in love with Punch and it's like a fever, how fierce it is. Punch's real name is Olivia, but no one calls her that anymore, not really.

"Check this one out," Benji says. He stands in front of the hole, the diary held out before him. It's just a regular spiral-bound notebook with a red cover and a bunch of stickers on it, and a warning—*KEEP OUT, DICKWAD*—done in a sure-handed script; Punch had done two years of Calligraphy in Mr. Mason's art class. Benji holds his free hand over his heart like some sort of orator. Benji, with his bleach-spotted sweatpants, the grime on his neck, the birthmark on his cheek.

He reads: "I had this dream about Mom the other night. She was looking for me in the cupboards, all over the place. In my room, the bathtub, where we keep the rags under the sink. The hall closet. But I was standing in the middle of the room the whole time, trying to get her attention. I cried so hard when I woke up." His voice is thick with mockery.

"Weird," Evan says, not sure what else to say. The intimacy of this moment stills him; reading Punch's diary—about a dream, about her and Benji's deceased mother—seems like Benji's way of hurting himself. Hurting his sister. Evan's job, it seems, is to lay witness, to be silent.

"She's stupid," Benji says. He tosses the diary to the floor and picks up one of his half-burned G.I. Joe guys, the arm fused to the body in a deliciously blackened mess, and throws it into the hole. Benji's father can be heard occasionally moaning from the bedroom down the hall. Sometimes too they hear the flush of a toilet, but mostly the moaning. With Benji's mother gone and his father like this and Punch off playing with Ouija boards and doing photoshoots in the graveyard, this is the small and final gasp of their summer: throw random things in the hole, tape Ground Bloom Flowers to Benji's G.I. Joes and then marvel at their melted, taffy-like disfigurements.

Evan will be moving to Portsmouth, Rhode Island, in a week. It might as well be across the world. It's a state Evan had never thought about a single time in his life before his parents told him they'd be leaving. This hushed, veiled talk of safety, of new beginnings. They have already rented a house there, sight unseen. Evan is both thrilled and terrified.

This will be his last Devouring, the last time summer will hold its grip on him and the people he loves. No more.

That's what his dad says, anyway.

Our last one, champ.

No more.

...

"Away with you," Benji says now, throwing another melted GI Joe down into the hole in their living floor. "May you find your wings, find eternal solace." Evan frowns at the floor, afraid to say anything. Benji is talking like Pastor Greg during the Devouring, and while he doesn't know what the word *blasphemous* means, he knows this feeling inside himself.

Down the hall, Benji's dad coughs again. There is the constant divebombing of flies throughout the house; Evan has seen Benji throw entire plates of dinner down the hole. The stink of rot here is like a decayed hand over Evan's nose. Tendrils of carpet hang over the hole in frayed blue strings.

Where did the hole come from? Benji either says he doesn't remember, or he lies. The story changes: one time it was that his father smashed the floorboards with an ax and the hole was there, ready. Or they had a piano and it fell into the hole and it's still falling and falling. Or it was just like that one night, Benji seeing it on the way to get some chips in the kitchen.

"A hole is a hole," is what Benji says.

He drops another burned G.I. Joe down and says, "You know she's got a boyfriend?"

Evan starts, drawn back to himself. "Who does?"

"Who do you think? My sister."

"Oh," he says, his heart lurching. Feeling a knife-twist of jealousy. Feeling a little sick. "Gross."

"He's a senior." Benji leafs through Punch's diary.

An arrow pierces Evan. If this boyfriend is eighteen, he can vote. Get tattooed. He can buy Peach all the clove cigarettes she wants.

He might have a car. He might try to take her away. Might not even ask Permission to do it.

"Weird," Evan says, aiming for a kind of cool, disaffected detachment.

Benji walks over to his father's recliner and sets the diary down in the ass-shaped indentation in the chair. He picks up an envelope that sits on the end table beside the recliner. A bill. He reads the sender's address, mouthing the words, and suddenly sticks it down the back of his sweatpants, rubs it around, then steps over and throws it in the hole. The flies are like another insane person in the house.

"Why'd you do that?"

"Evan," says Benji, "you got a lot to learn, my *little friend*." This little friend business has always pissed Evan off. He's four months older and forty pounds heavier than Benji.

Benji goes back to Punch's diary and pulls another page out. Doodles. A death's-head surrounded by black hearts. A hangman's noose, a dog smoking a cigarette, oh Punch, you are perfect and wise and pretty and so goddamn cool.

Benji throws it in the hole. It flutters down and disappears. His face as stoic as an undertaker's.

Evan has asked his parents if they've gotten Permission from Pastor Greg to leave. Wide-eyed, clearly terrified, his father had shaken his head no. Instead, his parents have sworn him to secrecy. That he must tell no one they're leaving. Evan has kept the secret. Except, well, for telling Benji.

"Let me read one," he says, as casually as he can manage.

He walks over to the edge of the hole, where there is a strange and shifting topography of debris. Plastic Coke bottles, unopened bills, diary pages, melted G.I. Joes, Benji's dinners, dark and unnamed things that Evan believes might be scorched clothes. Perhaps the furtive shift of animals, insects. Sometimes, glimpsed beneath, something that might be a mouth yawing wide. The sheen of flies roving over it all. Benji's house is dark, yes, but the hole is *unfathomably* dark. It's maybe three feet down to the hardpacked dirt of the foundation, and in the center of that, like a dark eye, is the hole.

Then they hear the bedroom door open and Benji's father pads down the hall. He steps out in blue boxers and an *International Beer Inspector* t-shirt. His beard is threaded with gray. Even in the gloom, Evan can see that his eyes are red. He stares at the two of them with his hands hanging down at his sides. His voice sounds rusty when he says, "You guys aren't lighting fireworks in here, are you?"

"No," Benji says, staring at the hole, frowning furiously. "We're melting them in the driveway."

"Where's your sister?"

"Touching some guy's wiener, probably."

"Jesus Christ, Benji." His father's haunted gaze settles on Evan then, his lips curling up into some approximation of a smile. "Hey, buddy."

"Hi, Mr. Boyle."

His eyes rove between the two of them. "Don't be lighting fireworks in here." He hobbles off, each footstep a scrape and bow along the floor before they hear the door snicking shut, the gentle, settling groan of his bedsprings.

"All he cares about is if I burn the house down," Benji says, rooting through his cardboard box of figures, "because that's what he almost did."

"He did?"

"Yeah, last summer. After. He drank a bunch of whiskey and listened to his Lionel Richie and John Mellencamp tapes.

Cried and cried and threw mom's clothes in the hole and sprayed a bunch of lighter fluid on them."

"Holy shit," says Evan. The curse feels dangerous, exciting. He's leaving in a week, seven days, they do not have Permission but still they're leaving, which means anything is possible. Nothing is off-limits. Maybe he'll be a cusser in Portsmouth. Maybe he'll start smoking cloves. Paint his nails black. Kiss a goth girl that looks just like Punch.

"Yeah," Evan says. "And the hole got mad. Screamed at him in a way that hurt and he had to jump in and stomp the fire out. His socks got burned off, it was so funny. That's why he walks like that."

"It didn't eat him?"

"No," Benji says acidly. "It was full, dumbass. From my mom. All the holes are connected."

Benji's house has always been a little scary, but it actually feels better now that Mr. Boyle has confined himself to his bed. The rooms seem to be slowly changing: it had always been a leaning madhouse of Mrs. Boyle's quilts and paintings and Mr. Boyle's paperwork and magazines and bills, his stacks of books, but things feel different now, since Mrs. Boyle was Devoured last summer. Things go missing now. By seven o'clock in the evening, the living room is plunged into darkness, as all the lamps have disappeared. Most of the lightbulbs. There was once an out-of-tune piano, its top used as a table of sorts. That's gone. In the kitchen, the family is down to plasticware and paper plates. The shower curtain has vanished, a few errant rings all bunched to one side of the rod.

The house has become like Punch's diary—piecemealed away, disappeared an inch at a time. Evan sometimes imagines the hole roving about the house in the dark, eating up the furniture, biting away at the Boyles ownership of the place. There are other holes in town—behind the foundry, down by the lake, where the bicycle shop used to be. And the football field, of course. But Benji's is the only house with one.

The front door squeals open, and there is Punch. Unmistakable, limned in blazing sunlight.

She blinks, waiting for her eyes to adjust. One hand visoring her brow, the other resting on the doorknob.

"What are you two dingleberries doing?"

Evan has already shoved her diary in the waistband of his pants, carefully pulling his shirt over it.

"Nothing," Benji says.

"Please don't tell me you're lighting fires in here."

"Oh my God. Why does everyone keep saying that?"

"Is Dad home?"

"He's in bed."

She walks in and peers down at the hole. Evan catching a dizzying scent of cloves and perfume. "You're still throwing shit in there, dude?"

"No," Benji says sheepishly.

"You know it won't help anything, right?"

"I know."

"It's not like she's coming back."

"I know that, *Olivia*."

She rolls her eyes. She has a small zit, up near her hairline, in stark relief against her jet-black hair, and that imperfection makes Evan's heart ache with an explosion of wanting so powerful it's almost grief. He also feels the stirrings of an erection, and to be caught with such a thing now, next to the Boyles' hole, with Punch's diary in the back of his pants, would be tantamount to self-immolation. He starts thinking of G.I. Joes in order to defeat it. *Storm Shadow. Zartan. Tomax and Xamot. Lifeline. Blowtorch. Barbecue.*

Punch says, "Pastor Greg told me to get you." Her eyes settle on Evan, and his heart thuds in his chest. "You too, dillweed. Everyone's got to come to the field."

Evan doesn't want to go to the field. He hates it there. He hates this part of summer. This terrible stretch of days, the heat, the understanding of what will come looming ever closer, like a hammer that has yet to strike the nail. He's sick of bearing witness.

But it is what it is. A hole is a hole. They've sang songs about the Devouring since kindergarten. They are reminded of it in Sunday school. There are fundraisers, carwashes, bake sales to raise money for the families of the Devoured, those who have made the supreme sacrifice.

Perhaps, Evan thinks, they're leaving in a week because the hole will be full then. No longer hungry. Less concerned.

Less watchful.

"I'll go with you," he says.

For a moment, Punch brightens, and she looks like a child, like someone his age, and his heart, that dumb muscle, kicks in his chest. *Snake Eyes, Destro. Lady Jaye. The Baroness.* "I just," he says, "have to go to the bathroom first."

He slips down the hall, past Mr. Boyle's bedroom. The family's bathroom is unfortunate. The lone window is latticed with a silver crack and looks out onto the throngs of blackberry bushes that have taken over the backyard. Peeling linoleum on the floor, shelving made up of splintered apple boxes drilled into the wall. Two different colors of mold climbing the inside of the toilet. Mr. Boyle's bedroom is next to this one and when he moans, Evan jumps. What is he doing in there? Is he still that heartbroken a year later?

Evan pulls Punch's diary from his waistband and holds it in his hands. To look inside would be the gravest invasion. Would kill the dream of the whole thing, somehow. Instead, he kisses the cover a single time and puts the notebook in the cabinet beneath the sink.

He can hear Punch and Benji talking in the living room, the soft dissonance of their words. He passes the dark mouth of Mr. Boyle's room again and casts a passing glance inside. Mr. Boyle is prostrate on his bed, a yellowed sheet twining snakelike around his legs. He cups his genitals through his boxers, as if he has just been kicked—Evan remembers Dustin Sotomayor getting kicked in the nads during PE last year and having to go home after vomiting, and he's remained mortally terrified of it ever since—and Mr. Boyle weeps silently, tears sliding from the corners of his eyes into his crinkly black-and-gray beard. His is the darkest room, darker even than the hole. Mr. Boyle's room is the place where pain goes to stretch its arms wide.

...

They step outside the Boyle house and Evan nearly staggers with the difference of the day. The swaying pines, the breeze. The *sunlight*. It is like being born, the newness of the world. This feeling coupled with a nattering guilt, how happy he is to be out of that house. Evan's home has the luxury of clean sheets, ceramic plates, an unbroken floor, a mother who hugs him, sometimes too forcefully. A father whose love is clearly suffused in every word, even when he is tired or angry. Benji's life is the hole and the memory of a mother who was eaten. Is Mr. Boyle cupping his unit and weeping into his own beard.

People are already on the field when they arrive. Grownups mostly, but a lot of kids, too. Punch walks over to a group of her friends without looking back. Evan and Benji fall in with a cluster of kids from school. Brandon Fiesman, a year older, grasps Evan's shoulder in a way that approaches brotherly. There is the slightest murmur among the crowd, but not much.

The field is used for games during the school year, but in summer the hole is ringed in yellow caution tape. It is roughly a hundred feet in diameter. Some summers it's larger, some smaller. This year's is average. It appears in June, widens, feeds, disappears by September. Sheriff Foster and his deputies have set up sawhorses, have formed a loose line in front of the crowd.

In front of the hole, Pastor Greg holds a microphone and wears a white button-up shirt and black slacks. With his widow's peak and pale, blue-veined arms, he has always creeped Evan out, especially after he took over as Orchestrator of the Devoured when Pastor Mike retired a few years back.

Pastor Greg is just starting his sermon; they haven't missed anything. Evan searches the crowd, looks for his parents, hopes for another glimpse of Punch.

"We are," says Pastor Greg, "beloved. We are blessed. We are chosen. These are the days of righteousness." His voice has that flattened quality when people speak outside through a PA. Evan keeps looking around, hoping to find his folks, wondering if the secret of Portsmouth will somehow be written on their faces. If it's visible on his. Benji wouldn't tell anyone, would he?

Evan sees Punch laugh and push her shoulder against a boy's. He's tall. He's wearing eyeliner and a black t-shirt, bracelets with spikes. The senior? Evan feels sick.

"We are bringing," Pastor Greg says, "light to darkness. This is the time of the grand sacrifice. Who among us is ready to shed the constraints of this world? To toss away the weakened veil of this body, that the soul might move beyond?"

No one steps forth. Murmurs ripple through the crowd, a sound like a snake writhing through dry grass.

Pastor Greg is poised to open his mouth again, to petition the town once more for what is already inevitable, when a pale arm is raised and someone threads their way through the crowd. Paster Greg brightens and the crowd parts and a grandma-looking lady with a bouffant of coppery auburn hair comes up to him. Bright pink lipstick and a pantsuit as yellow as a canary's, and Pastor Greg holds her, his chin resting on the top of her skull. He holds out his microphone to her and she says, in a voice husky with held-back tears, "I been ready, Pastor. Here I am."

"You've *been* ready," Pastor Greg repeats, smiling, gazing out at the crowd with eyes widened in awe, in jubilance. "You've *been* ready, Mrs. Lyden. Mr. Lyden gone, what? Eighteen months now, a heart attack, and you've been preparing yourself, haven't you, dear? Placing upon your soul all your spiritual armor. Offering a sacrifice so that the rest of us unworthy ones might live through another turning of the page. Bless you."

He looks out at the audience, and starts pointing at people.

"You, Priscilla, watched your Matthew battle the darkness, and Henry there saw his Claire do the just thing as well, and I see the Boyle children here, Benji and Olivia, who saw their mother stride down heaven's backbone just last year. Do I blame their father for his absence? No, I do not, and neither should you. Mrs. Boyle has shed the skin of this world, had donned a sword of righteousness in the next one. And now? Now Mrs. Lynden's *ready*, she says. She's *been* ready, friends."

A murmur among the crowd. A scattering of applause. A palpable sense of relief.

Pastor Greg ushers her beyond the Sheriff and his

deputies, beyond the white and orange sawhorses. He raises his arm and the crowd begins its incantation. Evan feels the air begin to change. Grow heavy. Thick with something that feels like menace but that he's been told his entire life is the embodiment of grace and goodness. Even Punch and her friends are chanting.

"Lashes upon," Evan speaks, sings, screams along with the rest. Their voices hit some shared note, an implied velocity of sound, and the air thickens further. "Lashes upon the house of the dark. Lashes upon the house of the dark. Lashes upon the house of the dark."

Some dozen feet away from the hole, Pastor Greg stops, but Mrs. Lynden is fearless, is ready, and she goes to the hole's ragged edge, prepares to leap as much a woman her age can leap, but her foot slides in the loose soil and she falls, half-spinning, her hands scrabbling madly at the soil.

Evan catches a quick glance at the look upon her face, and it is not righteousness anymore, it is not peace, it is terror, pure and unadorned. The look of a woman who realizes she has made a grand mistake. That terror makes her sacrifice seem garish and obscene. Seem small. This poor old woman in her yellow pantsuit, her pink lipstick, her wild, crazed eyes. The town chants about lashing apart the dark house of the devil, about smiting Him, and a wet and mottled ebony tentacle rises from the mouth of the hole, a thing dripping with clots of mud, and it plucks a screaming Mrs. Lynden into the air, and even before she is brought down into the relentless dark, Evan sees the blood blackening her yellow suit where she is being squeezed.

She raises her face towards the sky and screams. A tremendous gout of blood jets from her mouth. Her dentures pinwheel through the air. One of the denture plates lands on the shoulder of the man to Evan's right. It leaves a pink mark on the man's t-shirt as Mrs. Lynden is pulled down into the dark.

Some people are still chanting their incantations, though many have stepped back away from the hole, are shouting in fear or disgust. Pastor Greg walks backward, microphone at his chest, until he bumps against a sawhorse and a deputy gently steers him back among the crowd. From the hole there is a momentary pause and then a geyser of meat and red mist is funneled into the air. People are spattered. Scraps of pantsuit flutter down, glittering crystals of bone shrapnel hang dream-like before descending. A crimson cloud falling upon them all.

Pastor Greg wipes his brow and tells the crowd to disband. His voice is shaky. Blood spots his glasses, his face. "Let us thank Mrs. Lynden, and wish her good battle." His voice cracks on the last word. A brief squall of feedback.

Evan drifts away, dazed. He can't find Benji. But he sees Punch, and she walks over and offers him a smile that, oh, breaks his heart. It is a smile reserved solely for children. There's a wide world between the two of them, between twelve and sixteen, and it is impassable. Her face is spotted with gore. "I fucking hate it here," she says.

Evan can only nod.

She says, "You know you'll never leave, right? You didn't get Permission. You'll never get to go."

He licks his lips. Dread sitting on his chest. The understanding that Benji told. "You're wrong."

She looks over his shoulder at someone. "I hope so."

Then she touches him on the arm and walks away, and there is Evan, alone amid the thinning crowd, the hot reek of Mrs. Lynden's effluvia coloring the yellow grass of the field, gleaming wetly beneath the sun.

What sort of life *will* they live in Portsmouth?

Perhaps Punch is right.

Perhaps every house, every patch of ground, has some kind of hole in it.

Someone lays a hand on his shoulder, and he looks up, expecting at last to see his father. But it's Pastor Greg, looking severe, dour, pained.

"Evan," he says. "I need to speak to you. A rumor I've heard." He motions in the opposite direction, back toward the phalanx of sawhorses, to where his parents are standing too near the hole for it be an accident. His mom hunched and weeping, pressed against his father's shoulder, a pair of deputies flanking them.

And then Pastor Greg says, "Come on, son. This won't take long."

FEM
iN A
BLacK
LEATheR
JacKeT
PuNK Never Dies!
PUNK goes HORROR II
2026 WORLD TOUR

FEM IN A BLACK LEATHER JACKET

MICHAEL VARRATI

DRAG NIGHT AT CLUB SKUZZ was something of a new development, though queens had been stomping stilettos across the venue's grimy floorboards for years. When management finally made the occasion official, none of the regulars batted an eye, and the only complaints came from poseurs who probably shouldn't have been there in the first place. After all, drag, by virtue of its very existence, has *always* been a little bit punk.

...that being said, punk-specific queens are very much their own breed.

For them, it's not about make-up technique or lack thereof, nor is it about choosing to lip-sync to the Dead Kennedys over, say, Debbie Gibson. A punk queen, at her core, is about *attitude*. To wit, at Club Skuzz a gal could have a Lady Gaga exterior as long as she had a Lux Interior, capisce?

Management didn't care if you were a mess, just as long as your mess was authentic...a fact that didn't always sit well with the regular roster of performers. Truth is, there are some queens who, no matter their own personal level of subversion, hold their artform to a certain level of polish, and when their sisters don't pass muster, claws inevitably come out.

For Kiki, such petty bickering was just part of the landscape. A bit of sport to get you revved up before taking the stage. She knew her beat was far from the best, but if the dressing room conversation turned an icy eye on someone else, she was happy to join the fray. Better that bitch than her, right?

But on this particular evening, petty squabbles were the farthest thing from Kiki's mind.

The ground outside the bar was damp, the result of a recent rain that only intensified the sharp scent of the dumpsters unceremoniously pushed against Club Skuzz's farthest corner. The trash's proximity to the door was likely a health hazard, but no one was coming to check, and some of the regulars had convinced themselves it was part of the charm.

Beyond the dumpster was the entrance to the back alley that led to the stage door. It was here that Kiki had taken pause, staring with a frown at the myriad of inconvenient puddles littering her path. The narrow, uneven walkway was treacherous enough in the best of conditions, let alone slick, with her in heels.

She knew she should have waited to get dressed at the venue, but every time she did that, her boy clothes ended up smelling like they were baptized in Pabst Blue Ribbon simply by virtue of sitting backstage. Besides, Kiki was proud of the Siouxsie Sioux make-up she had managed to pull off that evening, and it would never have been possible in that shoebox of a dressing room with all the other girls getting ready at the same time. It was an oft repeated refrain from the queens that they were "tit-to-tit" back there. They always laughed, but there had been a few breast-plate collisions over the years that led to sparks, both figuratively and, in one instance, literally.

With a sigh, Kiki teetered forward into the shadows. It was a walk Kiki had taken many times, but she had never quite gotten used to the mud of it all. It also didn't help that the one naked light bulb the bar had deigned to install above the stage door had died sometime during the Reagan administration. Typical.

Kiki had almost made it to the door when something in the shadows caused her to stop anew: A single, orange dot amidst the darkness.

A sight every drag queen at Club Skuzz knew well: The burning end of a cigarette.

"Who is that?"

Despite Kiki's peering, whoever was standing back there had chosen a particularly murky spot to light up. Not that Kiki was phased by the inconclusive nature of staring into the void. This was just business as usual.

"Well, if you're not going to be chatty, at least bum a queen a cigarette? I'd ask Boom Boom, but you know that bitch only smokes menthols and if I wanted that mint-shit in my mouth I'd suck on the pine tree I have hanging on my rearview mirror."

By way of response, a plume of smoke hit Kiki right in the face, the result of a particularly pointed exhale.

"Bitch, did you just--"

Before Kiki could get the next words out, a well-manicured hand darted through the shadows and the smoke to seize her by the neck. Startled, Kiki struggled against the grip, even as the acrylic press-ons digging into her flesh began to draw blood.

From the darkness, the figure stepped forward, revealing themselves for the first time. Kiki's eyes went wide with recognition, then, in spite of herself, she spoke her mind:

"...it's you? *Ew.*"

It was the last shade Kiki would ever throw. The figure who had seized her yanked Kiki back into the black, and--

...

The applause is light, but enthusiastic, as a queen who's channeling Courtney Love takes her last bow and is replaced on stage by a grizzled Emcee. Though he's hosting the evening's festivities, it's clear from his deeply-faded Germs t-shirt and expression of passive amusement that he comes with the bar and his participation is more compulsory than committed.

From his place in the spotlight, the Emcee surveys the scene, and it's pretty underwhelming: A few regulars swilling beer from their posts at the bar, several drag groupies sitting at a table that's uncomfortably close to the stage, and a whole lot of vacancy. In the back, a couple of the queens who are part of the evening's line-up watch the proceedings, not terribly concerned about ruining the element of surprise.

The Emcee gives them a little wink before broadly gesturing to the performer who just departed, encouraging one last round of applause. It more or less works.

"How about that, huh? Don't see that in Cleveland," The Emcee says with an approximation of showmanship. "Anyway, next up here at Club Scuzz, we're excited to welcome this evening's headliner..."

Pulling an index card from his back pocket, the Emcee brings it up to his eyeline and squints, attempting to make sense of the scribbled show notes he definitely didn't make himself and which he most certainly didn't care to memorize.

Finding the words he was searching for, the Emcee's face falls into a visible frown before quickly recovering.

"...one of our own local queens who has really stepped up her game..."

The Emcee's tone suggests he doesn't quite believe this to be true.

"…please welcome to the stage, the one…the only…Edie Mamé!"

A fresh round of polite applause ensues as the Emcee clears the stage and a bass-heavy track begins to reverberate through the venue.

Seconds later, Edie Mamé herself emerges from the wings, and as far as punk bars go, she's an absolute *vision*. Clad in a black vinyl dress that's fastened with several well-placed safety-pins, she hits the stage like a form-fitted wrecking ball of ferocity.

As Edie gyrates to the primal cries of Wendy O. Williams, she lifts her claws skyward, the dark hue of her press-on nails framing the shock of color that rests upon her head. Counterbalancing the dark tones of her ensemble, Edie's wig is a towering bright pink bouffant that spirals up to the ceiling like a monolith challenging Heaven itself.

Even the regulars, whose eyes rarely stray from their drinks, can't help but stare.

However, not everyone's gaze is so adoring or kind. At the back of the bar, two of Edie's contemporaries watch with narrowed lashes. One of them, Boom Boom, matches her namesake in presentation and countenance. An explosion of mismatched hues at all times, Boom Boom is the human personification of a Fourth of July firework. Everything about her is big, and she likes it that way.

At Boom Boom's side is Glitz, whose general vibe is also reminiscent of a holiday emblem: A Christmas tree…albeit one that has been left on the curb in February. Brittle and barely holding on to her sparkle, Glitz thinks of herself as Club Skuzz's resident showgirl, whereas most of the clientele think of her as "still alive."

Mismatched a duo though they may be, in this particular

moment, Boom Boom and Glitz are undeniably uniform in the icy glares they direct toward the stage.

"I never thought I'd see the day: Edie Mamé headlining a gig," Glitz rasps over the bass.

"Last week she couldn't even get on the lineup."

"Gotta admit, though: She sure is good tonight."

Glitz winces at Boom Boom's words. It's true, and she isn't thrilled by the notion of potentially having to give a compliment to someone she has long dismissed as a perpetual booger.

"That's the problem, Edie's *never* been good. Everything about her act has always been second rate: Bad fashion, ratty hair. She couldn't put her makeup on if her face was a paint by numbers. And now this: New hair, new outfit, new act."

Boom Boom shrugs. "That wig sure is somethin'."

"If you like that gaudy stuff."

"I'm a drag queen...of course I like that gaudy stuff."

Glitz frowns. She never was one to be distracted by slapping Bob Mackie on a hog.

"I'm telling you, Boom Boom...something fishy is going on."

...

The sound backstage is muffled, but still more aggressive than the Emcee would like. Not that there really was any reprieve at Club Skuzz, but sometimes a guy just wanted to let his weed gummy hit in peace, you know?

Standing amidst the garment racks and wig heads, the grizzled elder punk takes a deep breath. It's meant to be calming, but instead the acrid scent of sweat-laden drag hits his nostrils like freight train.

The Emcee grimaces.

If you had told him at the start of all this that the queens would be more unhygienic backstage than the tobacco-crusted, liquor swilling, sweat-laden punk bands that passed through, he'd have never believed you. Now the Emcee knows better. This is the price of beauty, he supposes. Or whatever.

Sidestepping a mound of sparkly fabric that had been unceremoniously left on the floor, the Emcee makes his way to the back door and pulls it open. The night air hits his face like a welcome baptism washing away the sins of stale beer and moldy wigs. The Emcee takes a deep breath and savors the moment.

As a slow exhale escapes his lips, the Emcee allows his focus to return to the here and now…and the damp, wet world beyond the stage door. At first, he notes nothing unusual beyond the requisite grime, but then the slightest glint of something reflecting light from the inside back catches his eye.

The Emcee takes a tentative step outside.

…is that a shoe?

His eyes narrow.

No. It's a high heel…

…and it's still attached to a foot.

…

Inside, Boom Boom and Glitz have budged nary an inch, their laser gazes still locked on Edie's performance. To the shock of no one, their sideline commentary has also continued uninterrupted.

"Now that I think about it," Boom Boom says, "I've seen that dress before. Lulu has the exact same one."

"You don't say." Glitz pauses, a realization occurring to her at the mention of their sister. "Speaking of, where is Lulu? I thought she was performing tonight."

"Never showed up."

The voice comes from behind, and the duo turn to see that the evening's bartender, Dean, has sidled his way to their perch, gladly inserting himself in a manner that only bartenders are wont to do. The intrusion is welcome. Boom Boom and Glitz like Dean. Of all the members of Club Skuzz's staff, he's one of the only ones to share tips with them when the evening's earnings are light...and unfortunately, that's often.

"...no word or anything?" Glitz's question is aimed at Dean, but comes out more like a general musing to herself. "That's not like her."

"Yeah. Lulu and, like, half of tonight's line-up just ghosted." Dean says this without judgement, as if he's used to unreliability. The girls, however, are slightly more shocked. Drag queens missing a chance to make coin was unusual, indeed.

Boom Boom's eyes stray back to the stage.

"No wonder Edie's headlining, then. There ain't no one else here."

Glitz grimaces.

"This ain't no coincidence. Queens go missing and Edie gets the spotlight in a stolen dress? You know what that is?"

"A crime of fashion?"

"No, Boom Boom...it's just a crime. And we're going to investigate."

On the stage, Edie's number comes to a dramatic end. Taking her bow, the evening's headliner heads off-stage. With a knowing nod between them, Glitz and Boom Boom move to follow.

As the drag queens peel off, Dean watches them go with passive interest. The Monday night bands were never this fun.

...

Often, when stepping off the stage, there's a moment of relief. And, if things have gone exceptionally well, a brief period of elation, perhaps even a feeling of invincibility.

If Edie Mamé was experiencing any of those emotions, you wouldn't be able to tell from her expression. In fact, her face in the moment seems devoid of anything at all…a fact the Emcee might have noticed if he didn't have other pressing matters on his mind.

Stumbling back in from the stage door, the Emcee's face is the polar opposite of Edie's: Active and full of dread.

"Something's happened to Kiki."

The Emcee's words are less urgent and more disconnected, as if his body were in the room, but his soul was still outside with whatever horror he had just seen. He turns to the newly arrived Edie with the energy of a lost child, desperate for an adult to say everything is going to be okay.

Edie does no such thing. Instead, she just stops and stares at the elder punk, causing the gravity of his vibe to morph into awkwardness.

Concluding in his heart of hearts that Edie's passiveness can only be due to her lack of understanding, the Emcee decides to do what clueless dudes like him do best: He doubles down.

"…are you dense or something? Kiki's in the alley. She's hurt…I think she might even be dead. We need to get help. Now."

At the mention of help, Edie has her first real reaction.

The Emcee has just enough time to catch it peripherally, his brain not fully comprehending what he's seeing.

His scream is cut short as Edie lunges forward.

…

The sound is staccato, and so brief that Glitz and Boom Boom barely even register it as they approach the backstage area.

Indeed, such is the uncomfortable art of drag that cries and grunts from the dressing room are not unusual, and these two are on a mission.

Approaching the door, the queens each give a silent nod of encouragement…and bound inside with a sense of grandiosity befitting their station.

"The jig is up, Edie! We know that's Lulu's dress…and we're not sure how, but we know you're responsible for the other girls being no-shows!"

Glitz's assertation hangs in the air with the authority of someone who's never once doubted their own correctness. However, despite the dramatic flourish of their entrance, Edie does not stir. Seated at a make-up table and lost in her own reflection, she seems neither phased nor interested in the accusatory finger pointing in her direction.

Glitz shoots a silent look to Boom Boom, communicating her annoyance before bounding across the room and seizing Edie by the shoulder.

"What have you done with Lulu and the others? You're a two-bit dumpster queen wearing a mopped dress. We know you're up to something…so spill…or so help me god…"

Boom Boom moves to back up Glitz as her comrade leans hard into her bad cop routine, hoping that the only thing more intimidating than one accusatory drag queen is two. However, as Boom Boom steps forward, she catches sight of something that Glitz overlooked in her b-line to play Mariska Hargitay: The body on the floor.

…or rather, *most* of a body.

Though the clothes clinging to the corpse are immediately recognizable as the Emcee's, everything from the sternum on up is so thoroughly smashed into a chunky scarlet gravy, you'd be forgiven for mistaking this person for a sausage pile.

Boom Boom freezes in her tracks.

"Glitz..." Her words come out as barely a whisper, a combination of simultaneously being in shock and trying to bite back chunks.

Glitz, meanwhile, has not pulled her attention from Edie for a second. In fact, her vice-like grip on Edie's shoulder has only intensified. Perhaps because of this, Edie finally looks up at Glitz, as if seeing her for the first time.

"Help...me..." Edie's words are weak, distant...

...and completely unmotivating to Glitz, who looks at her with utter revulsion.

"Help you? Why would I do--"

"GLITZ!"

Boom Boom's cry causes Glitz to finally look back at her friend...only to see her standing over the gored body on the floor. It's a vision so immediate and sudden that Glitz can't quite process what's in front of her.

"Oh my god."

An inhuman snarl abruptly fills the room and Boom Boom, standing squarely with the other two queens still in her field of vision, screams.

Glitz snaps her gaze back to Edie...and her jaw drops.

There, atop Edie's head, the towering pink bouffant is quivering, the strands of tightly woven hair swirling autonomously upward like a thousand tentacles. It's an impossible sight... one that causes Glitz to release her grip on Edie's shoulder, and to stumble backward.

Glitz and Boom Boom watch as the wig, now vibrantly active, shifts and shakes, causing fresh divots near the apex of the do to split open, revealing eyes...or some alien approximation of them. Beneath these ocular impossibilities, a third opening splits the follicles, unveiling a cavernous mouth and a row of fangs comprised of the same fibrous pink fluff.

Now staring back at them, the wig does something wigs rarely do: It roars.

Glitz is the first to speak, her terrified utterance encapsulating the whole moment in a single word:

"WHAT?!"

With a great heave, the wig snaps forward, heaving itself off Edie's cranium. Ribbons of flesh rip from Edie's skull as the wig springs free, leaving the queen's body to collapse to the ground in an unceremoniously disposed heap. It's a death drop that Edie won't be getting up from.

The wig, flying through the air like a murderous tuft of cotton candy, slams into Glitz with a force unexpected from its size and shape. The older queen is knocked off her feet and to the ground with a scream.

As Glitz's back hits the concrete floor her legs swing up into the air, causing her heels to go flying. It's a sight that would have otherwise been humorous, were it not paired with the sickening crunch of bones.

Glitz's cry of pain is primal, causing Boom Boom, initially frozen in fear by the self-launching up-do, to shake off her stupor and rush to her friend's aid.

However, as Boom Boom nears the prone Glitz, she's frozen anew by the grisly sight before her.

Using strands of its own corporeal self to secure a spot on Glitz's face, the wig gnashes and bites, pulling larger and larger chunks of queen into its maw with every sloppy crunch. Glitz is dead, and to add insult to injury, the creature also ruined her make-up.

Revulsed and understandably terrified, Boom Boom turns to run...but that's the pitfall of stilettos. Sometimes they don't move with you.

Boom Boom feels the heel snap, and watches in alarm as the ground comes rushing toward her.

Proving her namesake to be correct, Boom Boom's collision with the floor is hard, and the wind rushes out of her lungs with a wet wheeze.

Behind her, the munching stops.

Boom Boom doesn't turn back to look. She knows what's there, and she doesn't want to slow herself down. Snaking a hand outward, Boom Boom's nails hit the concrete in a splintering display of acrylic press-ons as she tries to gain purchase and pull herself toward the door.

To her credit, she makes it a few noble inches, attempting to choke out a cry for help as she does so, but her breath is too shallow.

Ultimately, it's an exercise in futility, and as Boom Boom makes one more desperate reach for the far-too-distant door, she feels a strangely warm and hairy tendril begin to wrap around her ankle...

...and she can't help but think, *"...that wig sure is something."*

...

Back at the bar, Dean has just finished pouring a beer with underappreciated precision when he spots the door to the backstage swing open.

Passing the pint off to the intended customer, he gives the emerging femme fatale a small wave.

"You do what you needed to do?"

Boom Boom stops in front of the bartender and stares, passively. Atop her head sits a spiraled, opulent, and new pink wig. A slight trickle of blood drips down her temple.

"Absolutely."

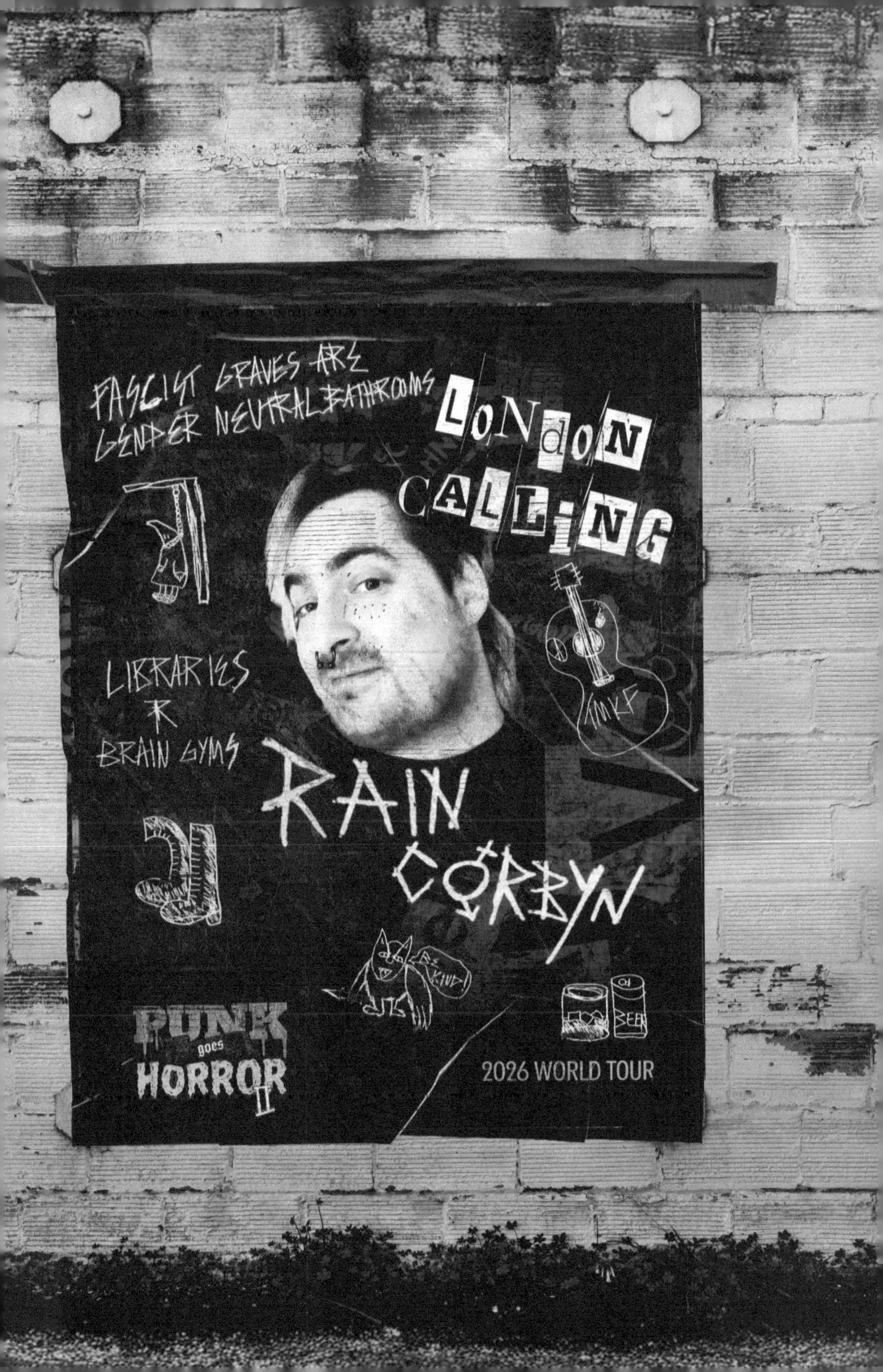
FASCIST GRAVES ARE
GENDER NEUTRAL BATHROOMS
LONdON
CALLiNG
LIBRARIES
R
BRAIN GYMS
RAIN
CORBYN
BE KIND!
IMKF
BEER
PUNK
goes
HORROR
II
2026 WORLD TOUR

LONDON CALLING

RAIN CORBYN

L AMP-LIT LONDON WAS A DOG-LICKED TOMB: above and beneath the bribe-greased streets were pigs, pigs, pigs. The river was a chewy bog, slouching, shameful, off to sea. London called me from across that ocean. It pulled me, less siren song than barbed hook, to those blindingly white cliffs that showed me exactly who would be welcome here. This was Empire's hall of mirrors: what sunlight broke through the miserable gray would ricochet off Dover, then off the ghostly faces of Albion's sailors come to land. If your face did not keep the glare going, a blinding litmus test of blood purity, then you were not coming home. You were just coming. Uninvited. Unwanted. Uncalled for by London.

Don't worry about my name. What matters is that I was once *of* these people, but I was never these people. They sent their best abroad, to seek their fortunes. Those men's sons would return generations later, broken, less-than, impudent. I was one such. I was far from a patriot to my own people, who had learned from our parents how to other, extract, maim, and forget. But Jesus, what these people called food was enough to make me want to break out a fife, musket, and War Coat.

These people can't even do explosives right. I had gotten

myself invited to a bonfire night celebration by an English rose I was hoping to put the squeeze on for one reason or another. The show was incompetent. It took half the city to get the bonfire started in their beloved drizzle, though I didn't half mind how the eventual fire glowed on Elizabeth's dewy cheeks.

"Say, what's the occasion, anyway?" I asked her, too loudly, a typical Ugly American. People turned. Elizabeth grabbed my forearm and laughingly shushed me. I took the chance to take her hand in mine. More quietly, "Sorry. I mean, who's that poor sap?"

I gestured to a wicker effigy at the top of the more-smoke-than-flame pyre.

"That's only Guy Fawkes," she said, yodeling his last name downward to express contempt or something. They may have come up with the English language, but they sure make it sound like a dying parrot in their own mouths.

"And we support him?"

"We support his burning!"

"Oh. Well say, what'd he do, anyway?" I asked, playing dumb. I didn't expect to get away with my mission, frankly. But if I did, I figured 'idiot yank' was a persona nobody here would question too much. Sure, I hung out with a radical set back in Alphabet City, but for the most part we kept our noses clean and only talked shop in private. Anarchist pillow talk is the bomb, you dig?

"He tried to blow up the King *and* Houses of Parliament in Sixteen-oh… something. D'jyou not know this?"

"Well gosh, I guess not."

"Do they not teach you English history over there? You've hardly history enough of your own."

"Yeah, well, you know what they say. Over there, a

hundred years is a long time. Over here, a hundred miles is a long way. But no. Never heard of the guy. So why did he have it in for the King…?" Again, I happened to know quite a lot about Guy Fawkes. Enough to know that, then and now, some bright minds believed there never was any Gunpowder Plot to blow up the King and his wig-shop of a government. Some hep cats think it was, what we'd later call, a false flag. A hoax made up to make a point about dissent, with Fawkes the primo patsy. A demonstration, just like the recreation we were watching that night, to show what happens to citizens who get a little too concerned.

I knew all of this, but I had to pretend. Playing dumb is a harder part of espionage than people think. It's actually a lot harder to act like you don't know things that you really do, than vice-a vers-a. To me, anyway. "Was this one of your Georges?"

"James. The first and sixth."

"Come again?"

"First king James of England, and the sixth of Scotland." She said this in a singsong voice, and I could just see her in a little uniform in class, proving the know-how that was expected of her as the daughter of a House of Lords poobah. Right before her lunch of boiled cabbage, eels, and no spices, I could only assume.

"Oh yeah. And why? What'd James do to old Foxy up there to make him so bomb-happy? As an American, I simply can't look with too harsh a light on royalty getting acquainted with the fine town of Smithereens. It's in my blood."

Liz shook her head at me and kissed me to change the subject. I knew it was because she didn't want to come right out and say, "Well, I'm descended directly from one of the Lords he hoped to turn into barbecue," but I wasn't about to complain about her tactics too much.

Ack.

On second thought... Turns out speaking isn't the only arena in which Brits are unskilled with their mouths. I had a Basset hound once who drank water like this. Gol-lee.

Around us, the crowd started to get excited, and I didn't think it was over my public display of love-making.

"Oh, it's the best bit," she said, pulling away and turning me towards the fire. I hadn't been looking forward to this "bit," but when in Rome, you go see people kill each other at the Colosseum. On cue, screams erupted from within the effigy of old Guido. "The traitors join their hero!" She said this like a witch out of movies. Gleeful in cruelty.

"So, what did *they* do?" I asked. I looked closer at the effigy and could see a half dozen people writhing and trying to beat their way out of the ribcage prison. A black police horse glowed sulphurous. Human ash was general.

"Oh, who cares, Marty?" That was the name I had come up with. "It must have been something dismal to be locked up in there and set on fire.

"You mean they don't tell you the crime, exactly?"

"We're not such sticklers for stuffy old scrolls as you lot with your Constitution."

"Yeah, well my constitution is failing me at the moment, sweetheart."

I never cared for screams. I mean, who but a lunatic does? But I'm saying they really get under my skin. A lifelong hangup just because of one childhood incident. What do you call it? A trauma?

We took a field trip as school children to see sausages get made, right? A generation of vegetarians, it made most of us. The churning, the grinding in the metal mouth of the machine, and the celery snap of a thousand bones breaking like nothing. But it was the screams that got to me. The abattoir was miles away, hardly as big as my child-sized hand over yon. But we could hear the screams. I never got over the sound of it, or the horror of the notion: a building just full of screaming beings.

This celebration reminded me of that field trip.

"Hey how about a drink, darling? I've got sights to unsee."

A few hours later, we were mercifully in a pub, one of this nation's more redeeming institutions. Regrettably, it was a Heritage Pub. Elizabeth tried to get me to dress in the traditional, expected attire: a bawdy pastiche of Shakespearean-ish garb. I wasn't too sour on all the heaving bazooms on display, least of all the ones seemingly trying to escape my date's dress. But still. Some histories aren't so sexy to revisit.

I thought of my lover back home and reminded myself that I was doing this for him as much as for the movement. I necked a pint of bitter, fast, to forget his delicate dark fingers. I slugged some dismal silty wine to remember what we'd done together in service of making tyrants afraid. I hit the brandy to forget the tears in his eyes when we admitted to each other that I'd been made, that our beloved New York was closing in on me, and that I only had time to pull off one more firework, so I'd better make it good, far away, and alone. Here in the boozy museum, I spent a fortune on some goddamned decent bourbon to remember what his mouth had smelled like when he told me he was proud of me.

We'd barely made it to Elizabeth's place before curfew, at which point the city's ghouls would be released to shamble through the ancient alleys and feast on vermin: rodent and human alike. We had just started up her stairs when, behind us, the doorman sealed the entranceway with something like a bank vault door. Elizabeth didn't want to start necking until the ghouls had been released. She said their moans covered up her own. Said

she was even in the habit of waiting until they were out to get to work on herself, on lonely nights. I thought of what it meant for a person to associate those barely-living making lunatic sounds with sex. I prematurely got the revulsion I often did after lays which were beneath me.

Some unknown time later, I was giving it to Elizabeth and it felt like taking medicine. She made a show of a wailing climax, and I couldn't help but assume it was for the benefit of the neighbors more than for me. I pictured her making naughty faces at them when she next saw them in the hallway, and it made me sick.

So after, I got up, lit a cigarette, and watched the damned's slow parade down whatever greasy street it was that Elizabeth lived on. And would die on. My smoke blew back into her apartment, settling into the velvet furniture like piss into a mattress.

"Quite a solution you all have for the Madness," I said.

"Well, we can't just kill them. They're mad, yes, but they've done nothing wrong."

"Right, not like those wicked insurrectionists in the bonfire. Remind me what they demonstrably did, again?" This was bad for my cover, but I couldn't help myself.

"You're worrying over nothing. Who ever heard of a paranoid cowboy?"

"I'm no cowboy, I'm from New York. It's as big a city as this here London."

"Tomayto, tomahto." I looked back outside.

"These poor souls' only crime was eating some bad hamburger a hundred years ago."

"It kept them alive... -ish. But mad, you know, absolutely. These nerve diseases are just dreadful."

"Should've bought American."

"Wasn't a comedian your leader at the time?"

"Isn't one yours now?" I knew I was acting bratty, so I turned over my shoulder and gave her one of my cockeyed best. She was flipping through an elevated fashion magazine. I saw outfits based on what I had to wear out of necessity back home. Torn jeans, moth-eaten tees with armpit holes that got an inch longer every year. I saw phony Doc Martens, polished so bright you could read the soap ads in their reflection. I couldn't see the prices on the page, but I could see too many digits.

"Do you think I'd look good in this?" She turned the page towards me to show some sort of triangular smock situation draped over a model who was all of ninety pounds.

"No."

"Well, you could at least pretend."

"I couldn't."

"Well." She lit one up.

"Call me a chauvinist-" I started.

"You're a chauvinist," she said through a mouthful of mulchy tobacco smoke. "And I like it. English fellows are always falling over themselves to ask correctly for what they would like. Not you, though."

"You know what I just realized? I know your name alright, but I haven't the first idea what you do." This was a lie, of course. What she did was the whole reason I'd made a point of running into her, literally, spilling my coffee on her and insisting on making it up until I got a date.

It worked. She got going about her fluff job at Parliament, though **not** *in* Parliament, naturally. That was Daddy's job. She was in charge of renovations and restorations: keeping the place looking modern while maintaining the historical architecture.

You know, wheelchair ramps in all the old secret passages. Lights that dimmed at a spoken command in the rooms where genocides were cooked up. It took her six cigarettes and some lazy mouth stuff to get to the part I was there for: the rumored warrens of emergency tunnels under the Houses of Parliament that got the big to-dos out through the sewers. Them out, or me and a whole bunch of dynamite in.

"Bullshit," I said, knowing this would piss her off and make her spill even more.

"I like how you say that. 'a-bwull-SHIT.' Like in a mob movie."

"I said I was from New York."

"It's not bullshit." She got this faraway look in her eyes that almost made me... pity her? If this was fondness, I'd throw myself to the horde outside. "There's a lift right from the center of the Lords' Chamber down to the sewers."

"Get out."

"Yes, that's its purpose. If there are terrorists or what have you, the Lords can get out quickly via the lift. It goes down an awfully long way, right in between tube tunnels, then down into an underground drydock."

"Which, presumably, is guarded 24/7."

"You'd think, but nobody's needed to use that exit for... well, since I've been alive. Not worth the wages."

"What if they do need to get out?"

"They won't."

"Oh yeah?"

She spilled all sorts of beans about the layout of the tunnels. Beans that'd never been discovered or even dreamt of, she spilled. She seemed to know the sewers like the back of her hand, a hand which had never held anything dirtier than a soup spoon. So, soon enough, I knew them like the back of my own hand. My hand which been through a dozen windows, two dozen jaws, even a door or two that looked at me wrong. Hands that had squeezed the ghost out of a man. Lighting up, she said,

"Secrets are dreadful to keep but lovely to share."

"Is that Wilde?" I asked.

"Wild? It's outrageous," she said, "and nobody knows about the tunnels but the Lords."

"Well, nobody except for you and me."

"You, me, and the pigs."

"Come again?"

"Thrice in a night is my limit."

"The pigs?"

"Of course. The London sewers are just teeming with wild pigs. Didn't you know this?"

"Come on. This is some 'feed the birds' Jack the Ripper mumbo, right?"

"Oh, no. I'm deadly serious. They clean up all the rubbish, just like the ghouls outside. Been there forever." Outside, I could hear the ghouls' slavering mixed with those phantom pig screams. I shuddered inside but kept a brave face.

"Uh huh. Well alright, nobody but you, the pigs, and me."

"Yes, and you're not going to do anything with that information." At this point we were both nude, with me sitting up against the headboard and she with her head in my lap. Saying what she just did, she laughed and looked briefly at me, then shut her eyes. She must have seen something rotten in my expression though, because a few seconds later she opened her eyes up, held her breath, and stared up at me.

She laughed nervously, then, "You..." I guess she saw more of whatever damnation was behind my eyes, because she made some kind of British noise and made to sit up. As easily as crossing my legs at a cocktail party, I got her neck between my thighs and squeezed. She made noises like the ghouls outside for the better part of two minutes. Then she stopped. Those ghouls would be gone by dawn, just four hours away. Her body twitched for most of the first hour. I stared at her, thinking about nothing at all, until she was still, the ghouls were silent, and I heard the downstairs vault door open. A bell rang somewhere. I posed her. I set up a lit cigarette in her hand and made sure the cherry caught on her expensive sheets. I left.

It's remarkable what people can do when they get together and set their mind to it. I didn't want to go to the dingy punk bar where I was instructed to meet my next contact. Or, rather, I very much did want to go there. Just not on business. It seemed too on-the-nose. You might as well have put a big sign out front saying "Raid Here!" But maybe that was the exact reason it was chosen. Who knows about the psychology of English criminals playing cat and mouse with Scotland Yard.

Inside it smelled like my bar in New York, yet just different enough to be uncanny. Like admiring your wife's ass and then she turns around and it's her sister. The passwords, the handshakes, the exchanges, this is all the stuff of spy pulp stories. When I was new, it made me feel excited. Legit. Now it just makes me clammy. But this is what you must do. If one person gets made, they're isolated from the others.

From the bar I went across town to an abandoned warehouse in which lay a wagon. In it, a half dozen identical fifty-pound crates, and a contraption that looked like a lawnmower engine. That piece was the only actual bomb. The rest just kept the party going.

From there, I went back across town to a boathouse with

a nice smooth launch for me to get my lethal cargo onto the Thames. The fog was thick, pea soup they call it, and I almost ran the explosives right into a lost ghoul who'd escaped the dog catchers. It was still twitching from my pistol shot when I got out on the water.

Boy, I'd like to find whoever invented rowing and kick his ass. Miserable work at the best of times, and these weren't them. Forget that I couldn't so much as see obstacles to paddle around them. Forget the mysterious wakes threatening to knock my load around. One wrong jostle and I'd be able to tell you what the moon was like from personal experience. Fortunately, I was not disturbed from my task of pushing ordnance the wrong way up the city's asshole. I can't claim any superior sense of direction, but something about my destination just called to me, like it did on that hideous steamer carving its way past Dover. When I arrived at the massive hole in the river wall, where noble shit floats into the city's fisheries, the fog parted for me like a theater curtain. Closing night indeed.

Back at that school trip to the sausage makers', there had been a whole long line of pigs, an orderly death march, leading into the screaming building. Rowing up the shitstream into the guts of Parliament, I felt like those pigs. I knew, of course, that my dying in the completion of the mission was acceptable, even likely. But the foreboding was more than mortal: it was profound, unknowable. Like important information was trying to come to me about what lay in wait in there, but my eyes and ears were just too small a funnel for it all. So I just rowed in, keeping half a worried eye on my explosive little baby.

The opportunity for escape through these tunnels was obvious. You could fit two, maybe three of my little rowboats next to each other in the channel if you had to. I pictured rich shits who had never seen their own rich shit in years, being forced to ride the brown log flume while some lunatic radical shrieked up above. Realizing I resembled that remark, I put the lid on picturing things. I didn't enjoy lighting a box lantern, given my cargo, but I couldn't see a thing. There were toilet holes periodically above me, and I realized too late that glancing upwards was an obvious mistake.

I scrambled through the gauntlet faster, and my oar glanced off of some half-submerged metal object. A diving bell, I thought, as the shriek of scratched metal rang through the sewers and echoed back accusingly. Christ. The screech wasn't fading. It just keened louder and louder, tinnitus's bitch mother, until I could hardly paddle for covering my ears. I plugged my scarf in them, and it helped enough to get me rowing again.

Behind me, a splash. Not the idiot sploosh of a turd in water, but something massive. Something the size of my boat. You'd think I'd have learned a lesson about looking places. But I was not the learning type.

I looked.

A pig, humongous and terrifyingly fast in water, sped silent and sharklike toward me. I picked up the pace, but the mutant swine launched itself from the surface, tusks and rotten lips parting the shitwater while the beast screamed like the nightmares I've had every night since childhood. Fear locked my joints, and I was rendered helpless as it pushed my skiff down one tunnel, then another, a sore-covered outboard motor vomiting up the sewage it swallowed.

I couldn't move, but I could think. The boar was moving me deeper inland, possibly closer to the Lords' Chamber, where I needed to be. All I had to do was get enough of a grip on myself to light the bombs and my mission could still be accomplished, mutant pigs be damned. Me with them, probably.

It pushed me to a four-way junction where two more car-sized pigs joined from each direction. They squealed in a wrong combination of ecstasy, rage, and hunger as noble piss rained down on my frozen form. Finally, they slowed, and I realized I was directly underneath the Lords' Chamber. The elevator was there, just like Lizzie said. The one I was supposed to load up with explosives, hit the timer, send up, then run.

A mountainous dirge of squeals.

I held up my lantern with a spasming hand, and shed light on the twenty-foot high rat-king of the swine. Before me, an incomprehensible amalgam of a whole herd conjoined at impossible anatomical junctures. Several of the pigs that made up its bulk had died, and were in various forms of decomposition in the great hematoma of pig I knew had been calling me here since what I saw at that abattoir. Around us, endless bones, picked clean by the fleshy apparatus of Empire. Humans, of course. Uncountable animals, nations, creeds, and bloodlines all represented. All had been flung down here when the kings above had wrung as much washed wealth from them as they wanted.

Something I might once have called God swelled in me, and I rolled away. I uncovered the bomb and slammed my hand on the activation button.

Nothing happened.

I gripped my lantern in one hand, and with the other I hastily ripped the lid off one of the crates I had so carefully protected until now. It was full of sand, and I knew the others would be, too. I had been set up. Betrayed by someone along the line of secret cells and whispers, just like Fawkes. But unlike Guy,

I would not be memorialized. I was not important enough to be made an example of. Just one of countless poor saps who thought they would be the one to make a difference.

One sequence of pigs appeared to function as an arm for the great mass, and it reached down and skewered me with a dead pig's tusks. I became a meatball on a fork. I screamed in pain, and what came out of my mouth was what I had heard on that day, and had kept in my heart since. A million screams came out of me. A million mouths opened in front of me.

Christ. Even the lions pitied Daniel.

veiNs
PUNK
goes
HORROR
II
2026 WORLD TOUR

VEINS

GRACE R. REYNOLDS

C RY FOR ME, BABY." The words slip through Magdalena's lips like silk on skin. Red. Glossy. Like a quiet prayer whispered in the dark that feeds tendrils of shadows curling at her feet. Illuminated only by a ring light behind her cell phone, Magdalena is the prima donna of this live stream. She dances for no one. She dances for everyone.

Magdalena's satin slip shines in this forgotten cellar, white as snow. It scarcely covers the collarbone which protrudes from her body at all the wrong angles, casting shadows on her gaunt cheeks. If one doesn't look too closely, she might be mistaken for a porcelain doll in a music box. Fragile, with limbs that only stretch so far before they crack.

"Cry for me, baby," Magdalena sings again as she looks at the phone. She sways her hips while tracing her form, letting her viewers imagine where they would put their hands, among other things. Cascading messages and favors from strangers on the internet make her smile. Her favorite nighttime playthings watch her. Judge her. Pay her to be a human puppet as they fondle themselves in the privacy of their own homes.

I love her eyes.

Wow, so sexy!

PUNK GOES HORROR II

You're so beautiful!

A star emoji pops up in the chat—a virtual gift equivalent to one hundred koruna. Five USD. Magdalena curtsies for her onlookers and pulls the hem of her slip up ever so slightly.

Magdalena kneels down and picks up a tube of lipstick like a microphone, the gold laminate worn from overuse. She untwists. From the camera's perspective, green doe eyes focus intensely on the rouge shaft that becomes erect between her pointer and thumb. A kiss emoji explodes on the screen. Magdalena pouts her lips and smears them over and over in that shade of *blowjob-red,* overlining the natural shape of her mouth. She looks into the camera again.

"Thank you, baby," she croons. She says it in that accent the audience can't quite place, but which is somehow universally known. Maybe she's Russian. Perhaps she's Polish. The way she rolls her "r" indicates she is undoubtedly some Slavic beauty from Eastern Europe. The kind of woman that seems to only exist as a fetish in the minds of mediocre men in search of mail-order brides. A woman they can claim for themselves.

More stars dance on screen like shooting comets. Magdalena arches backward, collapsing her body onto the cement slab. She pretends to be a synchronized swimmer in a pool of dust, ruddying that silky slip, looking up to heaven. An audience of dead moths and gnats rumble under the quake of her acrylic nails grazing the concrete. Shattered veins, hollow husks, and dead bulbs.

Her hips angle up as she extends her legs, opening them just wide enough to leave room for her audience's imagination.

Incredible!

Show us more!

I'd like to see her on her knees again if you know what I mean.

The crowd loves her; sees her. She is a brazen light burning for them in the night. Alabaster skin so tight that purple veins bloom under her eyes like belladonna. Magdalena is a gothic fantasy in a rat king's dream. Starving for dark romance and confessional poetry.

She is no one, and somehow, she is everyone. Searching for love and affection in all the wrong places online while lonely in a cramped, damp space. A self-made crypt where hopes and dreams go to die. She moves below her linen sheet like a ghost, sauntering in the afterlife, whose groans manifest in the creaking floorboards above and the furnace here, below.

"Cry for me, baby." Her refrain, haunting and melodic, is the chorus to her performance. The dirge of rage and sorrow that draws them into her pit.

Her phone sounds like a slot machine in a casino, jingling coins and bubbly ringtones. They can't stick their dick in her, but they sure can type their credit card numbers into their phones quick enough. Let them get off on the idea that if they just send her one more favor, she'll show them her naughty pillows and spread her legs open for the world to see.

And maybe this time, she'll make enough money to leave the sleeping bastard upstairs who lost his job, again, thanks to his love for the bottle. She could move out of this shithole town, a place whose name these, presumably, American men cannot pronounce. Everything east of the Vltava River is Moscow, right?

A knife emoji pops up on the screen. The equivalent of 1,000 USD.

Jackpot, baby.

Magdalena reaches somewhere off-screen for a kitchen knife. She holds the handle firm and waves it around to show how the light scintillates off it. She glides her tongue slowly along all eight inches of the blade, making sure to bat her eyes for the camera. Her tongue circles the tip quickly and burns with a fresh cut. Blood clings to steel and dribbles down her wrist, staining that beautiful, crisp white slip.

Oh my god, I can't believe she cut her tongue.

She's so fucking hot.

Want me to lick that up for you, darling?

Another knife emoji appears, followed by more stars. Magdalena licks the knife again, running its length between the slit in her tongue. The open wound stings and continues to stain the negligee. Her voice is husky, and she spits blood at the screen. "Thank you, baby," she says between crimson-stained teeth.

While strangers jack off to a woman they'll never meet "IRL," Magdalena continues to slice up her tongue because that is what these men want; what they *really* want. Silence; *her* silence. But if they want her quiet, then she will make them work for it. She will make them pay.

"Cry for me, baby!" Her shouts are louder, raspy and distorted, as more stars explode on the screen and she gasps, thrusting her pelvis for them to see. Have they noticed how close she is to her climax? She tugs at the lace lining her slip and straddles the floor once more.

Scissors, knives, and stars continue to surge amid hundreds of comments. Magdalena is cutting furiously, carving up the tiny straps on her shoulders, the fabric on her thighs, and the lace across her chest—they want to see what's underneath, but don't they want to see *her*? *All* of her?

The chiming comments come faster and faster, a hypnotic chant as Magdalena loses herself in performance. She pants; the chemical high of endorphins releases in her brain. All eyes are on *her* now. The impulsive urge to show them just how bright she can gleam in the glow of the LED ring is more important now than her foolish fantasy

She plunges the knife into the soft space beneath her breasts and screams

"THANK YOU, BABY!"

Her voice is hoarse, but through her pain, she is smiling. Laughing, even. Salty black streams of mascara roll down her face. Her tears are briney, like a ship out at sea, lost in the roiling waves of a storm. This is what they want, isn't it? To take the helm? To take control over a woman like her?

What the fuck?

Is this real?

OMFG YES!!!

Through blood-spattered glass, Magdalena can see a slurry of words and emojis. Can hear the chimes rising in crescendo. So many comments. Requests to join her on camera pop up and, while tempting, she declines. Adrenaline courses through her veins, and the rush of terror scares her. Excites her. She knows that pain and pleasure are two sides of every blade.

She pulls the knife out of her chest in one swift movement and shows it off to her viewers. Her fans. Online lovers who lust for the destruction of a woman *à la petite mort.*

Magdalena ignores the gaping hole in her sternum. Doesn't feel the burning pain of muscles getting eviscerated strand by strand as she continues to stab the soft flesh where men would cup her, grab her if they could. She has dissociated her mind from her body. Lets the question of why she feels most alive at this moment float away, into the dark.

This is fucked, can someone call the police?

We don't even know where she is.

Love me some blood play!

"CRY FOR ME BABY," she rasps. Her lungs are punctured, filling with fluid. Magdalena knows she was made for this because women were born from violence. A precedent set by God himself when he first crafted Eve from Adam's rib. Their nature wrought into the bones of men forever.

The slip is soaked. No remnants of purity remain. The imprints of men's desires seep into cracks of concrete and pool at Magdalena's bruised knees. She is a delicious red apple brimming with forbidden truths that she will find buried somewhere inside of her.

Magdalena reaches a hand inside her chest cavity and squeezes something wet between her fingers. Inch by inch, her intestines unfurl out of her body and onto camera. Her audience count hemorrhages, but that's okay. Her *faithful* followers will stay with her right up until the end. Loyalty is the greatest reward.

Stars. Knives. Scissors. Kiss emojis for slaughter. Payment just to see how far Magdalena will go. Forever on the precipice of self-actualization in the eyes of men who think they own her. Control her. That she is somehow better than her Western counterpart because they believe she is submissive. Naturally beautiful and unruined by feminist ideology. How foolish can they be?

STOP! PLEASE STOP!
What the hell is she doing?
KEEP GOING!

Magdalena is desperate now. She digs and claws those dull acrylic nails across the inside of her rib cage. Her heart pumps faster, her fingers slick as they fish for somewhere to grip. The rib is *right* there, but how does she grab it? She has to find it before her song ends. The emojis on her screen mean nothing when she knows the real prize is attached to the cartilage on her sternum.

Magdalena's fingers stop and rest around something hard. She looks into the camera. Her pupils are dilated, and the capillaries burst. All viewers can see is a smattering of red, uncanny eyes and a forked tongue flicking against her lips, like that deceptive trickster in the Garden of Eden.

Magdalena has found it. Her truth. She begins to pull.

Ribs are some of the strongest bones in the human body, second to the femur. It takes immense pressure, or trauma, to crack them. Magdalena is strong, though. She will survive this trial long enough for them to see. She will reclaim what is rightfully hers.

"CRY FOR ME, BABY!"

Her viewers realize this is no longer a live stream filled with sultry requests for money. This is a command. A show of force, power, and will over the men who decided to cast their gaze over her distorted figure. They will witness her overcome this feat of strength; this reclamation, or she will die trying.

Magdalena's head is woozy. Her head pounds from blood loss. Sweat trickles down the nape of her neck, and every instinct in her wants to purge her insides out as a final act of self-preservation, but she knows she can do this. She must do this. These dying voyeurs will understand that they cannot, will not, own her. That no man can and that she knows her autonomy will never be given to her freely. She will have to take it back herself.

Bone splinters in her chest. The pain is blinding, but her knuckles and fingers emerge from the gristle and viscera with a curved bone in hand. Magdalena holds it up for no one, and everyone, to see.

This is what they wanted, isn't it? What they paid for in the end. *Violence contre les femmes.* Penance for what an angry god did to the first man, long ago.

She throws the fractured rib at the screen and falls to the floor, the unwanted debt of creation repaid.

LOUD bARk
SPINELESS READS
MARINO
PUNK goes HORROR II
2026 WORLD TOUR

LOUD BARK

L.C. MARINO

I REALIZED I HAD TO KILL NICK the first time I saw him in public with his family. It wasn't because of the condescending, knife-edge tone in his voice as he spoke to his wife, or the heavy disappointment in each word he spat at his children.

What soured my blood was the hunger in his narrowed eyes as he watched his daughter walk from their table to the restroom.

His wife's eyes tugged at the edge of my vision for the briefest moment. She had to have seen me seething, but she dropped her gaze to the overpriced meal scattered across her plate. I couldn't clearly read her pallid, downturned face but I felt exposed, like she'd seen me for more than a random woman at an adjacent table. Had she also seen the way Nick looked at their daughter? Had she recognized my disgust?

She must have.

Why wasn't she confronting him? I wondered if she cared enough to protect her child. Perhaps she was complicit in her silence, choosing to protect herself rather than to protect her child. A blush of simmering disgust and anger spread through my chest and neck.

Shrimp cocktail writhed in my stomach as I closed my

eyes, and the image of Nick lusting after his daughter materialized in the morphing colors behind my closed lids.

You son of a bitch.

He'd stared at me like that when I walked past his table in Devon's Lair the night we met. The grimy, cracked, floor-to-ceiling mirror along the back wall reflected his unblinking eyes, his jaw slacked by bottom-shelf liquor. He'd been completely unaware I was hunting, waiting for the right guy to say the wrong thing and to enter my snare. Which, naturally, he did.

Once I had him, I intended to treat him like the other rich men who'd come before him. Allow him to overspend his way into a high-end beachfront hotel while his family slept in their carbon-copy Long Island home. Allow him to assume he had control of our situation as he spent his kids' college funds to bankroll our arrangement. If he played his role wisely, he'd pay dearly for a senseless affair and live. If he caused problems, my anger would overtake my resolve like a storm surge breaching a quay wall. Then, I'd kill him and save his family from his recklessness, his perversions, his iniquities.

His wife would make panicked calls to the police when he didn't come home or answer her calls. As the days stretched into weeks and the guesswork failed to accumulate into meaningful leads, there may be a news conference, a public plea for information. But cold trails sap motivations and his file would join the other unsolved missing persons reports in due time. They'd never find his car, his phone, his wallet. His wife would console their children as she struggled to give them hope in empty promises.

"Daddy will be home soon."

"He loves you. He'd never leave you."

"They'll find him soon, baby. I promise."

But he wouldn't return home.
He'd never loved them enough.
They'd never find him.
And they'd all be better for it.

...

Mom was the first to traffic me. She broke my spirit in the alleyways between the bodegas and the payday loan shops which infect the rougher edges of Queens. We never stayed put, always on the move, drifting with the ebb and flow of men who frequented the area for girls. Mom protected me only when threats risked payment. Otherwise, she sold my innocence for drugs and money.

A lifelong victim, Mom's own mistreatment started in her infancy, much earlier than mine. But rather than protect me from the same fate, she'd thrust me into the chasm of abuse. Occasionally, when she felt especially vulnerable balancing on the precipice between consciousness and passing out, she'd thank me for doing what she was no longer willing to do—sustain us. While my teen heart craved her thanks, my festering, endless anger suspended my empathy like a hostage. I'd lean past her fluttering eyes and whisper into her waxy ear, "I'll never forgive you."

In fact, those were the last words I ever said to my mother. She overdosed shortly before I turned seventeen. I left her soiled, drug-ravaged body behind the Suds N' Savings laundromat, a worthless pile of refuse discarded alongside the rest of the block's trash. Her passing came at a fortuitous time because I'd finally outgrown my youthful frame and tipped fully into womanhood. At least, that's how Jazmine felt about me. Jaz was the first person I told about Mom's passing.

"Let that bitch go. Having a pimp as a mother was a damn

curse. You're a grown-ass woman now and you're too pretty for this bullshit. You see that, don't you?"

I had crushed my Camel Light on the chipped curb between us and exhaled a chest full of cigarette smoke through my nose. "What do you mean?"

Jaz grabbed my bare arm, startling me with her aggression. I turned to her, the late afternoon sun breaking the buildings into shadows spanning Roosevelt Avenue around us.

"You're gorgeous, girl. I can't move up, but you...you need to leave this shithole and get to the next level. I'm talking big money and a whole different game once you learn the ropes. I got a cousin who can help you, but you gotta work directly for him before you can fly solo. You down?"

Accepting her offer changed my life and ended so many others. But I wouldn't have it any other way.

...

I wore a dress for the first time in my life the night Jaz introduced me to her cousin, Javier. I found the sky-blue linen dress in a dusty thrift store on the edge of Jamaica, then changed in the car on our way to a restaurant near Howard Beach. We may as well have been dining in the Hamptons. I'd never been to the south side of the island, let alone to a fancy steakhouse. I was more nervous about conducting myself appropriately in an upscale restaurant than I was about the proposition of entering an entirely new phase of life. Javier did his best to take advantage of my unease.

"Jaz was right about you. You definitely fit the bill looks-wise. Trust me, we'll work on the rest."

Trust me.

"I'm not worried. And don't take this the wrong way, but

I don't trust nobody." I had kept my eyes on my plate as I hoisted garlic mashed potatoes and filet mignon into my mouth.

"*Anybody*. You don't trust anybody." Javier corrected me. "And that's a good thing." A smile tugged at the edge of his thin lips as his eyes swept the smooth contours of my exposed neckline. I didn't care if he watched me eat. I felt my jaw muscles protruding with each bite.

"Right. You get my point. So, how does this work?" I asked around a partially chewed hunk of medium-rare filet.

"Well, I'll coordinate meetings between you and clients. Everything comes through me, so you don't have to worry about finding work. Does that work for you?"

"Hell yeah. That sounds wonderful." I replied.

"Good. Occasionally, I'll ask you to ride the trains between the city and Long Island. The commuter routes are packed with miserable businessmen dying for a change of pace. But my network of referrals should hold us over for now."

"So, these are people who know what services you provide?" I asked.

"Yes. But more accurately, they are rich men who know what services you provide, and they come through me to get them. I vet them, you serve them. I take a cut; you get the rest. Rinse and repeat. You good with that?"

I looked up from my plate to see Jaz leaning toward Javier in anticipation of my response. The busy restaurant buzzed around us, but the patrons seemed miles from our table, living in another world, an entirely separate reality. They likely discussed their mundane work week and life-sucking commutes, never considering their complicity. They *chose* to live like lemmings, wasting their time to enrich their mammoth corporations before plunging from the cliffs when they'd aged out of usefulness. They chased dollars, then pissed them away. I wanted their money so I could *live* for once.

"I'm in. When do we start?" I took a large swig from my glass of water and set it down as Jaz turned toward Javier. He nodded and she said, "Tonight."

Two hours later, Javier and I slept together for the first and last time. I suppose I shouldn't have been surprised that he was like most men, craving a fix for himself before thinking of others. He was gentle with me at first, but gradually grew distant and mechanical. In his eyes, I found the same sadness I'd always seen in the eyes of cheating men. Was he thinking of his wife? Or was he as far from her as he could get? Poor, rich, old, young— they all carry the weight of their sins in their eyes.

And they all regret me the moment they're done with me.

...

Nick was a textbook client at first. Our relationship started as a mutually beneficial arrangement. I had what he wanted, and he had what I wanted. But it wasn't long before I realized he was a whole other level of rich, a corporate monster who wasn't content with having the best car, the massive mansion on the Island, or the trophy wife and 2.5 kids. He craved more. There were no limits, no end.

Never one for common street drugs, Nick preferred ketamine. I'd heard of that shit on the streets, but never seen it for myself. It's a rich person's drug, an elixir for overachievers, not your common junkie. At least, that's what I'd always assumed. In the end, it's all the same, I suppose. A way to elevate, to escape. None of it appealed to me. I preferred sobriety over an alleyway death, unlike Mom. I needed to stay sharp like a syringe to maintain my control over the people using me. The downside of being sober lies in feeling everything, never escaping the easy way. I hide from my maltreatment the hard way, through a broken mind, as I always have. Not Nick. He geared up.

A textbook narcissist, he donned the armor of grossly contradicted and misleading religion. Nick often spoke of how God chose men like him above others. His divinely gifted fortune emboldened him to perform beyond the rules of men. What other explanation could there be for his exceptionally rare financial success? He'd grown his software company into a tech juggernaut, one of the first players in the race for data center dominance in the northeast. He saw his success as evidence of divine protection.

Because of his complex, Nick incorrectly believed he had all the power in our relationship. I was merely there for his pleasure. But realistically, I always held the power. I was willing to go farther than he ever would. I was willing to kill. At least I thought I was.

That night in the restaurant, when I saw him lusting after his preteen daughter, I realized *I* was the one with a higher purpose. I'd kill Nick for everyone he'd mistreated, for his neglected family, for every coworker or employee he'd wronged. I'd kill him for all of them. He couldn't fathom how much people hated men like him.

I spent a week debating whether I should go through with Nick's murder or if I should cut him off and enjoy my lavish lifestyle with the safe guys, the ones who willingly paid to obey my rules. By all rights, I had it pretty good.

But you can't cut a guy like Nick off. Guys like him do the cutting. You either roll with them or you don't, but it's their call, not yours.

PUNK GOES HORROR II

It was inevitable. Nick would be my first victim. Rather than avoiding him and finding someone less problematic, *I chose him*. I wanted to explore how far I was willing to go. There was safety in working with the higher end guys. Most of them sought a premium experience in their infidelity—something cleaner, safer, a little closer to normal than a random hooker on the streets could offer. I wanted to see how far I could take him before I killed him. How much would he spend? How long could he last in my process before he became too aggressive, got too bold and grew violent. Some of these guys weren't violent, they just had kinks. They wanted something weird or different than what their spouse was willing to do. I could give them an experience my domestic counterpart would never match.

But not Nick. He wanted more. He wanted to hurt women, to violate their trust and dominate their fears. Nick craved violence. Unfortunately for him, he'd met a woman who's hunger for violence exceeded his own.

...

I'd gone over my plan of attack a hundred times that week. I needed my first kill to be clean, untraceable, a potential accident. Nick needed to die and I needed to disappear without interrogation, so our usual hotel rendezvous was out of the question. But Nick wouldn't comply with my request to spend the night on his boat, insisting instead that we rent a beach house for the weekend.

We drove separately to the Hamptons on a Saturday afternoon. I never entered the home's interior, opting instead to wait for him on the back deck overlooking the Atlantic's steady, unrelenting assault on the dunes from a lounge chair. After an hour, I heard the back door slide open behind me, followed by the hard soles of Nick's boots thundering across the composite planks. I turned to greet him and my breath caught in my throat.

Nick's wife stood where I expected to find him. She wore sporty black cargo pants and a fitted black t-shirt. Spirals of errant chocolate curls spilled from a messy bun, pinned to her head like a crown. I must have looked simultaneously mortified and overwhelmed. Angela seemed completely at ease as she extended her hand to greet me.

"Hi. We haven't met yet. I'm Angela."

I struggled out of the lounge chair as I clambered to my feet, unsure whether to prepare for a fight or a cordial meeting.

"I'm sorry. I wasn't expecting you," I said, surprised by my own honesty.

"Right. Well, no worries. He's waiting in the car. But we need to have a girl's talk before we head in to see him."

"I don't understand." I eyed my escape route down the deck stairs ten feet to my right.

Angela smiled, her beauty compounding with the gentle spread of her lush lips.

"That's completely legit. Let me start over." She stepped closer, extending her hand again. "Hi. I'm Angela. I'm here to help you get rid of my husband."

My legs turned to numb stilts beneath me, and the ocean breeze threatened to blow me over. Angela grasped my limp, partially extended right hand. When had I offered her my hand? My mind spun. Angela gripped my hand in both of hers and continued.

"I know who you are. I've known for months. I was upset at first. Furious, to be honest. But I know he's not your fault. Nick's always been this way. But I can't allow him to...*be*... anymore, if you catch my drift. And you're going to help me *un-be* him." Angela's smile faltered.

"I'm so sorry." My words seemed impossible to find.

"You did nothing wrong. And it doesn't really matter anymore. What matters is that he's gotta go and you're gonna help me get rid of him."

I stepped toward the stairs, my eyes staying with Angela's as my instincts willed me toward flight. Angela stepped with me. She reached for my arm, but my defensive posture and narrowing brows must have caused her concern.

"You can't leave. I need you."

"I'm outta here, lady." I moved like a gust of wind towards the stairs.

"He hurt our daughter." Angela's desperate voice cut the day in half.

I froze on the top step, my fingers digging into the flat wooden handrails flanking my sides. I turned to face Angela and found a rage in her quivering face far exceeding my own.

"You know what I mean. I want him gone. And I know you do, too. I saw how you looked at him in the restaurant last week. Help us. Please."

I can't explain how I suddenly felt conjoined with Angela. Something wholly primal welled in me like a mushroom cloud, expanding, filling my entire being, urging me to action. Angela was a mother protecting her child, someone I needed when I was defenseless. I closed my eyes and squeezed them tight against the memories of men's shadows working above me in dark alleys while my mom turned away from me to count her money.

"Where is he?" I asked through teeth clenched so tight my jaw went numb.

"In the trunk."

...

We worked without speaking, the closed garage door sheltering us from the driveway winding between the dunes. Nick's desire for a secret getaway paid off. We had the entire beach to ourselves. No neighbors for miles.

I'm not sure how Angela got him into that trunk, but I didn't ask. I decided to keep things simple. I rolled him out of the trunk onto a plastic tarp and stood over him as he hyperventilated around a red shop rag that had been duct taped into his mouth. Angela stood beside me, towering over his quaking form. His eyes jumped between our faces, bulging orbs of disbelief and unbridled fear.

"We know what you did," Angela said, her voice twisting as a sob overwhelmed her. "I can't believe you hurt our baby girl." Angela held her tongue as anger overwhelmed her features, twisting her face into a quivering knot. "You deserve every ounce of pain you're about to feel and more, you sick fuck. You ride that misery all the way to hell."

Nick tried to argue through the gag but Angela cut his protest short by stomping his head into the concrete floor. A whimper slipped from his throat as blood pooled beneath his skull on the ocean blue tarp. Angel regained her balance and composure.

"I'll never forgive you." She spit a web of phlegm into his upturned eyes.

I placed my hand on her shoulder for support and drew my knife with the other. I never considered driving the blade into her.

I kneeled beside Nick, my hand shaking as adrenaline pulsed through my muscles. A metallic, primal scent of pheromones rolled from his body for me to consume. His fear excited me.

"Look at me."

He did.

"This is for all of us."

...

I quartered Nick's body on the beach as the sun set over a magnificently calm ocean. When I finished, I tossed his limbs into a rock-ringed fire pit amongst the dunes and let the flames work their way through him. Hours later, when only bone and ash remained, I strolled to the house and invited Angela to join me. We sipped tea in silence, warmed by glowing firewood and bone as the moon climbed the sable night sky.

"Nick listed you in his work phone as WM. May I ask your name?"

"It's probably best you don't," I said, probing the sand with a broken cat's tail stalk. "Don't take this the wrong way, but I don't ever want to see you again."

...

At some point in the night, I scooped Nick's ashes into a thin metal planter we'd found collecting wind-tossed sand and moonlight on the back porch. Angela left and I spent the rest of the evening tossing Nick's ashes into the sea under Mother Moon's star-clustered dome.

When his ashes ran low, I tossed the planter into the sea, watching it bob on the mirrored surface as I stared up into the night sky. Perhaps my mother was out there somewhere, watching over me. I rarely thought about her anymore, but in that moment, I needed her to hear me.

"I'll never forgive you."

I never spoke to her again.

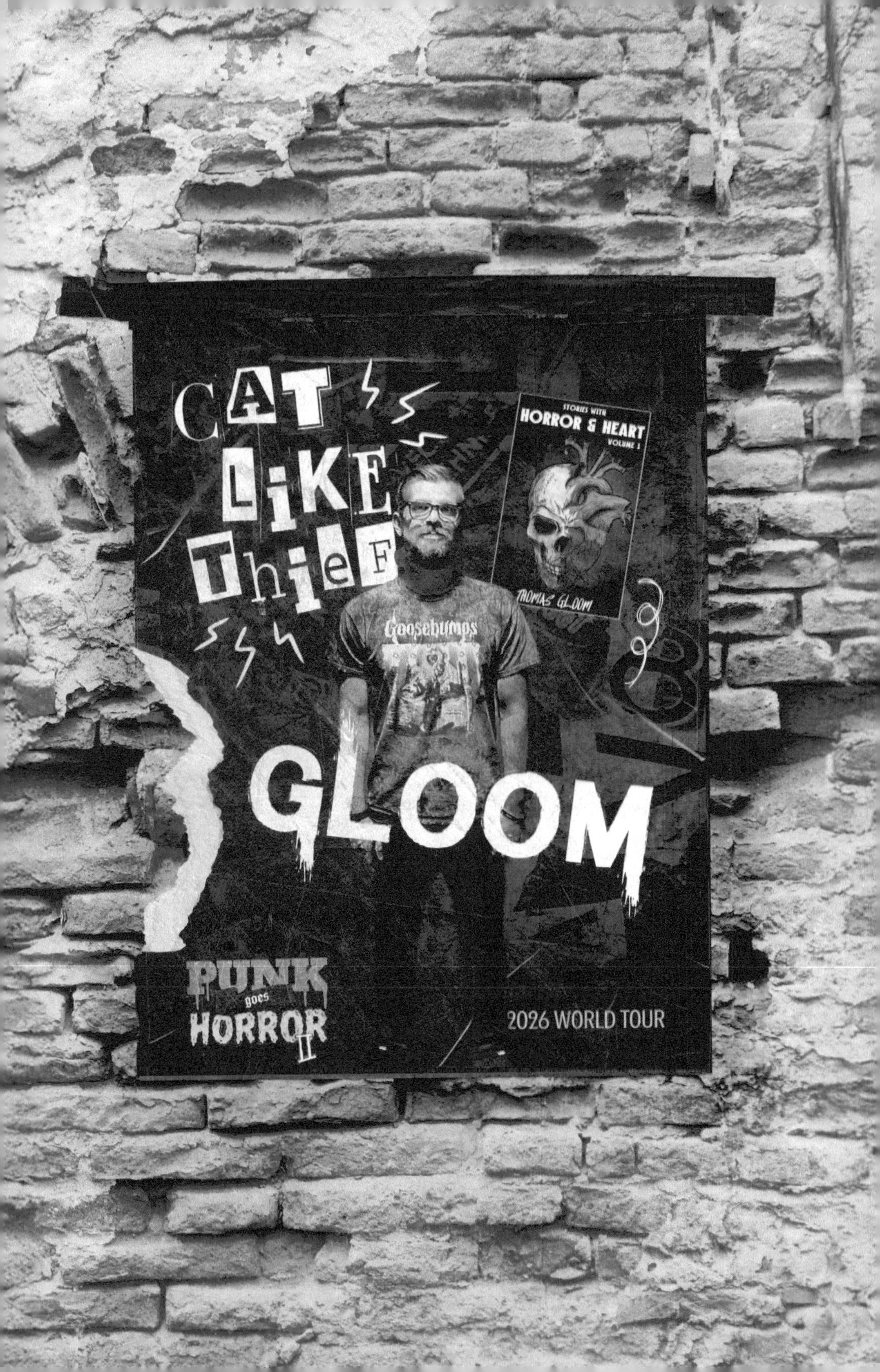

CAT LiKE ThieF
STORIES WITH
HORROR & HEART
VOLUME 1
THOMAS' GLOOM
Goosebumps
GLOOM
PUNK goes HORROR II
2026 WORLD TOUR

CAT LIKE THIEF

THOMAS GLOOM

NATE BUSTED INTO THE BLACK WIRE'S dingy bathroom, fell to his knees, and puked his guts into the urinal. The vomit shot into the ceramic bowl, splashing stale urine back into his face.

He'd never been one to spiral after a relationship ended, but this last girl, Mary, had done a number on him. Drinking had never been his scene, but from the day she broke it off with him he'd been on quite the alcohol and drug infused bender. It couldn't last much longer, could it?

Hoisting himself into a standing position, Nate opened his eyes wide in the hopes that the room would slow its spin. The lone light above the mirror and sink flickered as if holding on to its last gasp of life. Nate staggered to the sink, turned the cold lever, then splashed water on his face. A proper shower would be needed when he got home, but this would have to do for now. Too disgusted to look at his reflection, he scanned the walls above and around the mirror. They were covered in layers upon layers of graffiti and bright band stickers. Amongst the scattering of color, a bit of black caught his eye. Something was wedged between the mirror and the wall. Nate reached his hand out and then chuckled.

PUNK GOES HORROR II

In this grungy underground punk scene, which he'd been a part of for two decades, zines were all the rage. When creative people fell into this scene, they tended to do one of two things; they either joined a band or they created a zine to showcase their drawing, photography, or writing abilities.

It had been his freshman year in high school when Nate had attended his first punk show. The music scene in Birmingham, Alabama was finding its stride and a small downtown venue was hosting all-ages shows a few times a week (with most falling on the weekends, since their main audience had been high school teens). Nate was drawn to Cave 9 on that particular Friday evening not for the music, not for the environment, and not because he'd received an invitation from a friend. No, he'd gone to his first show because he knew Katie would be there. She was short, wore high-top Chuck Taylors, and had a constant "fuck off" attitude. To say he was infatuated would be an understatement. He sat directly behind her in English class, but hadn't said a word.

He'd spent weeks rehearsing the coolest lines he could come up with, but never let any of them escape the fortress of his mind. He knew they weren't *actually* cool. Katie would see right through them. On and on the arguments went in his head. By the fourth week of school, he wasn't sure if he'd learned anything about grammar, because he was too focused on fantasizing about Katie.

One day Katie leaned over to the girl beside her and mentioned an upcoming show at Cave 9. Nate decided right then and there that he'd figure out some way to arrive at the venue, shed his loser veneer, and sweep the girl of his dreams off her feet.

He did no such thing.

Nate *did* find a way to get to downtown Birmingham (he

lied to his mom and said he was attending a Pokémon card game tournament at a card shop two blocks away). He *did* pay the $5 cover charge to get through the doors (money his mom gave him for vending machine snacks). He *did not* talk to Katie (though he spent plenty of time staring at her from across the dirty, cold cement floor in front of the elevated platform stage). Yet despite the flop with Katie, something else happened that night.

By the time the last band took the stage, Nate had fallen madly in love with the punk music scene.

In those early days, it was as if each show he attended became building blocks to his new identity and purpose. Within months, he was no longer the shy, awkward, nerdy kid who couldn't help but trip over his own fears and anxieties. That Nate was dumped into a six-foot hole, and each strum of an electric guitar, each crash of a dented symbol, each bruising circle pit he entered was like another shovelful of dirt being dumped on top of his old self. Before long, the person he used to be was buried and forgotten. The new Nate was brash, confident, and rough as hell around the edges. At first. But as the years ticked by, these changes that had once given him so much vitality, began to suck the soul right out of him. Broken bones, broken promises, and broken relationships got scattered all along the path which had brought him to the place he now found himself... beaten, exhausted, and plagued with regret as he fought not to make eyes with his reflection in a disgusting dive bar bathroom.

Yet the zine in his hands made him smile. It represented creative possibilities, and fuck if he couldn't use the reminder that it was never too late for a reinvention. Nate stared down at the nondescript cover with its hand sketched artwork of skulls and stars. The title in bold, blocky letters read: SIXTEEN CHAPTERS. He turned it over and found nothing but a black back cover. The zine was definitely homemade, bound with staples and held together from much use with scotch tape.

Either this thing had been flipped through hundreds of times or it had ridden around in someone's messy trunk for years as they drove like some speed demon with nothing to lose, but everywhere to be.

He turned to the first page and was surprised to find mostly words. Judging by the cover, Nate assumed the zine would be a promo for doodles or photography, not writing. He skimmed the first few sentences and found what was clearly fiction. The words unveiled a gnarly and brutal scene, dripping with violence and gore.

Behind him, the bathroom door swung open and another drunk bar patron stumbled into the stall which Nate had just emptied his stomach contents into, then slammed it shut. Not wanting to hang around for whatever noises and odors would soon mix with the unpleasant environment already hanging thick in the room, Nate shoved the zine into the back pocket of his jeans and headed back out into the bar. Head down, he pushed through the crowd and toward the exit. He paused to take one more look back into the bar, stepped out into the night air, and bumped right into someone.

"Watch yourself, asshole," came the gruff response.

"You've got eyes too, prick," Nate said without hesitation.

The two men met eyes and laughed in recognition.

"Nate, I should've known. You live in your head more than in the real world, and one of these days it's gonna get you hurt. I was about to punch your lights out."

"You would try, Joker. And while I'd love to stick around to prove you wrong, I've gotta get home."

Joker laughed. "Home before midnight? You're going soft

in your old age."

"I've got better things to do then drink and fight with you," Nate said with a wink.

"Like that hasn't been your entire existence for the last few weeks." Joker shoved past him and melted into the crowd. As the bar door closed behind him, Nate didn't realize that was the last time he was ever going to see Joker.

...

Nate sank into the ratty old sofa he used as a bed and opened back to that first page of the zine. His forehead scrunched as he read, and the story left a strange feeling in the pit of his stomach. The tale recounted the sadistic murder of a man who eerily reminded him of Joker. Same dyed hair, same tattered clothing, same sarcastic attitude. The fictional character got into a heated, drunken argument with the wrong person and then wound-up dead in an alley outside a bar. The descriptions of the murder were a bit too visceral for his liking. What the page lacked in word count was made up for in the gory details of the victim's eyes being popped like rotten grapes by the thumbs of his attacker. He was stabbed over twenty times with a dull, rusty blade that sawed jaggedly through flesh instead of cleanly puncturing it. Nate tossed the zine on the floor, turned on the TV, then rolled over in the hopes that sleep would take him and quash the mid-level anxiety that was buzzing through his body.

...

Nate was awakened by the buzzing of his cell phone. It was a text from his friend Daniel (one of the few people still in his life who had known Nate before that first punk show), which included a link to a local news site. Nate clicked it, hoping the uneasy feeling tugging at his mind was simply the cobwebs of his drunken night.

Someone had been murdered outside The Black Wire. According to the article, the killing had occurred not too long after Nate headed home. In fact, it was probably close to the time he was drifting off to sleep. He shuddered. It's strange how close people can be to death without ever recognizing it in the moment. But the bar was infamous for weird and wacky happenings. One time, a woman had even given birth in front of the bar. She'd come in with her lush of a partner, and before he'd even finished his first drink she went into labor right there on the sticky cement floor. Later that same night, a guy who was showing off for some buddies opened a beer bottle with his teeth, but at his level of intoxication instead of spitting it out he accidentally swallowed it. He gagged and wretched, but it must've been wedged in there extra tight. Most people just thought he was acting like a drunken fool, which was characteristic for the guy, so nobody stepped in to help him. By the time folks picked up on the fact that this wasn't an act, he was motionless in the fetal position, turning blue. He died right there on the same floor the baby had been born on. The bar gave life, and took it away. But as far as Nate could recall, this was the first murder. The news report didn't list any names and stated that the investigation was ongoing.

Nate and Daniel texted back and forth, deciding to meet up at Waffle House. By the time Nate slid into the cushion-less booth, anxiety had, once again, taken a full-throated hold on his day. Daniel arrived a few minutes later, and they ordered their food.

"It was Joker," Daniel said as soon as the waitress stepped

away from the table.

"Huh?"

"Joker was the one killed in the alley."

"Bullshit," Nate said. "How do you know that?"

"I talked to Milton." Milton worked behind the bar of The Black Wire. "You know he's always got juicy details about all the wacky shit that happens there."

Daniel continued. "Milton said he didn't see any of it go down, but he talked to a handful of people that did. Joker was arguing with a guy over in the corner near the pool tables. But you know how Joker is, so nobody really thought much about it. There were a few shoves, but then the yelling died down so people went back to whatever they were doing before the excitement. A couple of minutes later, the two of them headed out the door and that was the last anyone saw of Joker alive. Milton also heard that Joker had been stabbed an excessive amount of times, and that his eyes had been gouged out."

Nate shuddered as the images and descriptions from the zine staggered like the undead through his exhausted mind. "Who was the other guy?"

"That's the other weird thing," Daniel said. His eyes shifted from side to side as if making sure that none of the other diner patrons were eavesdropping. "Nobody got a clear view of the guy. Most of the people interviewed just said that the guy was 'dark' or 'shadowy.' Whatever the fuck that means."

Nate didn't say much else to Daniel after that. Daniel rattled on like he always did, but Nate was deep in his own thoughts. This had to be more than a coincidence, right? But even if the story he'd read had predicted the future (or maybe even caused it), there was no way to prove it. Thus, he left the Waffle House without mentioning it to Daniel. Nate needed to read the next few chapters of the zine to be sure. He'd skimmed ahead. Seen that there were only sixteen chapters, as the title suggested. That wasn't too many, right?

...

The next few chapters were just as strange and unnerving as the first had been. The pages were full of death and destruction, all befalling characters who resembled people from Nate's life. In chapter 2, a guy who looked like Sean, a regular at The Black Wire, was run over by a speeding car right outside of the bar. In chapter 3, a man missing an arm, just like the owner of the corner store down the street, was shot behind his register as other customers watched on in horror. But it was the contents of chapter 4 that really got Nate's attention. And not just the attention of his mind, but his body too. He threw the zine down onto the couch and ran out the door.

Speeding down the road in his clunker of a car, Nate couldn't stop hyperventilating. The horrific images from each chapter were seared into his mind's eye as if placed there by a glowing red cattle prod. And if they were prophetic, then he had to do something to try and divert whatever Final Destination bullshit was at play.

Pulling into the lot, Nate parked his car, then ran toward the apartment building his ex, Mary, lived in. He banged on her door like a madman, knowing he should stay calm, but not being able to follow through.

After a few seconds, the door opened and there she stood—the Siren who'd shattered his heart. Seeing her face, even as it was sketched in anger, had a sobering effect on Nate.

He shouldn't have come back to her, and he immediately his impulsive decision.

"What the *fuck*, Nate?"

"Are you okay?" was all he managed to get out.

"Besides the fact that my ex, who I *specifically* told to give me some space, is banging on my door, unannounced and unhinged? I'm fine. Studying for exams. Please leave."

"I just," Nate stammered. "I was worried about you."

"Worry about yourself. You look like shit." And with those last words, she slammed the door.

Nate stood there debating with himself. He wanted to respect her boundaries, yet he knew he hadn't been able to make himself clear. Her life was in danger and he didn't want to leave her. He never wanted to leave her. Yet, no matter how long he stood there muttering—*don't leave her, don't leave her, don't leave her*—she wasn't opening that door again.

The drive home was long and cumbersome. Nate felt trapped inside of his head, and what he found there was insanity. What was the word Mary had used? *Unhinged.* It was the perfect description for his current state.

Had he got this all wrong? Was the murder of Joker all just a coincidence, as opposed to some strange dark magic tied to an old, crusty zine? Mary had been a special kind of weakness for him, and the thought of her in danger had sent him into a tizzy. His pounding head (most likely a side effect of it being the first day in weeks that he hadn't rolled off the couch and into the bottle to start the day) was contributing to his irrational behavior. He'd already begun to recognize the shitstorm his life had become before finding the zine, but it was crumbling even faster after reading the damned thing.

In Chapter Four, a young woman who looked strikingly

similar to Mary had died of smoke inhalation in her small apartment. Mary was a chain-smoker. Her tossing a cigarette into a trashcan without recognizing the cherry was still alive and burning was well within the realm of possibility. He saw it all so clearly... not just on the page of the zine, but in his overactive imagination.

Nate was less than a mile away from his shitty studio apartment and a crushing headache was pounding within his skull. He needed some beer, but the bank app on his phone reminded him it needed to be cheap. Good ole PBR should get the job done. Pulling into a parking spot in front of the 24-hour corner store he frequented for such missions, his heart sank as a flash of bright yellow fluttered across his path of vision. *Chapter Three. The dead corner store owner.* The greasy contents of breakfast threatened to travel from his stomach to his car's windshield.

A strip of loose-hanging crime scene tape acted as a barrier between the store's entrance and the sidewalk. In an act that had become frequent since Mary put an end to their relationship, tears filled Nate's eyes. The walls of his nothing-supernatural-ever-happens world were no longer just crumbling; the artificial facade had been blown to smithereens. He sat in the parked car, white-knuckling the steering wheel until the joints in his fingers screamed from the strain. At some point, without Nate's conscious awareness, the screaming went from his knuckles to his vocal cords. Something in him snapped. It was as if the door in his psyche labeled FEAR had been broken down by another four-letter word...

...

"Rage!" Nate yelled into the phone. He was back at his shitty studio apartment. The first thing he'd done when he walked in was grab the zine and toss it across the room. The second thing he did was call Daniel. "I was so scared this morning. That's why I didn't mention any of this to you at Waffle House. But now I'm just angry. There's gotta be a way to put a stop to this, and I'm gonna find it!"

He gave Daniel the whole rundown from finding the zine, to the eerie images inside, and finally to its seemingly prophetic powers.

Daniel had floated in and out of various music scenes through the years, caring less about the bands and more about the ladies who attended shows. Over the past two decades, he'd dated women with all kinds of interests. He'd sat in Ouija board circles, received tarot card readings, and even attended a couple of séances. The sex magic gals had been his personal favorite, but Nate honestly thought Daniel was willing to put up with just about anything if the bedroom vibes were stellar. He wasn't picky, but he also didn't believe in any of the supernatural mumbo jumbo, and he'd always made that abundantly clear to Nate each time he'd rattled off his latest sexcapade.

"I'm gonna burn the damned thing," Nate said.

"That's a good idea."

It was *not* a good idea.

...

Nate found out quickly that he couldn't tear, cut, or shred the zine. He dowsed it in lighter fluid, tossed it into an aluminum trashcan, and dropped a match inside. Nothing. The fire did flare up, but once it burned through the lighter fluid, the flames subsided and left the zine behind, seemingly unscathed.

In the midst of his attempted assaults on the cursed object, he received a text from Mary. She asked that he not respond to her, but wanted him to hear from her before he heard it from someone else. She'd dozed off with a lit cigarette in her hand not long after he'd left her place earlier. It fell from her fingers and set a rug on fire. She'd awoken to a choking cloud of smoke, but had managed to douse the flames and had aired the place out before the fire department had even arrived.

According to the zine, she was supposed to have died in that fire. Had Nate's arrival and knocking on her door thrown off the event somehow? Nate couldn't destroy the zine itself, but it seemed that he could at least alter its intentions. So that's what he planned to do.

Throughout the years, people had often asked Nate what the best show he'd ever been to was. And no matter how many times that question was dropped on him, he'd always stammered. A single answer had alluded him, because how is something like that even measured? When it came to his personal preferences of punk or hardcore, the music may have been the glue that held the scene together, but there were so many other pieces that formed the true image. He remembered the people in the pit or on the stage. He remembered the drugs and the alcohol (or in some instances, like those early straight-edge days at Cave 9, the lack thereof). He remembered the cuts and bruises from errant fists and elbows. But most of all, he remembered the attitude. The anti-establishment, "fuck you, I won't do what you tell me" mentality was the thing that had called most directly to Nate.

This zine wanted him to give up and give in. It was hoping that Nate would roll over and take whatever was to unfold based on the words and images within its musty pages. But that wasn't going to happen. He'd skipped ahead to the last chapter. It had depicted him, a shattered and empty shell of a man after all that had transpired through the previous fifteen chapters. It also depicted him replacing the zine behind the mirror in The Black Wire bathroom for the next unsuspecting sucker to find. Fuck that. Control was what the zine wanted, and so Nate was going to take it back.

...

The years ticked by with increasing rapidity, yet Nate never gave in to that constant pull to grow up, act his age, or leave the scene like the majority of his friends. Being the last man standing was a badge of honor he wore with pride, and maybe even a bit of obstinance. Seen as a pillar in the local punk community, he did what he could to introduce wide-eyed newbies to the raucous noise of both the past and present.

In a shocking turn, about a decade back, The Black Wire closed its doors only to open them again a few months later as the newest music venue in town, all while retaining its original name. The bathroom remained dingy, but no longer did any cursed objects lie in wait behind the mirror.

The zine remained in Nate's possession and he read it through once each year. The cover always stayed the same, but the chapters changed with each read-through, bringing new horrific premonitions in the form of words and images. Nate's body became covered in burns, scars, and other painful reminders of battles waged against the curse to keep its stories from becoming realities. And he'd keep up the defiance until his last breath. The zine had desired to steal the air from his lungs, but it had failed. Instead, Nate found new reasons to keep on fighting.

And now, flipping through the ragged pages, he knew he'd find sixteen more.

i'M shiPPiNG TO BosTON
NerdyWordsmith
PUNK goes HORROR II
2026 WORLD TOUR

I'M SHIPPING UP TO BOSTON

SPENCER HAMILTON

D O THE GODS GAZE UPON MY return to the Olde Towne tonight? Are they huddled together in their teeming masses and shivering at my shaved skull, the *No Control* tee, my one motorcycle boot kicked on the dash of our van as we climb the ventricles of Boston's heart?

They fuckin' should be.

The rest of the band aren't talking to me. Took them twelve stops on this tour to figure out I have nothing to say to them. My throat wouldn't come unstuck anyway; it feels coated in wet cement mixed with molasses, cloying and bittersweet, but that's all right—bitter is my kind of sweet.

Bitter returns. Bitter crowds. Bitter chronic pain, pulsing hotly where my foot once was, the left one, like a mocking bassline.

We chose Boston as our last stop because our show here last year had been really the only time we felt like we'd *found* something. Something ugly and mean and sweaty from doing what punk does—swelling the house floor with a wave of connected, collective rage. Everybody in the place had slammed into the others to kickstart the heart of this thing. Music, escape, rebellion, call it what you want. We'd finished that set, stood breathing down at all those screaming faces, and we all looked at each other and, still on that punk frequency, we'd all thought: *Maybe we can do this thing after all.* And then: *None of us ever doubted we could.*

We *had* all doubted it, of course. Before that show, I'd already planned to leave. Get my cash from our percentage of the door, tell Jonah to fuck himself with a chainsaw, spare the others a middle finger or two, and leave the scene forever.

But then that Boston show, in a refurbished stone cathedral, had pulled me back in. And then . . . well, suffice to say, I'm coming back to settle a score. If I have to, I'll climb into the maw of The Thing That Blood Bleeds herself and take back what's mine.

...

The venue is one big Gothic spike, piercing the veil and holding this beautiful city together just for us. Its ceiling soars miles above the lights rig; I can't see past the unblinking eye of the spotlight. Below the stage, the crowd swells. It's a *sea* of punks, churning at my feet, ready to part if I command it. The mosh pit opens up not even two verses into our opener, and with every song it grows and grows, a maelstrom. A blood-red, beer-and-piss-smelling mist hangs above the moshers, and tonight is the greatest night of every single kid's life in this unholy place.

My teeth clack into the metal mesh of the mic as I scream—

"ALL YOU FUCKS TAKING ALL THE LUCK!"

—and somehow, cutting through the blaring amps that vibrate my bones, through the reverb of my own voice bouncing off these black, stone walls, I hear the crowd scream back—

"FUCK YOUR LUCK, I'LL TAKE THE PAIN!"

—and I can't help this idiot grin, none of us can. I remember, we all do, that this band used to be a *family*, joined together by the love of the music, and what the hell happened to us anyway? So we didn't score a multi-million-dollar record deal? Nothing we've put out there's gone platinum, there's been no massive world tour to fund a drug habit so prolific that we sear our name into the punk rock mythos? So fucking what.

Just as I share this moment with the band, about halfway through our set, my left leg twinges, and it all comes rushing back.

"So fucking what"? that phantom limb says. *That's not what you said to that priest last time, and that's definitely not what that priest said to you. He said exactly the fuck what. And when he knew he had you, he said exactly the fuck how. You followed along, and now you've got this titanium peg and nothing to show for it and—*

"MY WORK CARVED IN THIS SKIN, BUT YOU PRAY TO HIM?!"

The crowd, like all the best ones, *feels* my sudden rage, tastes the bitter hate, and works itself into a frenzy. The moshers roar full-throated, eyes rolling like spooked horses, and they throw more red on the splash zone. I can feel my bandmates' gazes on me, but I ignore them now. Fuck them. Fuck family. All I need is myself, my crowd, and what's owed to me.

One way or another, it ends tonight.

...

"I've never seen anything like it, man."

"Goddamn, bro, did we step through the time-wall or some shit?"

"Every. Single. Song. Crowd loved us."

"Band vote that we move to Boston, like, yesterday?"

We were moments removed from the encore of that first Boston show. The rest of the band was living on that third rail, feeling the electricity of a once-in-a-lifetime set. I was feeling it too, of course, but as I followed them out of the green room to the tour van, I could already feel myself retreating to the chalkboard in the back of my mind that read, in spiky, hungry letters, *HOW DO I GET MORE?!* The others could see it on my face, no doubt—spending weeks at a time crammed into a rank van together will do that, you just learn each other's tells—and I could already feel their disappointment that I couldn't just live in the rush with them. My lead-singer resentment flared up, and I stopped hurrying to follow them into the rain. They sure didn't wait up.

And in my mind. Scribbling.

HOW DO I GET MORE?!

"A rapturous performance tonight, my son . . ."

The voice was so close I felt it on the nape of my neck. I whipped around, but all that stared back was the black throat of the backstage exit tunnel. The heavy metal exit door slammed shut behind Baldy Q, the last of the band, and I was alone.

"Someone there . . . ?" My throat closed around the question mark, and a sudden bitterness flooded my mouth. I barely suppressed a gag.

Nothing answered.

"Who said that?" I racked my brain for the name of this place's stage manager. Connor? Kyle? K-something, maybe. "We good to go, yeah?"

A voice definitely responded to this, but it was so faint. I spared a glance back at the exit, a last thought spared for my bandmates, then retraced my steps down the back tunnel.

The green room was even smaller than what we expected from these places. The apse, or whatever the Catholics called it, no more than a glorified closet really. And it was empty, just as we'd left it: a small, sagging sofa and stone walls covered in decades of overlapping band posters like the MISSING pin-ups of a ghost town.

And that voice, past the apse: ". . . my son . . ."

I was committed now. Fuck the others. That blackboard scribbling in my head needed to be fed some chalk. I kept going, through the green room, up some tight, uneven stone steps, until I came out onto the stage proper, looking out at an empty theater.

The rig of lights was dark but still emanating heat. The rest of the space, to my surprise, now glowed from countless minuscule flickering flames. Candles populated every available spot on the floor and wall, waxy sandcastle towers melted into the stone like toadstools. Center stage, they gave way to a circle of clear space, upon which someone had drawn an unfamiliar symbol with neon-orange gaffer's tape: a cross between a pentagram and the Evil Eye.

"Join me, son. For a word."

Standing on the pupil of the eye was, I couldn't believe it, almost laughed: a God's-honest Catholic priest.

"You might be a bit lost, Father," I said, and realized it was the first time I'd actually spoken to a quote-unquote "authority figure" from any church.

"I am neither lost nor found, Fritz."

This made me smile, and I picked my way over to him through the landmine of candles. Our insurance claim definitely wouldn't cover burning the place down. "You know my name. You catch our show? I wouldn't have pegged you as a punk head."

The priest smiled in return, and here was my first sign of

danger: beneath cracked lips his teeth were rotten, crooked; the ones he still had jutted from gray, bleeding gums. I looked closer at the man as I stepped into the circle with him. His head was shaved, and the robes that I'd at first taken as typical Catholic fashion were actually black strips of gauze, loosely wrapped around his skeletal figure and hanging like curtains.

"Who are you? And, um . . . excuse the language, but what the hell is all of this?"

"Ignore the candles. Nothing but ceremonial trappings. But pay attention to my words. Listen carefully, and I can promise your life will never be the same."

...

Now, a year later, screaming into this microphone, I have to admit: the dark priest may have spewed a lot of bullshit that night, but that promise—*your life will never be the same*—he kept.

"MOM AND DAD PROMISED DREAMS WORTH CHASING—"

The crowd chants back: ***"—WELL, MOM AND DAD SUCKED OFF REAGAN!"***

The only thing that night gave me, besides a handicap parking pass and an opioid addiction, was the motivation to keep the band alive. And that's what I did, somehow convincing the others to give The Not-To-Be-Describeds one last Hail Mary. Jonah and Max and Christian and even Baldy Q gave up asking what happened to me that night and agreed to hunker down for at least one more album.

So we did the work. Holed up in a decrepit cabin somewhere and wrote our hearts dry. It had been the hardest few months any of us had survived. More than once Baldy Q had to be revived from a puddle of his own puke, and Christian hid every sharp object in the cabin toward the end, but we came out of it alive, mostly (maybe) intact, and with an album that each of us was, somehow, in some way or other, actually *proud of.*

I urged the band to put it out without fanfare, that the punk thing would be to just release the thing, no marketing or ad campaign or press junket. Let the fans find it and hold it for themselves, and let the music say the rest.

I thought I had insider information, you see. I thought I'd paid up in full and The Thing That Blood Bleeds was sated and ready to hold up her end of the bargain. Every day after we released the record, I woke up thinking *Today's the day my name is carved right onto punk's forehead.*

But every day, nothing happened. Nothing but a maelstrom of pain and anger, anger and pain, and me at its center.

...

"So is this, like, a cult? Am I about to be inducted into the Illuminati?"

The dark priest's fucked-up teeth had peeked out for a bubbling chuckle. There was definitely something wrong there, a bronchial fungus growing on the walls of his lungs.

"Hardly. The entity I speak on behalf of prefers its sheep to wallow in ignorance while growing fleece for her bedchambers."

That made a certain kind of sense to me, but I still treated it all like one big joke. Told myself it would make a good laugh with the band later. But you see? With that thought, I'd already forgotten my plan to quit the band that very night. Some part of me saw a pact with the Devil and *hungered* for it to be real. Truthfully, some part of me saw it as my birthright.

"Old man, my bandmates are gonna wonder where I got off to, so maybe give me the elevator pitch version of whatever it is you're selling."

"It's that exact impatience that sets you apart from the rest," the man said. "It is what brought you to her attention."

"Her? Like . . . a Satanic groupie?"

The priest's grin soured. "She will not permit mockery within these walls. If you truly want what she sees in your essence—a hunger for fame, for glory, to be worshiped as a rock god—then you will meet her with reverence."

I laughed. "Someone might have laced your stash, bud."

Before I'd even spoken, as if my laughter had stirred the stale theater air, a ripple swept across the sea of candles, their flames flickering, flickering, then—*WHOOSH*—extinguished.

Darkness.

Then . . .

I met her face-to-face. The Thing That Blood Bleeds.

At least, I'm pretty sure I did. I remember a vague presence, a cold fear, then . . . an erection? Laugh if you want, I know how it sounds. But my memories of the rest of that night are murky at best. Flashes of clarity like images in a deck of Tarot cards:

The rough stone handle of a serrated knife, gripped in my right hand.

A promise of fame, world tours, sold-out arenas, millions and millions of dollars, and all my wildest dreams my reality. All that was required was a sacrifice. A limb, given freely.

The blade, flashing in the night, its teeth biting into my left leg, just below the knee.

What I don't remember is feeling any pain. Not until I came to, somehow dumped on the doormat to our cheap motel room. I remember *that* pain very well: sudden, brighter than the sun, angrier than any lyric I ever wrote. Jonah opened the door at the sound of my screams, and then there was a lot of yelling, screeching tires, and I was bleeding out in the too-bright reception room of the ER.

...

"—KICKING DOWN THE DOOR FOR WHAT'S MINE, POUR ME A SHOT OF STRYCHNINE—"

That's the kids in the front singing my own lyrics at me, because I've blanked and I'm just standing here like an idiot. Where am I—no, *when* am I? I'm back in Boston, that's for damn sure. My stump is screaming bloody murder, and the show has turned sour. By now, the beer cans on the floor outnumber the dissatisfied crowd 10-to-1.

"Dude, what the hell is your problem?"

That's Jonah, screaming into my ear over the blaring amps. The others are charging onward, not missing a beat, but they're all glaring at their fuck-up lead singer.

"Get your shit together or I'm throwing you out of the set," Jonah yells, and I can see it on all the faces staring up at us now: everybody heard that. Everyone in this place knows I'm blowing it, and the crowd is seconds away from turning ugly and throwing shit to get us off the stage. Punk is a volatile combination of democracy and street justice.

Street justice. That's the whole reason you're here, remember, Fritz?

Vengeance, you might call it. I don't fucking care. Do you know how to scratch a burning pins-and-needles itch all over a leg and foot that *isn't even on your body anymore*? Can you imagine what that does to a person, to the id, to your idea of what constitutes your self—are you your whole body, your brain, your nervous system? Are you your various identities draped on your carcass to signify your gender, your politics, your fandom, your devotion to punk?

Is this peg leg a part of me? Is the severed leg still me, slowly digesting in a scam god's eldritch gullet?

Fuck your judgment. I was promised something in return, the id to beat all ids, and now I'm just a sad cripple who once tested the mouthfeel of an unregistered Glock 19 and whose band probably knows all about that and are secretly disappointed it was just a test.

...

As we exit the stage—skipping the encore this time; the crowd would crucify us if we tried—I can feel the others' glares burning into my back. My stump leg feels molten, like its prosthesis keeps stepping in tar. But I need out. I'd crawl off the stage if I had to.

And Jonah, Max, Christian, Baldy Q? They'd leave me there to crawl. They're seconds away from kicking me out, I can just feel it. I duck them in the green room, doubling back and hiding in a custodian's closet with the mops and bleach.

Hurrying off the stage like that, and down those stone, chipped steps, in this current body—that comes at a cost. My stump feels coated in fire ants forming their own mosh pit. The pain pulses hatedly up my torso, my gut clenched with nausea, my scalp boiling sweat.

My painkillers are in the van. I'll have to weather this storm.

That's my last, desperate thought before I slump against the door and everything goes black.

...

I gasp awake, choke on the acrid breath, and the door gives, spilling me and the musty mop out to crash against the back tunnel wall. I let gravity do its thing until everything's settled and I can catch my breath.

Silence. Time feels like a needle jumping a scratched 7-inch.

I'm alone.

I limp back down the hall, back up those cursed steps, and onto the stage. I half expect the place to be decked out with melty candles again, but it's dead as a graveyard.

"Hello?"

My voice bounces against the cathedral walls and is eaten by the silence.

Déjà vu: rancid breath on the back of my neck, but when I whip around nobody is there.

"What seems to be troubling you, my son?"

Out of nowhere he's right there, just downstage of me. I stumble and almost fall backward from the surprise, and that's when I notice the candles. They're all there, just as before, lit and melting over the stone as though they've been burning awhile. I just manage to stay within our circle clearing. My boot and peg straddle the center of the neon gaffer's Evil Eye.

My surprise sloughs off like a second skin, and the righteous anger returns with a vengeance. "Don't play innocent, you toothless fuck. Did you think I'd just forget about your end of the bargain?" I say, clinging to my rage like a life jacket.

"And did you think," he says, grinning, "there was a return policy on feeding your flesh to the queen beyond the veil?"

"She sure as hell ate it, though—"

I rap my knuckles against the part of me that's carbon fiber and titanium, sending the fire ants into a frenzy. Fueling my seething, petulant hatred. It jolts my bones, tuning forks of clarity, and that scribbling chalkboard of the mind says that it's me that I hate.

"—and I've lived with the consequences long enough to shit out the best punk record of my career, and you know what? It sold for *shit*. Seems to me like I'm doing all the work and paying for it, too, and you and your little pet are just another religious grift."

That whore déjà vu, again: a wind sweeps through the cathedral. This time, however, it comes with a rumbling earthquake from beneath that vibrates up my peg leg. The multitudinous candles begin to topple, their flames joining, spreading, until the house floor is a lake of fire.

"Why are gods always so easily offended?" I try to say, but my voice is lost to the noise. The priest stands beside me, and we look on as the mosh pit of fire churns, a river of frothy, bubbling wax, flowing faster, faster, into a maelstrom. I'm staring into the eye of the whirlpool. Waiting.

For her.

But before the mosh pit can open up, something far more terrifying than the bitch who ate my leg sneaks up on me. A voice, close to my ear, and not the priest's.

"We thought it was drugs, but . . . Jesus Christ, Fritz."

Jonah.

I turn my back on the seething lake, and they're all there. Jonah. Max. Christian. Baldy Q, his drumsticks in hand. We all came back to the stage for our encore after all. This used to be my family. Now, them standing in a loose formation outside of the gaffer's tape, they feel like my judge, jury, and executioner. Their expressions flicker between existential horror and abject disgust.

"The music was never enough for you, man," Jonah shouted.

I scoff. The anger is boiling up my throat. *Fuck* Jonah. "Is your 'love of the music' fulfilling to you? Really? I don't remember our landlord accepting a chorus in cut time as payment for rent."

Jonah scoffs right back. "You're so full of shit, man! You expect us to believe you did a blood sacrifice so you could pay some bills?"

Baldy Q points a drumstick at me, screams, "FUCKING SELLOUT!"

I slap the scarred oak stick out of my face. "Oh, you think that's such a *dirty* word. Grow up! All we ever do is try to sell our shit. You're telling me you *wouldn't* sign a million-dollar record deal? Being rich and famous suddenly makes the music fake?"

They just stare at me. I notice the dark priest has disappeared, off to do his master's bidding elsewhere, and with him goes my chances of fame, of fortune. All of it, everything, is ruined. My stump pulses with excruciating pain; I shift my weight.

"I DID THIS FOR THE BAND!" I'm screaming now, the best full-throated screams of my career. "I did what had to be done to put The Not-To-Be-Describeds on the map!"

"You did this for yourself," Jonah says. "You did this for groupies and adoration and validation. You think the punk scene would rep our shit if they knew about this?"

"DO YOU KNOW WHAT THIS IS LIKE?!" The chronic pain, as if hearing its name, surges forth, a colossal wave to submerge me into oblivion, and I almost give in right then and there. I can't stand still anymore; I bend, contort, so I can rip my stupid prosthesis from my stump. I may be in so much pain and feel so much rage that my vision is blotting out, but I've gotten good at balancing on one leg like a fucking flamingo. I brandish the prosthesis at them, one at a time, peg-end first. "Do you know the constant, never-ending river of pain I've been in? It never lets up, man. Not for a second. Not for sleep, not with drugs. Pain is my life now. And you know what? I'd do it again if it meant world tours with my brothers."

As I say this, spotty vision now blurred from hot tears, I feel a massive, Stygian presence rising behind me. There's a magnetic force drawing us together, Ahab and his whale. I want to turn toward her, crave it in my delirium, but my bandmates are ruining it all. Seeing their heads rear back as they take in The Thing That Blood Bleeds, their expressions stretched in rictus horror, does little to cheer me up.

They compose themselves and share a look between them, collectively backing away as Jonah proclaims, "Fritz . . . we're all in agreement. Your values do not reflect those of The Not-To-Be-Describeds. We've decided that you are out of the band."

"You're not punk, bro," Baldy Q says, and like he does at the end of every encore, he chucks his drumsticks. But not into the mosh pit. Right at my face.

As I lose my balance, the cursed peg leg slips from my grasp and clatters to the stage floor, coming to rest halfway outside of the bastardized pentagram of tape. Some spell has been broken. I feel it. We all do. The bond that tied us all together. Fate's thread, frayed, seconds away from the snap. I flail around, desperate to see her—

And there she is. The Thing That Blood Bleeds. As indescribable and unwieldy as punk itself, towering above all. Glistening black, her countless, ever-rolling eyes hungry for more of me. Striated rivers of thick candlewax and flame flow around her, thick gobs dripping from her maw and hitting the stage with a *hssssss!*

I wheel my arms wildly to keep from falling—

And fall nonetheless. Off the lip of the stage, toward the mosh pit.

The Thing That Blood Bleeds. She swallows me. Into the black.

My pain, where once was my foot, sings.

Whole again.

ASESINOS

"Until they become conscious they will
never rebel, and until after they have
rebelled they cannot become
conscious."
- George Orwell, 1984

PELAYO

"He determines the number of the stars and calls them each
by name." — Psalm 147:4

PUNK
goes
HORROR
II

2026 WORLD TOUR

ASESINOS

CYNTHIA PELAYO

THE COLD FOUND THE GAPS IN MY COAT. It edged into the seams and slipped down the backs of my ankles and settled into my boots. I should have worn more layers, but I hated the heavy feeling of so much fabric pressed against my skin. It made me feel like my limbs weren't my own, like I wasn't really real.

"You need to wear layers, mija," I could hear my mother say whenever I complained about January in Chicago.

I suppose I'd rather feel cold than not feel like myself.

The file arrived on my desk at 9:47 AM.

I remember the time because I'd just burned my mouth on my coffee and finally felt warm after that walk from my car in the parking lot to my desk. I pressed my thermos against my lip, letting the metal soothe the sting, and trying to make sense why the file in front of me was so thin.

As an investigator for the Cook County Public Defender's Office most files were stuffed full of documents. Intake forms, arrest records, receipts, affidavits, parking tickets, anything and everything and more.

My job was to locate these people and to find where they had been lost in the system.

Up until recently, this had been a fairly simple job. People don't just disappear, not in the system. But in recent months, it had become more difficult to locate some of their whereabouts.

Of course, complications occur. Cases can be catalogued incorrectly or even delayed because of typos. Sometimes things can also be misplaced.

My email pinged. A system wide announcement with just one sentence and no further explanation.

If someone is not in the system, they do not exist. Mark the record as reconciled.

I returned to the file on my desk. It had no arrest number. No detention ID. No court date scheduled or missed.

All I had were a few handwritten lines on a sheet of white paper which included a spouse name and contact information.

Date: June 8th

Luis G. Alvarez

Age thirty-four

Address: 337 W. 26th Street, Garden Unit

Employment: Construction

Outside my window, the CTA bus hissed to a stop on Clark Street. A man stepped down into snow that had turned to slush. I watched as he trudged toward Daley Center, shoulders hunched, head down past the massive abstract sculpture that no one could accurately describe besides just calling it the "Picasso."

Was it a bird?

Or some type of primate with wings?

No one in the city really could tell you.

Even columnist Mike Royko once said, "Its eyes are like the eyes of every slum owner who made a buck off the small and weak."

The small and weak, I thought, and found it fitting that the sculpture didn't even have a real name.

It's officially untitled, like many of the people who now come across my desk.

I read the lines again and again.

This man had been missing three days.

I called his wife. This phone rang until it went to voicemail.

"This is Nora. Leave a message."

I didn't.

By noon I'd run his name through every database I could access.

County. State. Federal. Cook County Jail.

Luis G. Alvarez was nowhere.

Nothing came up indicating he had been detained, processed, or even transferred.

I continued searching because gone is not a legal status.

More reasonable explanations were entertained: a clerical error or processing lag times. Also, that G in Luis G. Alvarez could be the missing piece. So, I searched for additional possibilities, Guillermo, Gabriel, Gerardo, Gaspar, Gustavo.

Nothing.

Gone.

At two o'clock, Yolanda stopped by my desk. My supervisor. Fifty-three years old, grew up in the Back of the Yards, and worked her way through UIC Law School's part-time JD Program while raising two kids alone.

"Anything?" she asked.

"Not yet."

"The email this morning," I started.

Yolanda repeated every word. "If someone is not in the system they do not exist. Mark the record as reconciled."

"But..."

She turned on her heel and returned to her office.

...

The building where Luis G. Alvarez lived was a brick three-flat with a wrought-iron gate that hadn't latched properly since probably around 1989. Next to the front steps was a small shrine to La Virgen de Guadalupe, faded plastic roses gathered at the base, as well as several unlit white candles. Her face calm behind the cracked glass of her enclosure.

I knocked at the basement unit.

Nora opened the door. She had dark circles under her eyes that said she hadn't slept in days.

I showed her my badge and told her I was with the System, that it was my job to locate Luis.

"They took him."

"Who?"

"The System."

"The System?"

"Don't you all communicate with one another?"

I supposed we didn't.

"How many were there? What did they look like?"

"Six. They just looked like...people who didn't want to be noticed."

She recounted all of what she remembered.

No uniforms she recognized. No badges shown. No

warrants produced. One of them was wearing a Bears hoodie. They told her to stay inside. They said they were helping.

"Luis went with them because he was scared. What choice did he have?" she said. "He kissed our son goodbye and then they left."

I looked past her into the apartment, shoes lined by the door, coats hung on a rack. Their son's school bag was in the middle of the floor, and somewhere in the house I heard a child crying.

"He doesn't understand," Nora said.

"Understand what?"

"That his dad's never coming back."

"We'll find him."

"But you took him. You are part of the System. And you don't even know where he is."

I told her that I was sorry, that I really believed we'd find him.

"Did they say anything else?"

"We'll bring Luis back if we can confirm."

"Confirm what?"

She looked at me like I'd asked her to explain the value of human life.

"They didn't tell you where they were taking him?"

"No."

"They give you their names, business cards, anything?"

"Business cards? You think those guys carry business cards?"

"I'm sorry."

Helping. Confirm. Grateful.

Words can wear disguises too.

I wrote down what more she could provide, date, time,

day of the week, the color of their van.

"Silver or grey."

"Which is it?"

"Does it even matter?" Nora said. "They're both the same."

I wrote until my hand ached. Men with no names. A silver-grey van with an out of state license plate. When I asked what state Nora said she wasn't sure, but she was certain it didn't belong here to Illinois.

I filled pages with facts that would mean nothing in any database I could access, but at least they were details she remembered and I could remember as well.

As I walked to my car, it felt like what had happened to Luis was starting to spread throughout the neighborhood.

It's not that the words were spoken aloud or even written down. People had heard about how the System was changing the rules, rewriting them as hours passed.

The news about Luis could be felt, communicated with a look, in the way neighbors passed each other on the street, steady and cautious. It was seen in the way people lowered their miniblinds and turned off their lights as a stranger walked past their house.

The only word I heard linger in the air as I opened the car door was -

Asesinos.

Murderers.

That night, I filed an official inquiry. I used polite language in a neutral tone. This was the careful, sanitized process I'd learned in my years of trying to align systems with the people they processed.

A response came the next morning as I was finishing my coffee.

No record of Luis G. Alvarez in federal custody.

No enforcement action documented at location stated.

No further information available at this time.

This had to be a mistake. I responded to the email with some of the key items I'd learned during my investigation: **Nora.** Her account of the men in the van.

I dialed Nora's number, but got a busy signal.

...

I drove to the office and went downstairs to the Records Department where Daria owed me a small favor from a custody case last winter.

She had a smoker's voice that sounded like broken glass being swept up in a dustpan, and the expression of someone who'd made peace with disappointment long ago.

"What do you think about the update?"

"The System didn't talk to you about it?" She said.

"No, I've been out on an investigation."

"They're supposed to talk to everyone."

"About what?"

"We're not supposed to talk about it."

"We're not supposed to talk about that email?" I laughed to myself. "What are we supposed to say if someone mentions it?"

PUNK GOES HORROR II

Her eyes flicked to the ceiling behind me. I looked and spotted the black sphere. "When did they install cameras down here?"

Daria's focus returned to her monitor. "If somcone is not in the system they do not exist. Mark the record as reconciled."

"I get that," I said. "but I need help."

"I don't really think you understand what's going on."

"Please."

I handed her the name and indicated I was investigating a discrepancy. She eyed me for a moment. Then, she typed each letter carefully, as if the keyboard may punish her for checking.

"What do you see?

"Nothing under Luis G. Alvarez. Gone."

I insisted she try something else. "Maybe Luiz Alvarez? No G?"

Daria opened her mouth to say something but then returned to the keyboard.

"No."

"There are other variations we could try."

Her eyes glanced back to the ceiling. And once again she typed, each letter delicately, as if the screen might shatter each time she hit return.

Luis G.

L. Alvarez.

L. G. Alvarez

Alvarez, Luis

Alvarez, L.G

"He's gone. The file is reconciled."

I stood there, staring at his name and those lines. I knew I'd spoken to Nora. She was real and she knew Luis was real too.

"What do you mean gone? Reconciled?"

"Luis G. Alvarez does not exist in the system," Daria said. But he did exist.

I thought about the child I heard crying in that garden apartment, about the Virgen de Guadalupe shrine, how guardians at one's doors couldn't even protect them.

"I spoke to his wife."

"Are you sure?"

"Daria…"

She exhaled through her nose. For a moment I thought she'd say no,

Instead she glanced at the camera, angled her body to block the screen, and typed a sequence of numbers I'd never seen.

"There was a search," she said, quieter now, her lips barely moving.

"Was?"

"Log shows the name queried three times yesterday. Then it was wiped."

Wiped? Not deleted. Like, the name never existed.

"That's not supposed to happen."

She toggled to a blank screen. "Things have changed. Lots of things aren't supposed to happen."

Daria stood. "I'm taking my lunch break."

I noticed her shoulders were trembling.

"You alright?"

"Yes," she answered right away.

She reached for her coat hung behind her, eyes fixed on the camera.

"You ever read that book? The one everyone quotes when they want to sound smart about being afraid?"

"Orwell?"

She didn't answer. Just looked at me, and then she was gone.

...

Over the next two weeks, more files appeared on my desk. Always thin and containing just a sheet of paper with some lines scribbled in blue ink.

A woman named Sofia Reyes who missed her hearing. I met with the judge who had issued a bench warrant, annoyed at the inconvenience of her absence. The next morning the official inquiry returned:

> *No record. No enforcement action documented.*
> *No further information available at this time.*

A man named Hector Ortiz who stopped showing up to his construction job. His foreman told me he marked him a no-call no-show and then called it in. The next day familiar results arrived:

> *No record. No enforcement action documented.*
> *No further information available at this time.*

A teenage girl named Maribel Torres who vanished on her walk home from school. The police officers at the station at 26th and California confirmed she'd been listed as a runaway. The report I woke up to claimed otherwise:

> *No record. No enforcement action documented.*
> *No further information available at this time.*

The city continued to move as disappearances rose. No one wanted to discuss them, these people or their lives. Yolanda stopped by my desk one morning and told me the System had asked all managers to personally relay the message to their teams:

"If someone is not in the system they do not exist. Mark the record as reconciled. If the official inquiry after an investigation confirms the individual does not exist in the system, again, they are to be reconciled."

"I don't understand," I said. "If my investigation shows I've spoken with their family, friends, employers then how can they be listed as not existing? I have reports from people all across the city that their loved ones were taken by groups of men claiming to be working for the System."

"I will repeat. If someone is not in the system, they do not exist. Mark the record as reconciled."

"But..."

"We do not question the System," Yolanda said before returning to her office.

Soon, people just stopped opening doors when I knocked. Phones rang and rang. Text messages were left unanswered. At the bakery on Fullerton, the one with the fancy conchas, the woman behind the counter looked right through me. She used to save me a chocolate one. People in the neighborhood who knew I worked for the System no longer spoke to me.

At work, I noticed how language had quickly changed meaning.

Disappearance was now Non-Verification.

Absence now Administrative Delay.

Fear turned into Community Rumor.

Helping morphed into Harboring.

One night I arrived home and found a piece paper taped to my door.

STOP TRYING TO LOCATE PEOPLE
WHO DON'T EXIST.

My hands shook as I removed it.

Inside my apartment, I locked the deadbolt. I stood with my back pressed against the door, my heart banging against my ribs.

That night I dreamed of a large hall lined with coffins, and within each one there were stacks of files, reports, case records, and manila folders bursting with details. Paper spilled across the floor, covering the surface. Each and every document was stamped RECONCILED in red.

When I woke, I found a voice message from an anonymous number.

The voicemail was warbled and electronic, but the words were clear:

"Answers can be found in the Archives Building."

There was a pause, followed by a burst of static.

*"They can make sure a person is gone now
but they cannot erase someone's beginning."*

Early the next morning I found myself sitting inside my car

outside the Archives Building, located miles outside of the city

I sat there for a long time, taking deep breaths and long exhales. I tried to find comfort with the steady sound of the heater blowing warm air, and knowing the cold and the frost creeping along the edges of the windshield couldn't get me, at least not until I stepped outside.

Every system keeps records. Systems believe their documentation processes equate a sense of righteousness and superiority. That a paper trail will validate the reality they've crafted.

However, every system that rewrites history wants to keep original copies somewhere. Conquerors always want proof of what they've conquered.

That's the arrogance of a system.

The basement of the Archive Building smelled like damp and mold. I'd been down there once before, years ago, searching for a document an attorney swore didn't exist. The fluorescent lights buzzed like angry cicadas.

Shelves leaned toward each other, in exhaustion over what they've been demanded to support. My footsteps echoed down corridors.

When I reached the Main Archive, I was as surprised to find a security guard as he was to find me here.

He didn't ask what I was doing. He only asked me to provide my badge, which I presented and he scanned. I could only hope no one would check the record to indicate I'd been here, but I knew better. Records are always inspected.

In the main archive room, I found an old computer, one so old there was no existing software update for it, but this was to my benefit.

The cursor blinked green against the black screen.

I typed Luis G. Alvarez's name and then hit enter.

There it was. All of it. Birthdate. Elementary school. High school. First job. College. Marriage certificate. Apartment applications. It was all there, the history of someone who had once been. I scanned. I read until I reached the final entry:

Case opened: Detained

Case closed: Reconciled

The screen stuttered. Then it displayed a single line:

SUBJECT CONFIRMED: GONE.

"Gone? Where are they going?" I asked the room knowing I'd get no answer.

I hit print. The old printer whined, shuddered, and spat out the page.

The overhead lights flickered. I grabbed the paper and turned toward the door.

A figure stood in the doorway, blocking the hall light.

Daria.

Daria looked thin and pale in a way that wasn't just because of the harsh fluorescent lights. Her eyes were sunken in her head. Her hair was missing in patches. She leaned against the doorframe as if that's all that could support her to stand. She held her left hand clamped to her right shoulder, fingers curled inward as if she didn't want me to see her fingers.

"Daria?"

"You shouldn't have printed that."

"What happened to you?"

"I went to lunch."

I took a step toward her.

"Don't. You'll make things worse."

"Worse than what?"

"You have a choice," she said. "Throw it away. Get the hell out of here. Pretend you didn't see anything."

"If I don't?"

Something raw moved behind her eyes, panic.

"You'll become like me. Someone who isn't real."

"You are real. You're standing here in front of me."

"The men will come for me soon."

Footsteps echoed in the hallway.

Daria's head turned.

"Go," she mouthed.

I ran.

At my car, I found a manila folder under the windshield wiper.

Inside, an official document from the system.

People of the State of Illinois vs. my name

Charge: Obstruction of government operations. Charge: Tampering with public records.

The allegations described actions I hadn't taken, meetings I hadn't attended, documents I'd never touched, or had access to. Everything listed was precise, with dates and detailed explanations. All of it false.

FAILURE TO APPEAR WILL RESULT IN DETAINMENT.

The hearing date and time was scheduled for the previous day at

9am.

Impossible.

"No..." I said.

My hands shook. I dropped the folder. Pages scattered across the wet and snowy asphalt. I knelt to gather them, my breath coming in ragged clouds.

That's when I understood.

They didn't need a reason. They could determine your guilt at any moment and create its design. All they needed to do was wrap it in procedural language. The System would do the rest.

I got in my car and drove to my office building in the city anyway, because some part of me still wanted to believe in procedure and process, in words arranged in the right order, and a reality that we could all agree with.

The security guard in the lobby looked up when I approached. I'd known him all of my twenty years working here.

"Hey Eddie."

He pushed a clipboard with a sign-in sheet in front of me. "Please sign in."

"It's me."

Maybe he was tired. Maybe I looked haggard. Maybe I just needed to mention something familiar.

"How's your grandson?"

"Do I know you?"

I held up my badge. "I've worked here for decades."

"Scan your badge."

I did.

The reader blinked red.

"That's invalid."

"I was just here yesterday."

I tapped it again.

The machine protested.

"If you have no business here you have to leave the building."

Behind me, the revolving door spun and cold air swept in.

Across the street, I spotted the silver-gray van. A man in a Bears hoodie leaned against the driver side door.

I rushed out the back entrance to avoid them and reached my car.

I sped down the expressway, glancing in my rearview mirror the entire drive home. Snow began to fall, softening along the city's edges, making everything look cleaner than it was.

When I parked at my apartment my phone buzzed.

A text message appeared from an unknown number.

YOU ARE TOO LATE

I thought about Luis, Nora, Sofia, Maribel, Hector, all of them. I thought about all of the names I'd known and would never know. I thought about all of the people I talked to who could corroborate that these people had one day woken up, gone to work, school, church, out for a walk or a meal with friends, and had never returned.

Each of them told me stories about a group of men who approached and took away their loved one. And that is where the missing person's story concludes, at the end of the question of:

Where are you?

I thought about Daria in the doorway, sickly pale. The day she helped me and the book she mentioned.

Yes, I'd read it long ago, like many of us have. But did we really understand what that author was saying?

That the state doesn't need to kill you if it can simply correct you out of the record. How language becomes a trap. How fear makes collaborators out of ordinary people, and how our very memory becomes a crime.

I walked up to my front door and turned the key.

...

By morning, my world entire world changed.

When I tried my badge at the office, this time the card reader flashed **RECONCILED**. I was escorted off the premises.

Personal emails I tried to send? Bounced.

When I dialed Yolanda's number? It was disconnected.

Daria's number was no longer in service.

I didn't know where else to go, so I went to the police station to ask for help. The desk officer looked at me like I'd asked for directions to a place that didn't exist.

"Do you have documentation?"

"No…"

"We can't help you," he said. "You don't exist."

That night I found an eviction notice pinned to my door.

I opened my laptop and searched my own name.

Nothing returned.

I searched again. My name plus dates. My name plus my former job title. My name and where I attended high school. My name and my ex-girlfriend's name. It was like I was forcing myself to be remembered, but there was nothing.

I searched the Secretary of State website.

Driver's license: error.
Voter registration: page not found.
Bank account: USER NOT FOUND.

My phone buzzed.

ARE YOU READY TO BE RECONCILED?

I got up. Found a notebook, paper, pen, the things that don't need a password or server or anyone's permission, and I began to write.

Luis G. Alvarez. Sofia Reyes. Hector Ortiz. Maribel Torres. Daria. I wrote about each and every one. I wrote about what I knew and what I had been told.

I wrote until my hand cramped. Names, dates and details. The kind of proof that doesn't live in databases. The kind of evidence that survives only in memory, inside of other people.

Outside, a silver-grey van drove past slowly.

My chest ached. I wrote faster.

I kept writing.

When the notebook pages were full, I tore them out carefully and put them in envelopes. I addressed them not to officials, not to courts, not to any system that could validate, revise, and correct them but to people. To real people, because it's people and not systems who can validate - I was someone and I was here.

One letter went to a journalist I'd trusted since my second year on the job. Another to a priest at St. Hyacinth who'd helped me find a witness once. The librarian at the Logan Square branch where I'd teach English As a Second Language a few times a year. A teacher at Benito Juarez High School who'd testified for a client's kid.

Not instructions. Not plans. No systems. Just people. Names and witnesses. Someone who could remember.

If language had become their evidence of annihilation, I'd make language evidence of birth. Because it's not necessarily the large waves of spectacle or violent uprisings that have the ability to reshape the world. Change also comes via insistence, and in these small and quiet moments of defiance as we know destruction approaches our door.

In the gray before dawn, I walked through the snow and mailed the envelopes from different boxes across the city. My footprints were the only marks on the sidewalks. People were now too afraid to leave their houses.

I thought about this world, and how it's held together through a consensus of systems, and how all of those systems must be aligned in order to agree upon what is truth. And I thought about consensus and how it could be broken by our human refusal to be forgotten.

When I arrived home, the van was there waiting, and while I was afraid, I held onto some comfort that I would be remembered.

T.H. Wall.........Fuck Them All To Hell

Cat Voleur.........Wow, I Can Get Sexual Too

Patrick Barb............Pillars

Chris Panatier...............Dismantle Me

Laurel Hightower...............Black Me Out

john wayne comunale.....Born On A Saturday Night

D.C. Phillips.................Rebel Yell

Justin Montgomery..........Don't Reach For Me

Brian Asman.................Wrong Way Kids

Clay McLeod Chapman.......Hidden Track

To lay out the context, plain and simple- each story in this anthology has been inspired by a PUNK or Punk-Adjacent song of the author's choosing.

Here's a list of the songs and musicians who inspired our writers. For legal purposes- we have no official affiliation with these bands or songs. Each story in this anthology represents our author's own artistic interpretations of the moods, themes, or emotions they feel when listening to these songs. Lyrics, tales told, and exact messaging remains distinctly separate from those songs being paid homage to, but we hope that if any of the original artists come across this "album," they'll understand how inspiring they have been to us. And we hope readers discover a banger of a new band thanks to all this.

Fuck Them All To Hell -- Stray From The Path

Wow, I Can Get Sexual Too -- Say Anything

Pillars -- Sunny Day Real Estate

Dismantle Me -- The Distillers

Black Me Out -- Against Me!

Born On A Saturday Night -- The Mean Jeans

Rebel Yell -- Billy Idol

Don't Reach For Me -- Knocked Loose

Wrong Way Kids -- Bad Religion

Hidden Track -- N/A

FUCK THEM
ALL TO HELL
WALL
PUNK goes HORROR II
2026 WORLD TOUR

FUCK THEM ALL TO HELL

T.H. WALL

I PREFER THE BELLY MEAT SLOW ROASTED until the skin crackles and crunches, served over rice and bathed in its own rendered juices. However, I think the secret treat most folks overlook are fingers, fried and slathered in lemon pepper. Chicken wings from the old days never tasted so good. They came up with a lot of recipes for the rich after the revolution…

…

The drone of crickets drowns out the tinkling sound of glass. I reach my hand through the hole in the window by the front door and unlock the handle. The swing of the door clears the window debris from the foyer. Moonlight streaming in behind us lights the hallway. The silence belies the sound of music from within that had drawn us here from the street. Our boots squeak on the tongue and groove wood floors. Flashlights illuminate paintings hung in the hall – not print copies of famous masters, these, but actual artistry. Either this place had been overlooked when the uprising began, or whoever lived here had hidden the paintings and waited for the rioting to calm before daring to hang the works again.

I motion to Cam and Brenda to fan out as I make my way into the kitchen. The orange light on the stovetop. The smell of

PUNK GOES HORROR II

boiled potatoes. We weren't wrong.

Someone is still hiding in here.

I turn to the left and see what must've once been a breakfast nook, but the table legs have been broken off. Chairs surround a collapsed remnant of what would have been a pleasant spot to read the paper and drink coffee. By the first chair, a doll lays listlessly on the rug. My daughter would have been too old for dolls by now…

My eyes are drawn to a brief sparkle by the kitchen sink as I turn my flashlight over the room. I spy a wedding ring with an over-large stone by the faucet. Perhaps someone had taken it off to wash dishes and forgotten it in the rush to hide. After a quick glance to assure myself that I'm alone, I slip the ring into my pocket and keep moving further into the house.

I meet Brenda at the stairs and shake my head. She makes a circle motion with her hand, and both of us climb to the second floor, the stairs creaking underfoot. At the top, a whirl of movement whips at me from the side, and a sharp pain lances through my arm. What used to be a well-dressed man, turned feral by hunger and fear, has come from behind a door to stab me in the forearm with a screwdriver. I smash my assailant in the face with my flashlight. The crunching of bones reminds me of the security guard who broke my arm with his Maglite when we were teenagers, sneaking past the Creekstone gate to prank those grand houses with their fancy Christmas lights…

Brenda pulls my arm away from the bloody pulp of what used to be a man's face. I must have blacked out after I hit him the fifth or sixth time.

"Stop fucking up the food."

I let the broken corpse fall from my hands. She's right. I can't be getting too aggressive now that the supply of bourgeois

pigs is dwindling. The feasts are less frequent these days.

Cam wraps the body in a tarp to drag it back to base while Brenda and I continue searching the second floor. The master bedroom seems cavernous in its quiet emptiness, and each hallway and bathroom seems to deny the presence of anyone else. But where there's one rich bastard, there's usually a family. And I couldn't allow them to be found.

"We should head back – there isn't anyone else here."

"What are you talking about? We haven't even finished sweeping the second floor."

There's a scream from the side room. Brenda and I rush in to see Cam, done wrapping the body apparently, holding a woman and child at gunpoint. The child – a little girl – has foam at the corners of her mouth. She flops limply in the arms of the woman. Cam spits in the doorway.

"So you'd rather poison her than have her grow up to join the revolution. You're sick."

"Fuck you," comes the reply, filled with bitterness and contempt.

"I'm going to skin her dead body in front of you. I'll make you wear her face as a mask while we crucify y--."

The crack of my rifle cuts Cam's threat short. The woman falls forward over her daughter's body, half her head missing, blood and brains splattered across the wall behind her.

"What'd you do that for"

I don't answer as I walk into the room to check for anyone else. Looking down at the dead pair, all I see are the bodies of my own wife and child flashing in my vision, their bodies similarly disfigured and tangled in each other's arms. The gun in my hands feels oddly familiar.

"We should leave these two. Just take the man with us."

PUNK GOES HORROR II

"What's the matter with you? Are you crazy? We can't leave these fuckers here – what will we use for the feast tomorrow? Granted, the kid is probably toxic thanks to whatever this bitch dosed her with, but her mom looks marbled just the way I like…"

I can't listen anymore. Cam's warnings about the commissar's report echo down the stairs behind me, but the memory of gunshots drowns him out. Back on the ground floor, I stop to catch my breath and steady myself, reaching to the carved balustrade for support.

How could I have been stupid enough to shoot her?

The standing order to bring prisoners back for "judgment" was published everywhere at base, and I had been put on warning before. I'm sure to be reprimanded when we get back, or worse this time. This is my sweep detail after all.

Back in the living room, Brenda and Cam meet me with the bodies of the man and woman, bagged and tagged. Just as we open the door to head back to base, there's a retching sound from upstairs.

"What the fuck was that?"

Leaving Cam downstairs to cover us, Brenda and I make our way back up the stairs to see the little girl come crawling and coughing onto the landing, her eyes rolling wildly, the foam still dripping from the corners of her mouth. She tumbles down toward us, making no effort to break her own fall. I move quickly to block Brenda's rifle coming up.

"No. This one we have to take back with us. She needs a doctor

"The doctors are gone. Better to end her suffering now."

I ignore Brenda and kneel down to pick the girl up in my arms. Her emaciated frame is so light. Her eyes lock with mine and seem to plead wordlessly for help as she convulses and

gasps.

"She's coming with us anyway."

"You know this is unorthodox."

"Brenda. It's a fucking kid."

She throws up her hands in frustration. "I'm not lying to the commissar for you again. It's your funeral."

I know she's right. My nostrils flare with the remembered smell of smoking flesh, and we head back to base.

...

The road back to headquarters is quiet as my team pulls our wagon between abandoned cars. The silence is only broken by the occasional gurgle and squirm from the girl laid out on top of the canvas-wrapped bodies of her parents.

The 4th People's Constituent Milita headquarters is housed on the campus of a community college. The entrance to the base leads to a small hill in the center of campus surmounted by a bonfire. The flickering light from the flames makes the shadowed outline of the guillotine on a platform halfway up the hill seem to dance across the gates as they open for our entry. The polished trapezoidal blade briefly flashes in the dark, a wayward spark leaving a blue floater in my vision. The guillotine's operators, the people's righteous anger, take great pride in keeping our meat cleaver nice and sharp for the cutting board.

We pass tents filled with sleeping militia members, the proletariat at long last awakened by the call to lose their chains and eat the rich. Three years ago, the downtrodden had finally had enough of the inequality, mistreatment, lies, and corruption all around them. They had risen in revolt, throwing the world into disarray. And in that disarray, they gorged themselves on the elites, consuming those who had gluttonously hoarded their

wealth at the expense of the masses.

Part of me wonders if the revolution might eventually begin to eat its own once it runs out of the remaining wealthy pricks.

We turn left at the auditorium and go our separate ways. Cam and Brenda will take the bodies we harvested to the kitchens for preparation while I carry the limp form of the girl to the medical station. Before she turns away, Brenda leaves me with one last glare. Her look is disapproving, but also…smug? Surely, I must have imagined the smirk right at the end.

The medical station is set up in the classrooms once used to teach teenagers to become nurses. It was abandoned in the initial uprising, but now it's been repurposed for treating the wounded members of the militia. Unfortunately for us, most doctors had been among the "professional classes" that were eaten in the second wave. It was understood that nurses were members of the working class, and it was to them that the revolutionaries turn now for medical support.

"Can she be saved?"

The charge nurse equivocates momentarily before promising to do his best. He takes the girl to the back room of a rundown anatomy lab. Vague instructions to pump the patient's stomach are shouted from behind the closed doors. Returning, he asks me what the girl's name is. I try to think back to the bedroom to recall any details about her. The memory is hazy with disjointed visions of the mother with half her face gone. Or, no. Had it been my wife with the look of sadness and acceptance in her eyes as I pulled the trigger?

…

"Call her Jane."

I don't stay to hear how it turns out for her.

The commissar will be waiting to hear my report in the administration building, and it will only be worse for me if I don't head there immediately. I slide my hand into my pocket to feel the cold metal band of the wedding ring from the sink, and I wish I had time to stop by my bunk to hide it.

In the quad, a light drizzle begins to fall, but the bonfire still burns on the hill illuminating my path across the traces of a desire path leading to the administration building. One could imagine the laughter and voices of young students meandering their way across the grass to their classes, unaware that the uprising would begin at a vocational college a lot like this, the next state over. The violent government reprisal would inspire millions to rise up. To reject the old world order in favor of a better one. "Let them eat genetically enhanced protein bars" came the quip from the president at the time, a billionaire former podcaster and fitness guru-turned politician.

I had watched on live TV as they slathered him in barbecue sauce before sticking him in a smoker for six hours. They say he came out red and caramelized after the screaming stopped.

The administration building was clearly built before most of the rest of campus. It still shows the wood and brick façade of the original architecture, a style that got replaced by metal and concrete across most of the other structures. It may have been warm and inviting to its students once, but now the mold growing on the doorframe and the dripping leak in the foyer combined with the claustrophobic feeling of cold humidity squeezing my wet clothes to my body only gives me the sense of impending calamity.

"What the fuck do you mean he just shot them?!"

The commissar has a voice like a foghorn, resonant and

bassy. It echoes in the halls over the squeaking of boots on linoleum and the shuffling of papers in offices.

In the conference room, I find a chair beside Brenda and Cam, already seated and making their report. The commissar stands, imposing, next to a large table lined with microphones that have long quit working. Behind him are half a dozen adjutants and officers adjusting maps of the surrounding communities and editing patrol schedules. One of those schedules had sent my team out to the neighborhood where we found the house today.

"He even admitted afterward that he knew he was violating the standing orders."

I had figured Cam would be the one to inform on me. I didn't expect it to really be Brenda also.

"And where is this bourgeois girl you brought back from the patrol?" The commissar eyes me angrily.

"I've left her at the med station. They're going to try to pump her stomach to clear whatever drugs her mother gave her."

"You know we have limited supplies as it is. It would have been more appropriate to euthanize the child. You certainly seem to have had no problem summarily executing her parents."

"That was different."

"Just tell him who you really are. Why you couldn't follow through."

I stare open-mouthed at Brenda.

"I told you I wouldn't lie for you anymore. I'm tired of being reprimanded and excluded from the feasts because you aren't a real revolutionary. I know why you ignored the orders. The kid looks just like Jane."

...

Suddenly I'm back in my old home. In my memory, it's smaller than it really was. Truly, it had been a mid-sized mansion. Much too large for a family of three. It had been important to me to have it built as large as possible as a status symbol. My partner in the brokerage had just bought a yacht, and I would not be outdone. When the revolution began and the mob came breaking through the gates at the front of the neighborhood, my wife and I had hidden upstairs with our daughter, Jane, while our neighbors were dragged screaming into the streets, torn apart and devoured raw.

When the crowds came bashing on our front door, my wife had looked at me and pleaded not to let them take us. I nodded, loaded my father's old handgun, told them I loved them, and then…

I was supposed to use the third bullet on myself afterward. But maybe it was the shock of seeing them laying there on the floor, or the guilt of having done it myself, or pure cowardice. Whatever it was, whatever reason or reflex, I didn't join them. Instead, I hid. From behind the bookcase, I watched as the sea of justice broke down the front door, surged up the stairs, and washed over the bodies of my wife and child, carrying them out with the surf into the street, never to rise again from the depths of the people's holy rage.

When I emerged from my hiding place, I joined the mob in their assault of the next gated community. The chants were easy enough to learn and shout in unison as we marched from door to door. The violence and pressure of conformity pressed my individuality from all sides, molding me into a part of the whole. For them it was liberation. For me it was numbness. A way to sublimate, or at least distract from, my shame.

I never told anyone until one night on a two-person patrol

with Brenda, the story just kind of…

"What are you, some kind of sympathizer?"

"Worse. He's one of them. He was a capitalist before the revolution."

Before they can even turn to look at me again, I'm gone. I don't remember how I got back out onto the quad, but I hear shouts from behind me over the rush of blood in my ears and my own wheezing breaths as I run back across the grass.

"Get him!"

"He's a traitor!"

"Fucking liar!"

I duck around the medical building to try to lose my pursuers. I need to think. I could try to go back for the girl, but who knows if she even made it, or if I would be able to carry her out with the whole base after me. Maybe if I could get to my bunk, the jewelry I had been collecting since my first patrol could be enough to bribe my way out of this…

Cam rounds the corner and grasps at the back of my shirt.

"Gotcha."

I twist hard and slap his hand away to break his grip. No time to get to my bunk now.

Fuck it. I sprint back toward the hill near the entrance. There are fewer people here away from the buildings, and maybe I can slip out before they close the gates.

I nearly make it.

Cam and a squad try to encircle me, but I spin and dodge under the arms of one of them to head up the hill toward the bonfire. Towards the guillotine. The light rain has stopped, and the muddy ground slides underfoot. On my hands and knees, I crawl the last few feet to the edge of the woodpile. Tendrils of steam rise from my wet clothes thanks to the heat of the flames.

To my left, the fire. To my right, the executioner's block. And directly behind me is Cam.

"You can't run, and you certainly can't buy your way out of this. There's no one to cover for you now, you lying sack of shit."

He reaches out to seize me, the same move as before.

"Gotcha."

It's my turn to say it. I snatch his wrist and pull. His momentum causes him to stumble and fall forward.

The latch falls into place with a click, and all it takes a quick pull of the lever for the blade to fall. Cam's head rolls down the far side of the hill into the crowd gathering below.

Strong hands grip my shoulders and force me to my knees. There's a sharp blow to the back of my head, and for a moment all I see is white. Then brown. When I come to, my face is pressed into the mud. I blink away the muck as best I can. The squelching steps of boots presage the commissar striding into my field of vision. Brenda is at his side.

"I think this is a trial that will take but a moment. On behalf of the 4th People's Constituent Militia Brigade, I hereby charge you with high treason, murder, assault, disobeying lawful orders, and I'll even toss in mail fraud for good measure. But most importantly, I accuse you of committing the unforgivable sin of avarice. How dare you have hoarded so much when others had to make do with so little. A witness has already testified to your confession. All in favor of a guilty verdict?"

The chanting chorus fills the night air. Guilty. Guilty. Guilty.

Brenda's face is inscrutable in the dancing light of the bonfire. The commissar leans down to me and whispers in my ear.

PUNK GOES HORROR II

"Don't be afraid. Fear spoils the flavor."

Two men drag me to my feet and another cuts my clothes off with a knife. The ring falls out of my pocket to the laughter of the onlookers, a final shiny confirmation of what they already knew to be true.

I shiver in my nakedness. What is this? Fear? Shame? Just the cold and wet? I'm struck from behind again and tossed to the ground. I see them bringing buckets and stakes up the hill before I black out. My last thoughts wander to the kid I left behind in the medical building. Maybe it doesn't redeem me for what I've done, but at least I tried.

The unique feeling of being rubbed down with an oily substance brings me back to consciousness. My hands and feet, I can't feel them. Looking down, I can see that they're bound tightly with ropes. Bony fingers pull me onto my back, crinkling the nylon tarp underneath me. A woman comes over with a brush dipped in vegetable oil and paints my body with rough strokes. When she turns back to scatter handfuls of ground spices over me, I try to wriggle away, but I'm pushed back onto the tarp. Hands reach out to rub the spices into the oil. The rough grit of the salt cuts my skin. After, they stretch my arms above my head, and the bonds on my wrists and ankles are tied to a long pole against my back.

It's a roasting spit.

The chant from the crowd swells around me.

"Do not struggle. Accept that this is inevitable. The revolution is the recipe. The carcasses of the rich will fuel our struggle with the fat of their excess. You will finally give something back to the world."

Brenda edges into my field of view. Her lips curl in disgust and she spits in my face.

"I thought you would have just committed to the

revolution after all this time. But I now know that's impossible for you. The greed in your heart has rotted it so that even if you don't have your wealth anymore, you can't stand to see anyone else thrive. Fuck you."

The commissar now looms over me.

"Any last words?"

"What about Jane? Is she ok?"

"Jane?"

"The kid I brought back."

A scowl crosses his face. Then, a wicked smile.

"The girl. She survived. The nurses pumped her stomach and were able to stabilize her. We'll take her to the reeducation camps tomorrow. But now, they say she needs something substantive to fill her stomach since it's empty."

There's a spike of pain in my side. I lower my chin to see a cooking thermometer protruding from my rib cage. He grips my cheeks with both hands and wrenches my head around to see a pair of revolutionaries carrying the young girl up the hill to the bonfire. We make eye contact. Is that...hunger...in her eyes?

I'm hoisted up by the spit and balanced across two stakes. By my feet, Brenda begins to lazily rotate me like a chicken on a rotisserie. The warmth from the fire that had been a pleasant reprieve on my naked skin against the night air now feels uncomfortably hot, growing hotter and hotter until I can't stand it anymore, and I begin to cry out. As the flesh on my belly blackens, the fat dripping, popping in the flames, the smell of my own slowly cooking body overwhelms me.

Delicious.

WoW, i CAN GeT seXuAL
PUNK goes HORROR II
2026 WORLD TOUR

WOW, I CAN GET SEXUAL TOO

CAT VOLEUR

IT'S NOT AROUSAL. NOT EXACTLY.

But I am *excited* when I hear the sound of the messenger go off. I know better than to check it—there's only one person who'd be reaching out this late—but my body is simply not my own.

I can't remember how long I've been lying here, heavy past the point of mobility, waiting for the worst part of the high to wear off. I must have been here awhile, seeing as I have to peel myself off sweat-drenched sheets to make it over to my desk. Countless hours that I've spent moldering away, and now she's cured me with a single

< hey >

I'm alive again. Tingling.

Her avatar looks pixelated on my ancient monitor, the blurry face not even a full inch across. The selfie was bad to begin with, and my piece of shit desktop isn't doing the girl any favors. So, it's definitely not arousal. And it's not her getting me all worked up like this, that would be pretty fucked up. The best I can figure is that it's some sort of Pavlovian response that makes the fabric of my boxers stretch tight as I sit down to message her back.

< hey >

PUNK GOES HORROR II

Were this just a normal night, I would think about this shit better and not be so fucking quick to answer. I promised myself I was gonna stop chatting to Mara. She's basically just a kid, and that doesn't feel right, what with me being an up-and-coming star and all. I may be stoned to shit, but even I know the optics are bad.

Would that I had something better to do than text chat back and forth with a teenage fan. But I don't. I say every time is going to be the last time, but here we are again. It's almost as though she can sense when I'm at my weakest and most miserable.

When my buddies aren't answering, and the weed is bad, and my high is starting to go morbid, it doesn't seem like such a bad thing we're doing.

Past a certain hour of the night, we're the only two people in the goddamned world. I'm almost grateful for her presence, because it means that I'm not all alone.

< *wat r u up 2?* >

I'm thinking about every mistake I've made in my life. How I got here. How sad it is. How I'll be remembered. How fucking bummed I'll be if I die before my band really takes off.

< *nothing much* >

I hope that it sounds cool, even though I know for a fact it's pathetic. Would 'not' have sounded less committal than 'nothing'? Maybe the singer of her favorite band should be too cool for full words. But then again, she may be hoping to get

a taste of my pretentious, lyricist side. That's all I'm good for, really—a tortured poet with a big, throbbing vocabulary.

< *Gross.* >

Why should I give two shits what some brat thinks about my digital linguistic mannerisms? I blame the drugs.

< *wanna chat?* >

I shouldn't, but I do.

This is how it always starts—there's nothing so wrong with chatting—and it always seems to get away from me. It would be easier to stop now, before we've really started.

Yet I find that I'm already sending a response.

< *sure* >

My fingers feel so alien that they may as well belong to someone else. That sort of excuse would not hold up well in a court of law. I don't think my history of substance abuse would do well in the court of public opinion, either.

< *wanna call?* >

No.

I don't.

I shouldn't.

The last time I called her—

I cut off the thought. It's better not to think about what exactly happened. It's enough that I felt like a piece of shit after,

and the lingering shame is enough to warn me off now. It reminds me that I should say no, absolutely not.

But then again, what's the alternative? If I don't have her, I'll just go back to bed half-stoned, all-zombified, and lie awake trapped in this Hell until the insomnia loses the chemical war being waged in my imbalanced brain.

< sure >

I'm quick to put the monitor back to sleep and grab my phone. I try not to reflect on how strange it is that I have her number saved. That we've done this before. That we're doing it again.

I *finally* hesitate.

It isn't too late. Nothing more needs to happen. Only I could really use the company right now, maybe a laugh. That's all this needs to be—a laugh.

So I call.

Ring!

I put the phone against my ear.

Ring!

I fall back on my bed, letting my head crash hard into the pillow. Maybe she'll help me relax enough that I can finally get some decent fucking sleep. Better decisions will be waiting for me in the morning, if I make it.

Ring!

I tell myself this will be the last time. I try to mean it.

"Hello?" she answers. Her voice seems different tonight, and I hate that I can tell a difference.

"Mara?" I ask.

"Of course," she says. "It's me."

Her words are coming out sort of breathy. Deep. Almost

gravelly. She sounds … *older* … than I know her to be, and not half so innocent as on our last call. I wonder if she's started without me.

"What are you doing?" I ask.

I promised after the last time never to let it go that far again. It's amusing—a little funny sometimes, listening to the mild sorts of things that a girl like her fantasizes about. But listening to her explore herself for the first time on the other end of the line…

I'm not letting it go this far if she *already* has a hand down her skirt before I call. That's out my control—if anything *she's* taking advantage of *my* loneliness. There's a tickle of something between my legs and I shift my hips involuntarily as I wait for her to answer.

"What do you want me to be doing?"

Her words are a cold tongue, licking heavy and wet down my spine: sensual, but wrong. I feel chilled right down to my rotten core.

I don't like how adult she sounds in this moment. Not that I want her to sound younger—I'm not some kind of pervert or anything. I just find it alarming how good she's gotten at this over the course of a couple calls. She's trying to seduce me and I'm not exactly laughing about it anymore.

"That depends," I tell her.

Even *I* don't know where the fuck I'm going with this. The sultry, leading nature of my own voice makes my stomach churn. My skin is alive and crawling with anticipation. I'm mortified and excited, and for some unholy reason my body is responding to the overstimulation with an uncomfortable stiffness in the last place I want to be caught stiff right now. I need to get out of this whole mess.

PUNK GOES HORROR II

"Depends on what?" she whispers.

My dick twitches in response to her tone. It's a rush to know she'd do anything I asked, but it's a damn terrifying thing to think I might be about to cross some lines for *her*. I've got to put a stop to this. It's not a joke anymore. I'm having the sort of thoughts now that could get me ten to life.

"On what you're wearing," I hear myself answer.

Why did I say that?

What the Hell is wrong with me tonight?"

"A dress."

Disappointment. Relief. She's not naked. She's not masturbating. This could be—is—just a normal call. Innocent, even.

"Cool," I try to brush it off. "Nice." I don't mention the part where her modesty has stopped me from going to a dark place. Where she may have just saved me from eternal damnation.

"It is nice," she says. Her tone hasn't changed at all—this fucking teenager sounds like she's out here with the sole intention of putting porn stars to shame. "It's black. And lacy."

Lingerie?

But no. *No.* That's another bad thought. I don't need to be thinking that sort of thing. Egging her on. I've sobered up just a touch, and I'm beginning to regret that I called.

I give her what I intend as a noncommittal grunt of disinterest, only to hear how vulgar the noise sounds in my throat.

"It's the sort of dress," she whimpers, "that you could bury someone in."

She moans.

It's a loud, long, trembling cry of ecstasy that seems to echo through the speaker. Through the haze of horror and

excitement and disbelief, it occurs to me that if *this* is her idea of dirty talk, she's in need of some serious help.

The idea that I may not be the best person to assist is fleeting.

She chose me. She came to me. Maybe, in a strange way, it's my duty to help her before she goes out into the real world and tries this on some sort of freak. There are a lot of real sickos out there into some depraved shit. Someone might really hurt her.

I listen to her heavy breathing as she comes back down, filled with a new sense of self-righteous purpose.

"Are you alright?" I feel like a better person already. It's a really good thing, actually, that I'm the one who called and not some creep who would take advantage. I can still talk her off the edge of whatever sort of fucked up fantasy she's got that involves being buried.

"I feel better now," she tells me.

I'll make sure she stays better. I can do that much, at least. It's not like I'm some sort of pedo or freak or someone who would even ask for something in return. There are a lot of guys out there a lot worse than me. Maybe I can build up her self-esteem so she learns to avoid them like the metaphorical plague.

"Good girl," I croon, feeling like a fucking saint.

"Do you like that?" she asks. "Listening to me?"

"Why don't you tell me what *you* like?"

Fuck, I am on a roll. If I made it a point to be this considerate all the time I could probably get myself a wife. Or at the very least a woman my own age who would go down on me from time to time.

"I like when you call," she says.

"Yeah? What else?"

"I like hearing your voice when I touch myself."

PUNK GOES HORROR II

Amateur shit, but harmless. This whole thing we're doing is *basically harmless.* "What else?"

"I liked it when my Daddy found out about us."

My mouth is suddenly very dry.

We're not doing anything wrong. I haven't done anything to her. But I don't know if her father would necessarily share that opinion.

"Mara—"

"Yes! I like it when you say my name."

"What do you mean he found out about…"

"About us," she says. I can almost hear her smile through the line.

I need to extract myself from this situation immediately. No more helping. No more preparing her. No more good intentions with questionable good deeds. No more anything.

"Listen," I say, trying and failing to keep the panic from showing in my voice. "I'm sorry if you imagined more between us than there was, but there isn't anything for him to know." The words taste familiar on my tongue.

She laughs.

She laughs so loud that I can almost feel her breath on my neck through the speaker. "Oh, *I'm* the one imagining things? Tell me, where do you think you are right now?"

What sort of sick game is she playing?

I'm at home in my apartment on the same piece of shit mattress that the last tenant was too lazy to toss out. It's dark, with only a few lights from my tower illuminating the walls, but I know where I am.

For some reason, I find I don't want to insist. That feels too much like playing along, and I don't want to feed into the idea that her delusions have anything to do with me.

"Mara, I think you need to get some help."

"Weren't you going to help me?"

Shit.

How does she know about that? I never said that out loud. Did I?

No.

Even my dumb-ass self would know how bad it sounds, despite my purity of intention.

"I never said that."

"You thought you would though, didn't you? Thought you would prepare me for the cruel world?"

How the fuck is she inside my head?

The lines of the walls and ceiling are swimming. I feel lightheaded. There's smoke in the room—but I know everything I smoked earlier should have long since dissipated. Is my vision this bad? Am I hallucinating? Sick?

This whole thing makes more sense as a fever dream than as a real moment in time. Maybe it's all a nightmare. Only, it feels so damn vivid.

"Mara, I'm not feeling so hot right now. I think I'd better—"

"You sounded plenty hot and bothered a minute ago when you asked what I was wearing."

"No, I'm serious."

My surroundings have taken on the aesthetic of a vintage cartoon—out of focus and staticky. I can see swimming lines of heatwaves. Something's definitely not right.

"Do you want my help?" she asks.

"I think I'd better just call you back."

"I think that you'd better touch yourself," she coos. "You'll feel better if you relieve a little bit of that pressure. Try it,

see if that doesn't cool you off."

I try to hang up on her, but my limbs have gone heavy again. Maybe I'm not as sober as I thought. I'm burning alive in here, but somehow she's right. There's still an uncomfortable pressure in my balls that feels worse and worse the more she talks like this.

"I don't think that's such a good idea."

"I would die for you," she whispers on the other end of the phone.

"I know," I tell her.

The worst part of this is the itch rising up in me. It's a sort of creeping, crawling sensation that's spreading and intensifying over my crotch as we talk. I *do* want to relieve that itch.

"So do it," she commands. "Touch yourself...for me."

There's a quality in her voice that's hard to place. It's not the pleading desperation present in our last call, nor is it the sexy whisper curated for this particular conversation.

It's a sinister sort of...resignation? Futility? Omnipotence?

To my horror, I can feel my arm moving down my body. This is not a command I gave it, but rather my hand seems to be moving on Mara's volition.

"This is for you," I tell her, as if that makes this any better. It's awkward, holding the phone in my good hand as I lift my hips up to better reach beneath the elastic of my waistband with the other.

"I like your voice," she continues, unprompted now. "I've always liked your voice...the words you write and the way you sing them." Her tone is teasing, but it doesn't matter. She's basically white noise to me as my fingers finally brush against—

"What the fuck?" I scream.

I drop the phone, my disgust a stronger motivation than my morals. My left hand has made contact with something wet and writhing where I had expected there to be skin. I withdraw as quickly as I can, only to see fat, white maggots slithering along my palm.

There's the distinct *pop!* of the call disconnecting. I barely have time to register the sound before I've turned my head to the side and am puking up my guts. The floor is swimming in and out of focus, trembling through a thickening cloud of smoke. I can feel my brain pounding in painful rhythm along with my heartbeat. I can hardly draw breath through all the sticky-sweet globs of stomach acid that are clogging up my nose.

Ring!

Not now, I want to tell her, but I can't.

I'm sorry if you imagined more between us than there was.

Ring!

I remember it.

The frantic phone calls.

Over and over again.

For days.

Over and over, the constant ringing and sobbing voicemails as she tried to get my attention. We'd just been fucking around a little, and then she just had to go and take the damn thing too far.

Ring!

And then the silence.

PUNK GOES HORROR II

The calls stopped coming all at once.

Long months of awful silence followed before I found out what had happened to her. When her dad called me and told me what she'd done to herself. What she'd said about me in her note. How she had printed out and kept all our messages.

He sent the police to talk to me after I blocked him, but all the while I was getting angry messages and threats from burners. He started trying to talk to my band mates, started hanging around outside our shows, screaming and shouting to anyone who would listen that I was somehow responsible.

Ring!

I'm back on the floor. Each shriek of my damn phone feels like a nail being driven deeper into my skull.

I prop myself up as best I can with a gelatin forearm, trying to find the damn thing. That whole situation with Mara and her dad must have been some sort of nightmare or some sick joke because she's alive now.

She's *calling* me.

Ring!

My fingers find the cool plastic of my case and finally I'm able to answer the call.

"Make it stop," I plead.

"Do you remember, then?"

"Yes," I stammer, "but-but no. You're here. You're still *here*. You're alive."

There's that laugh again that echoes three-hundred and sixty degrees around me instead of coming from my speaker. "Oh

baby," she says. "Neither of us is alive."

I know two things for sure.

One, this bitch is fucking crazy. And two, her dad must be responsible for whatever the Hell is happening to me right now. That fucker has been stalking me for weeks, trying to get justice for something Mara did to herself, and she's still here. She didn't even really do it, apparently.

The weakness in my body, the burning of my room, it's all urgent again. Never mind what sort of sick suggestions my broken psyche might be susceptible to, I'm scared about how far this man will really go. The smoke in my room feels thicker.

"Is my apartment on fire?"

"Oh, I love this part," she says with the casual endearment of someone watching a favorite movie over for a hundredth time.

"What part? What the fuck are you…?"

But the question withers and dies on my tongue. This isn't my apartment anymore. This hasn't been my apartment for a long time. I couldn't stand to be here after everything—couldn't even afford to be here once the rumors started.

"I love the look of panic on your face…that feeling as it all comes rushing back to you."

I don't love it. I barely have the strength to keep myself propped up against my pillows. I'm absolutely melting and my guts are somersaulting all around my insides and I can still feel those fucking *things* crawling over me.

"Tell me what he did to me!"

She must find my attempt at intimidation as pathetic as I do because again, she's laughing. "*He* didn't need to do anything. Your band didn't want fuck all to do with you after they figured out what sort of shit you were up to."

"No."

PUNK GOES HORROR II

They'd had my back when I was facing harassment. When I was being stalked.

"They had zero tolerance for grown men who go sniffing around little girls."

"No," I say. "I'm not. I wasn't. I just wanted to—"

"To help me? When you weren't laughing at me or thinking about my underwear or stringing me along to stroke your ego?"

"It wasn't like that."

My band would have known that, even if no one else in the world believed me. They would have. Right? My band has always been my life.

"What did *you* think it was like? Because I thought you *loved* me."

"We never even did anything!"

A couple of messages. Three or four phone calls. I never even touched her. She was the one who did all the touching.

"You knew exactly what you were doing."

"I never touched you!"

"But you wanted to, didn't you?" she asks. "You told me I made it up, but you wanted to touch me."

Of course I did.

She was all over me, and she was young and hot, and she wanted me and it felt good.

"Funny how I wasn't too young until *after* those calls. Funny how you wanted to see the pictures until I told you I loved you."

I'd forgotten about the pictures. I'd forgotten why I finally tried to tune her out.

"Mara," I choke out. I mean to apologize, but the words don't come.

"It wasn't just your band, either. It was the fans. Your career ended before it even started. Because it doesn't matter how talented you were, there's no room on the scene for trash like you."

I shake my head, but the whole room shakes with it.

"You want to know the sad part?" she asks, like this whole night isn't the saddest thing that's ever happened to me. "If I had been alive, I *still* would have defended you. I'd have done anything for you."

I throw my phone against the wall as hard as I can manage. I can't listen to her voice anymore. I roll over onto my back, already exhausted by the effort.

First thing's first, I've got to get the bugs off me. The itching is truly enough to drive a man to madness. Summoning all my strength, I reach down to strip off my boxers. The fabric turns to dust beneath my fingers.

I force myself to squint down at the writhing mass of larvae that has replaced my manhood. They're all fucking and feeding and breeding on my skin—only my skin isn't really *skin* anymore. It's nothing but a sticky, reddish brown layer of decomposing tissues; it's melted clay trying to return to the earth.

I try to brush the demons off my genitals but my whole world erupts in pain. The slimy remnants of my nether regions congeal to the goo left coating my finger bones, and the entire mess tears free from my frame. Stars obstruct my view, and I can't think of anything else until I've given the tiny suns time to sink back into the onyx of my tunneling vision.

My bed is gone.

The sweltering apartment that I used to live in, and my computer, and my guitar, and my phone, they're all gone.

There's nothing in the world but the blackness of this small,

wooden box beneath the dirt where I have been laid to unrest. Where I will not be remembered.

This is Hell.

I am in a Hell of my own making—a sentience after death where I can barely move and there is no release for the aching pain of my phantom appendage. I lie here, and I am slowly overcome by the creeping remembrance that I did this to myself. I overdosed in my piece of shit car years after I'd unknowingly taken the stage for a final time.

I'll be remembered for Mara, and not my music—if I am remembered at all. Even when I try to recall my name, I can feel it slipping off the tip of my acidic tongue.

Ding!

It's not arousal. Not exactly.

But I am *excited* when I hear the sound of the messenger go off. I know better than to check it—there's only one person who'd be reaching out this late—but my body is simply not my own.

PILLARS
PUNK goes HORROR II
2026 WORLD TOUR
WEIRD·DARK·HORRIFYING·PATRICK BARB

PILLARS

PATRICK BARB

IT WASN'T SO MUCH THAT WE, the citizens of Sonny's Vista (population: 1,011), were *changed* by the pillars— those stone-like columns, flawlessly smooth and whitish gray like impenetrable fog, all rising to perfectly matching heights, each spaced evenly apart from its neighbor, in numbers great enough that they outlined the town's perimeter. We certainly weren't changed in some mystical, magical fashion. Rather, it was the emergence of these mystery pillars from an indeterminate source underneath our feet that helped us understand who we were meant to be all along. They reminded us of deep and fundamental truths we had forgotten. We were a town, a community.

We are *still* a town, *still* a community.

So, when it comes to our relationship with the pillars, it's not so much about what *they* can do for us. Indeed, we've only been able to discern minimal advantages and the majority of those have proven not at all widely applicable. Together, as a town, we have come to understand and truly appreciate the fact that the pillars chose *us*. Sprouting up one May evening after the schools had let out for the summer, these pillars could have grown from Hell or from a hollow earth lost world kingdom, or from dreams of gods that existed before God. They could

have chosen to surround any other village or town or city—just imagine them around some sprawling cosmopolitan monstrosity of urban oppression. But we were the town that the pillars chose.

In the main, we view our connection to the pillars as a relationship of equals. Of peers. We choose to accept the pillars as part of our community. All because *they* have chosen us.

Of course, there are some of us who wish to give ourselves even more agency in this exchange. Simply put, some wish to claim *we* were the ones who made the choosing possible in the first place. *We* chose to make our town, to shape our community, molding it in such a way that it became a place where the pillars would have no choice *but* to appear.

Father Albert...we're sorry, we know he went by Al, just Al, after the pillars emerged...he'd said it's all a matter of semantics. "It's easy to get caught going around in circles if we're not careful," he'd say. "But the truth of the matter is, we are here, the pillars are here. We are here together in this moment. That is as far as the truth will take us. The rest comes from faith, belief."

Earlier this morning, we pulled Al's body from The Creek—whose proper name most of us have forgotten and that we long ago settled for referring to exclusively as "The Creek." It's the one that runs back behind the Brownrigg Place. That was last night—when Al must have gone and got himself killed. The outsiders, the invaders, and those who do not understand and thus want to destroy the pillars, they'd lured him away, stripped him bare and laid his clothes out in front of the pillar he was supposed to be guarding. Like some mock offering, some faux sacrifice. Al's beaten, bloodied, broken body appeared pale, flabby, and unremarkable when viewed through the slimy top layer of murk across the creek water's surface. One of our number who helped pull the body out from the creek said it felt

like touching a balloon stretched tight over lumpy, home-cooked mashed potatoes.

Doubtless, that vulgar bon mot came from Davey Roebuck, the punker-poet-laureate of the eleventh grade at Sonny Day Senior High. Mohawk dyed blue, ears gauged with lobes dangling like Silly Putty. He had a sneer that many of us once thought permanent, that he's since replaced with a serene expression, his lips parted slightly, as if permanently on the verge of giving away the most intimate secrets of the universe.

Prior to this impromptu eulogizing, we'd all last heard from Davey when he and his father Greg radioed in a warning from the opposite side of town—reporting the approach of a caravan of vehicles driven by more would-be pillar destroyers. Taking turns, both Roebucks had glimpsed the invaders through Greg's high-powered field binoculars. The wannabe destroyers approached our town from the west. Soft-spoken Greg, a Scoutmaster in the time before the pillars, was heard screaming and swearing on the line by all of us back at base camp, this string of invective transferred from their patrol outpost to our HQ in the old Armory Dance Hall, where Christmas lights were strung between rifle notches in the old building's brick facade.

Someone, amused by the old Scoutmaster's frustrated outburst, must have gotten bored, because they connected the two-way radio output into the speakers at our makeshift concert venue. Scoutmaster Greg's curses were then paired with awkward three-cord shredding by Pablo Enriquez, whose papa worked as a janitor because our school administration didn't ask too many questions about after-hours staff or double-check IDs, and soon all of us in the building were throwing our bodies around the wide-open dance floor. Arms windmilling, sweat droplets engaged in silent sprints across our bodies, all while

fists flew and our bloody-mouthed smiles grew and grew some more. Every breath taken by the Scoutmaster mid-walkie-talkie-rant was punctuated by our communal grunts and growls, words and meanings indecipherable even to us—the ones who made them.

But, back to that other pillar, the one at the edge of the Brownrigg estate. You'll know the place we mean because once you're there, you can't miss the still-standing, but no longer sustaining, farmhouse. It's been long abandoned across a couple of generations, following the family's departure from Sonny's Vista in the 1990s. The Brownrigg Pillar, which we seem to have given a formal name to, thanks to its connection to the death of one of our own, remained undamaged despite the attempted destruction by the outsiders.

Which, of course, is not surprising. Not when you know the pillars like we do.

Not a mark, not a scratch, no graffiti tags, no scorch marks from attempted burnings. Those who would destroy the pillars have, at the very least, learned that lesson and don't often try such tactics anymore. They understand that the pillars surrounding our town are not so easily bested or destroyed. Most times, nowadays, the ones from outside park their vehicles and stand a good distance from town limits, and then shout and mock, teasing us without mercy or quarter.

All because the pillars chose us and not them.

They mean to draw us out. They'd love to see us move past the pillars, past the safety of town. Because, once we're past the pillars, once we've gone astray...

"There's nothing we can do for them," Deputy Mayor Yolanda Garrison said about Mayor Terry Rosen and his wife Tina and their two teen twins Tommy and Tamara. The First

Family of Sonny's Vista, they'd been out of town—a vacation to Disney World, or maybe Disney Land—when the pillars rose all nonchalant and remarkably unremarkable. On their return, their SUV— packed full of suitcases and overpriced gifts from Mickey Mouse gift shops— rolled closer and closer to the pillars at the edge of town. The nearest resident on the Sonny's Vista side of the pillars was Old Freddy, our local wino who sleeps by the tracks and sometimes watches after a dog named Snapper that he claims was a wolf before he tamed him. Freddy came to the town meeting after the events in question and, between long, purposeful swigs from his 40 ounces of Mad Dogg 20-20, he told us what happened.

"Damnedest damn thing I seen," he said, holding himself remarkably straight and tall, without needing to lean against a podium or brace his hand against a wall, especially remarkable given the near-toxic alcohol fumes wafting from his dirt-clotted clothing and mud-streaked, blistered skin. "Once Mayor T and kin got close 'nough where they had a good eyeline to the pillar, it's like somethin' went and changed inside 'em all. Like a switch got flipped. Mayor's face went beet red, almost dang purple, looking so mad I swear I saw veins popping out his forehead. And his missus and the children won't much better. Through that windshield I seen 'em all foaming at their mouths. Like mad dogs. Like a goddamn Old Yeller. That's when Mr. Mayor's car went shooting forward, like it was a damn bullet, man. No slowing, no nothing, they just plowed straight on into the pillar. And that car of theirs, it got crushed against it like someone stepping down hard and full-footed on a empty soda can. Except that sound their car made was so much worse. Nails on a chalkboard and cats in heat and below that screaming, crying. Inside, they sounded like babies, how they scream and cry with their whole bodies

because they haven't had a chance to understand the concept of disappointment. I heard all that…and then nothing."

The late Mayor's vehicle was sheared in two against the pillar, and both halves were crumpled, tossed back from the impact point. No one has ventured past the pillar to retrieve the bodies or the remnants of the vehicle. Animals have been spotted outside the pillar perimeter, sometimes considering the wreckage, but ultimately giving it a wide berth. They stop short of direct contact, of scavenging, or feasting on the smashed and bloated dead. The wildlife seem smarter than the human life, that so-called civilized world meant to exist outside our pillar-protected town.

Mayor Yolanda was sworn in once Old Freddy finished his story. She and the Town Council established what we've all come to call the Pillar Laws. (1) No one from outside the perimeter is allowed to try to come inside Sonny's Vista. (2) Every able-bodied man or woman above the age of sixteen is required to patrol the perimeter for at *least* three hours per day, so we make sure the pillars remain in place. (3) Anyone who leaves or even steps beyond the pillars may not return.

We all agree that they're good laws. You see, we made the laws together. They're ours. Just like the pillars are ours. Folks outside, they don't, they can't, understand this. So, first they tried to destroy what we have. Then, they mocked it. Lately, they've tried to make us all feel shamed.

"But how can we feel shame for something we love?" teenage Sissy Tenenbaum asked, cupping her hands around her mouth and shouting her query back at a ranting zealot with a megaphone who stood across from the pillar that marked the edge of her family's property, the line separating town from our next-door neighbors in Forrestville.

The megaphone man had no reasonable response to this query. Certainly nothing that any of us would wish to remember.

When tactics of destruction or aggression fail to move us, because we are united, because we are connected under the silent guardianship of the pillars, the outsiders drop to their knees on top of the leaves and dirt or on sidewalks and cracked asphalt roads, all before begging us to let them in, promising that they will "be good," and worship the pillars like they think we do.

None of them understand.

Again, consider the theories put forth about the makers of the pillars. Was it aliens? Angels? Devils? Are the pillars actually time machines cloaked to resemble these stone monoliths? Are there passengers inside, staring out and gawping at us, observing us as we go about our lives, trying to make sense of daily challenges that somehow some way persist even in the face of the uncanny?

Yes. No? Maybe…

But those questions aren't ones that *we* have ever thought to ask. No, we've encountered these questions by way of mad megaphone rantings and ravings, along with scrawled manifestos tossed across the border as paper airplanes, all courtesy of those from the outside. It's as if they can't help but ask themselves these unanswerable questions about the pillars. And then they're making themselves enraged by the non-answers they've concocted.

It's a farce. A mummers' game. How fair can it be when they've chosen to be both Inquisition and tormented?

Despite their seeming imperviousness, we guard the pillars. We just don't know how long they will last. They could leave us ten years from now, or tomorrow, or they could be leaving right this very moment. Mayor Yolanda and other town leaders

remind us to be vigilant, because those who would destroy the pillars may still find a way to do so.

And we have, all of us left in Sonny's Vista (population: 1,010), decided that this is a good and noble course of action. The pillars chose us. And we, in turn, must continue to make a community worthy of being chosen. We are intertwined like chain link fence diamonds, spreading from side to side and stacked one on top of the other.

Of course, we are not free from sin when it comes to the pillars. How could we be? When you have only extrapolations and interpretations devoid of answers, how could we ever hope to avoid mistakes?

The worst of these came from a group of us who missed the story Old Freddy told at the meeting. This foursome of young men and women—a band visiting from Forrestville and crashing on the couch of local concert promoter Mason Morrow—had questioned whether or not they were worthy of the protection afforded by the pillars. Bearing the juvenile band moniker of DICKPUNCH, these itinerant musicians grappled with very adult questions of existence, fairness, and justice.

"Are we supposed to be here? We aren't from town, but we are *inside* the town. Do the pillars want us here?" Those questions, posed to bandmates in private via lead singer, Brendan Boners (birth name Brendan Banners), were echoed by his bandmates. Later, when the surviving members came to us and we embraced them as part of our town, we all expressed regret that they hadn't come to us sooner.

Bassist, drummer, lead guitar, the trio decided Brendan should take the lead in their search for answers, just as he did on beer-splattered stages and inside the smoke-filled bars of the circuit they traveled. And Brendan Boners went right along with

this plan, showing a willingness to sacrifice himself for the good of the band. "We tied him to a pillar, facing out to the world beyond. It was hard work, especially because we tried to keep as much of our own bodies inside the town limits as we could. Later, exploring in the woods, one of us found old buck antlers and tied them to Brendan's head, cinching this new addition tight with looping strands of cold, greedy barbed wire. We smashed his arms and legs, despite his protests. 'I won't try to escape. I won't try to run. Please believe me,' he told us. However, after each blow struck, we laid our hands upon the pillar and felt a sense of inner peace and connectedness, an ethereal, harmonic vibration, as though a higher power played the three of us, making us a part of a three-cord ballad. We came to trust in the pillars and nothing else besides."

At this part of their story, so many of us nodded. We were still learning to trust each other at that point. We still hadn't come around to the idea that we were bound by the pillars, and so we were bound to each other.

"We slept beside the pillar, still within its protective boundary, while Brendan faced the world and bled and sobbed and suffered. We woke the next morning to the pungent scents of bloodshed and piss, leaking in equal measure from our makeshift Judas Goat, the sole repository for the sins of a world before and beyond this town's boundaries both physical and temporal."

When the remaining bandmates finished speaking, we explained that their story was *ours* now. By vowing to make their story our own, any fault or sin would fall equally upon all our shoulders. That was the moment that we went from population: 1008 to population: 1011.

...

PUNK GOES HORROR II

Later.

We uncovered the above document, a record of our early days in Pillars' Vista (from that time when the old names were still in use, but slowly fading). Here in Pillars' Vista (population: 1,231), we trust in the pillars to keep us safe, to keep those who would destroy us at bay. Patrols are now once a week, a rotating roster of citizens participating. Some of us skip the proceedings and our new mayor Brendan Banners Jr. says nothing to reprimand us or to inspire us to any renewed commitments to our pillars.

Still, there is something—a feeling, a shared consciousness, or perhaps a mass delusion—that draws us all to the perimeter of town as the sun is rising on a new day. One of our number (with an aptitude for numbers) mentioned that the number of our citizenry now matches the number of the pillars that encompass our existence. Many of us found this amusing. Many of us cast wary glances around, worrying of signs and portents that we couldn't hope to comprehend.

When we looked out past the pillars, something new caught our eyes. After so many years of silence, a long period of peace from the would-be destroyers, we finally faced something new. Piles of bones, fragments of rusted, ruined automobiles, a skeleton wearing a makeshift deer horn crown, the debris and detritus of a frustrated other. All of these and more have been gathered by those outside. With the focus of an army of artisans and steady hands in sync, they've made these piles rising from the ground, shooting up toward the sky.

We recognize these columns for what they are.

Because they couldn't destroy *our* pillars, they have made their own. Patchwork, hodgepodge, imperfect creations. From a far enough distance, we suppose they might look the same as the

real things. But move close enough and you'll see, it's a pose, a fake, a phony.

Our most ancient citizen, the tremor-ridden gentlemen we have called Fred for years and years now, he spoke at the revelation of these false pillars. "Let them have their fun. Let them make of their world what they want. They don't understand that the pillars are not simply columns. They're not monolithic structures growing straight up and down."

It's hard to tell whether the quavering voice bears witness to prophecy or is simply evidence of the aftereffects of sobriety come too late in life to reverse alcoholic ravages. But Fred is us, as much as any other one inside Pillars' Vista is us, and so we understand what he means.

The pillars don't just stand alone. They have a purpose. They hold something up. They keep it aloft, raised over our heads. We are ready now.

Ready to raise our heads, tilting back farther, farther, farther still. Flat hands over brows to block out the sun, we will see what these pillars have held for all these years.

And we will ask if this roof, ceiling, or whatever it may be is equal to the task of keeping us protected from whatever may be trying to reach us from above.

disMANTLE Me
fizzgig
PUNK goes HORROR II
2026 WORLD TOUR

DISMANTLE ME

CHRIS PANATIER

THE FLY SITS IN THE SHADE OF THE PASTA SHOP, watching a couple having a date on the patio. This is the fly's favorite place in all of Melbourne to sit. Despite the warm air, the shade is always cool. The leftovers are always plentiful. And the man server is the most beautiful thing her many eyes have ever seen.

He hasn't appeared yet today, but he is the one who works when the sun is high, so he's bound to arrive soon. The couple read their menus, sometimes flapping them when other insects swoop in to harass. The fly pivots on the windowsill and watches the door, *waiting* for him to emerge, a glorious, shining man with sun-shimmered skin and eyeballs of dreamy, sky-deep blue.

The couple also watches the door, but for them it isn't about seeing the server man himself. It is because they want him to bring them a drink of water and then to take their order. Neither of them, nor any other human, is capable of the love the fly has for the man server.

A shade across the door, and then—Oh! There he is! The fly rejoices, buzzing her wings in the frequency of elation and affection, exposing her heart for all to hear. Oh, how she fancies the man server.

PUNK GOES HORROR II

He comes from the inside of the restaurant with two glasses of water already dripping with condensate. He wears slim black pants over his long legs, and the fly imagines him with four more just like them. Six legs and a pair of wings and together they could take to the sky. But even as a fly man, he would keep his luscious skin and noon-blue eyes, and she would show him her world of infinite size and smells. Then, in her dreams, breeding.

The man server asks if the couple are ready to order their food. The man person orders first, asking for a cheeseburger and French fries. This is a boon for the fly. Such a meal always results in crumbs of bread and crunchies of potato. Sometimes even a crumble of beef. The beautiful man server turns to the woman person and the fly sees that she has noticed him. Her watery eyes gaze hungrily upon the man server like he is a fresh pile of dung. Her teeth bite at her lip. Her fingers twirl at bits of her beach sand hair.

The fly vibrates her wings in the frequency of warning. The same tone she uses when other flies encroach on a claimed bit of cheese.

The woman person is not attuned to the fly's tones, however, and she continues to open herself up to the man server, finally placing an order for tomato soup and grilled cheese. Good choices, thinks the fly, *for a child.*

The man server returns inside. The fly hardly notices, so divided her attention has become on the interloping woman person.

The fly launches from her sill, shooting across the patio to the couple's table. She buzzes them in angry loops and circles, making them swat and dodge, and the fly laughs her laugh that they cannot hear. She lands on the woman person's shoulder and defecates prodigiously. She flies up to where the part in her

hair exposes a bit of scalp and consumes a flake of the woman person's dandruff. It is tasty, but not so delicious as the woman person would like the man server to believe. When a hand comes up to investigate the sensation, the fly easily avoids it and returns to the sill, laughing her little laugh.

The man server arrives with the food. The woman person thanks him effusively and strikes up a conversation. How long has he worked at Basil, is he from Melbourne, does he live nearby?

The fly scoffs, for she already knows his life. She has heard the man server tell other customers. He has worked at the restaurant for eight months. He was pupated and hatched in Melbourne and has lived here all his life. His home is nearby, in fact, as the fly has often followed him down Swanston Street, where she spies at him through his bedroom window until he pulls the shades for sleep. The fly knows more about the man server than the woman person ever will.

On hearing his answers, the woman person giggles and shrugs her shoulders, making herself cute like a maggot. Her date, who sees that he is no longer the focus of the woman person's attention, excuses himself for the bathroom.

The fly has seen this move before.

He isn't coming back.

The woman person doesn't seem to notice that her date has vacated. When the man server returns to fill her water glass, she resumes conversation with him as if she had arrived alone, telling him of her home, her job as a banker, her passion for yoga. The fly understands this dance very well.

She watches the man server's reactions. Is his smile a friendly, accommodating type, angling for tips? Or is he genuinely charmed by the woman person's bold advances? It is hard for the fly to tell.

PUNK GOES HORROR II

The woman person asks for an espresso to-go and the man server dashes off. The woman person checks her reflection in a circular pocket of sky she keeps in her bag. The man server returns with the coffee and leaves the check. Smiling, the woman person signs the bill, her face glowing red like a cat's hot asshole. She strolls away with a self-satisfied grin on her face as if she's just come across a fresh pile of rodent scat.

Good riddance.

By the next day, the fly has almost forgotten about the woman person until she sees her again, bouncing up the sidewalk through the kaleidoscope of her six thousand eyes.

The fly pivots in place, dancing between the door to the restaurant and the oncoming problem. The woman person sits in the same spot as the day before. Her legs extend from the hem of a short dress in courtship display. The woman person is adept at attracting mates. The fly hates her.

The man server emerges and the fly flutters one wing for him. It is her best affection display and not easily performed. But he does not respond.

He goes directly to the woman person, whose brightly colored lips move in a way designed to make the man server think about mating with her. The fly leaps from her sill in a fit of humming rage, darting at the woman person, diving at her face, making her flail and slap. Hopefully the man server will notice this and think that the woman person is formed of excrement.

A laminated menu cuts through the air, narrowly missing the fly. She spins off on turbulent vortices, disoriented and confused. The attack had not come from the woman person, but from the man server. The fly regains her equilibrium enough to flutter down to a nearby chairback. Already, the man server has resumed chatting with the woman, a big smile on his rugged

face, menu rolled up and slapping the palm of his hand. To the fly's dismay, he does not seem to believe the woman is made of shit.

The pumping vessel that runs along the fly's abdomen is broken by the man server's betrayal. Flies don't cry, which is good. Tears from six thousand eyes would desiccate her into a husk.

Instead of crying, she waits patiently on her sill for the woman person to finish her lunch, then follows to her little bungalow. The fly watches through a window, raging. Were she ready to lay eggs, she would deposit them in the woman's skin and allow her babies to eat of her flesh. *Flystrike*. But then, the fly wants better for her offspring than this whore-painted megafauna. She buzzes her wings in the frequency of threat and shoots back to the restaurant.

…

The woman person returns every day to resume her courting dance. Some days the man server sits down to talk. They often hold hands beneath the table. They embrace. They touch mouths, sucking on one another's fleshy red probosces. The fly is overcome with sadness, understanding deep down in the twitching hairs of her abdomen that waiting for the man server to love her is a gnat's errand. They will never be together. He will never accept her. They will never mate and reproduce. Still, even with her time running out, destitute of his love, she reflects fondly on their time together.

The time when the man server picked up a piece of cake and took a bite out of it to prompt a laugh from the crying child who had dropped it. The fly had vomited performatively to keep the fun going, but no one had noticed.

The time when he chased down a pair of criminals who

ran out on the bill. The fly had pursued as well, buzzing at their eyes and distracting them long enough for the server man to catch them.

Until now, they had been something of a team.

She flies to the local wharf where fish are brought in each day from boats. Out back is a mountain of discarded heads, tails, fins, skins, and so on. Vultures circle. There are billions of flies here—a glorious selection of mates, were a fly to care about such things. But she cares only about mating as quickly as possible so she can get back to Basil, where she will spend her final hours before laying her eggs.

She settles on a discarded chunk of groper and is immediately bumped from behind by a horny male. His pheromones aren't her preference, but they bleed the truth: he is a fly, not a man. And she is a fly, not a woman person. Fantasies cut loose from hope, she allows him to mate with her, all the while thinking only of the man server: his long black legs, his eyes of wonder, his skin of dreams. Ah, yes, dreams. Dreams are as close as she will ever get.

She leaves the wharf. Soon her eggs will be ready. She'll find some fresh excrement to lay them in. Maybe an odorous trash pile.

But before that, she returns to the restaurant to admire the man server one last time. She watches from the windowsill for hours, but he is not there. Maybe he is not working today. She is tired. There are eggs growing in her belly, almost ready to be laid.

The restaurant grows busy. Man servers and women servers rush about as the dinner crowd fills in, but none are him. Her love is not there. If he was, she could perform for him one more time, tracing a pattern through the air he might understand.

And maybe, just maybe, he would know that she didn't care that he tried to kill her with a menu. That she understood why he did it and forgives him. They can bury it. Move on.

With the sky turning purple, she leaves her sill for the last time. Maybe one of her babies will find this same spot, once she's gone.

Strength waning, she concludes that the man server must be at his home and flies there to say goodbye.

Her body calms when she sees him inside, bathing in the warm glow of a lamp. He is reading a book. He is smart and sky deep. If only she could put herself into his thoughts.

An arm slithers along the back of the couch and the woman person leans into him. He kisses the top of her head. They touch glasses of red and drink. The fly breaks apart inside. He doesn't know what he has done to her over these last weeks. Doesn't know that he has reached out, taken hold of her body, and dismantled it. She can't watch any longer. She pivots on the sill and faces the empty night.

She readies her wings to fly, but something stops her. Voices from within. The window is cracked. The woman person asks a question. Does the man server want to reproduce? He smiles and says sure, maybe someday. The fly knows he would make a good father. His legs are long and his skin is a pond before the rain.

The fly stays, watching her love in the company of the woman person. They talk and touch each other and drink the red. The fly is tired, but she is determined.

The lights go off. The woman does not leave the man server's house. The fly enters through the open window and watches from a piece of furniture as the two humans do their courting ritual. Looking back on her many days with the man

server, she wonders if they were wasted. But they were not. Even now, as he mates with another, the fly regrets nothing.

The pair conclude in a flurry of motion, then fall asleep. The fly ponders what she has witnessed, feels the gears in her brain slowly clicking into place. So, the man server is ready to be a father after all.

She flies down from the furniture and alights in his hair. So deep is his slumber that he does not notice. Traveling to his quivering lip, she feels his hot breath. Her vision goes slippery from the wine of it. His snores are animal. A glorious beast.

When the door of his throat is open, she dives inside, slipping past his tonsils, shooting down his windpipe, wet and black. Down and down she crawls, her feet dragging lines through the mucous-lined walls. Below her, his lungs begin to rumble. The man server coughs. He coughs and coughs, but this only draws her deeper into the warm and humid branches of his breathing tree. Air roars. Pulse pounds.

Life rumbles within her. This is it. The nursery.

The fly hooks her feet to his flesh and penetrates the spongy lung tissue with her ovipositor. Squeezing the segments of her abdomen tight, her eggs gush into him, nestling snug into their membrane pocket. Soon it will swell and pop, bursting forth with their squirming children. Thriving upon his flesh, he will be the best father.

Another cough shakes the world and a gust of air catches her. Then she is out, laying wearily in a ball of phlegm. Exhausted, she gazes up from the man server's hand. He peers down from above, sleepy eyes searching.

The lights come up and his mouth turns down. White tissue is balled from a roll and descends from above. The fly salutes him with one wing as the paper smashes her to paste.

bLAcK
ME
oUT
HIGHTOWER
PUNK
goes
HORROR
II
2026 WORLD TOUR

BLACK ME OUT

LAUREL HIGHTOWER

HALLOWEEN WAS NEARLY TWO MONTHS GONE, but the blood looked real.

Claire took in the ghost town vibes of her oldest hangout, pulling at the heavy strap of her bag, trying and failing to get it up over the bunched shoulder of her long coat. She hadn't wanted to believe it, but her boyfriend Evan was right: the scene in this town was dead. She took in the deserted corners of her adolescence, the futzing neon spelling out senseless half-truths. Flickering overhead lights and empty stalls where once there'd been noise and lights and joy and *life*. Seeing the mall like this, hooked up to machines and breathing its last, she almost wished she could put it out of its misery.

"Don't go if it makes you sad, babe," Evan told her when she bundled up to brave the pre-Christmas cold and traffic. "The kids have plenty under the tree."

And he was right, they did. But Christmas Eve mall shopping was one of Claire's oldest and most treasured traditions, and she wasn't ready to give it up. So here she was, one of the lone, last shoppers, headed for teenaged Claire's holiest of holies: Hot Topic. It sat right across from a kiosk selling swords and axes of all things—she perused for a minute or two, her eye on

a scimitar her daughter absolutely didn't need, but would look cool as hell wielding. Maybe for her birthday in the summer.

Claire turned away from the weapons and took a second to survey the store where she'd bought both her prom dresses and the black lace gown for graduation that had nearly given her mother a heart attack. She'd been half afraid the place would be closed, another victim of the latest economic downturn, but the metal grate was up, the entrance dark but open. Everything about the place was dark, it was part of the appeal. Claire's aging goth heart warmed as she approached, noting the red liquid that appeared to drip from the dim window display. It coated the arms of a trio of black Christmas trees someone had decorated with silver skulls and chains, interspersed with ornaments featuring pop culture critters she didn't recognize. A lifelong Halloween freak herself, she respected the store's refusal to give up their year-round spooky vibe. She loved Christmas because of the kids, but October was where her soul dwelt.

Her heart surged into her throat when a hand shot out from the darkness and barred her way. A skinny kid who looked the same age as her eldest son loomed over her, his hair in long black spikes, eyeliner running down pale cheeks.

"Ma'am," he said, his tone a studied offense, a sneer curling his pierced lip. "You really don't want to go in there."

Claire sighed, a flash of anger tightening her chest. She knew how she looked to this kid, with her high waist jeans, practical mom purse and one of Evan's old Patriots t-shirts peeking out from her wool coat. She was an *old*, part of the establishment, man. She could have told him stories of the shit she and her friends used to get up to, and bit back an urge to tell him her tattoos were cooler. But she *was* an old now, and okay with it—she didn't need to prove her street cred just to buy a

gift for her stepdaughter. So instead, she raised an eyebrow and pushed past him. "My money spends the same, dude."

The boy's sneer widened to an unpleasant smile. He lifted the hand that had blocked her way and glanced over his shoulder into the gloom of the checkout counter. "Your funeral, lady."

Claire rolled her eyes and tried to let them adjust to the dim. As they did, a deep unease roiled her belly, her shoulders going up. There were too many people in here, none of them giving Christmas shopper vibes.

Three kids were on their knees in the corner against the far wall, out of sight of passersby. Claire couldn't see their faces, but their body language was tense, frightened. The girl in particular, her shoulders shaking, hands trembling in her lap, fidgeting to pull down the hem of her checkered miniskirt.

Claire turned slowly, sensing more bodies, and saw a big man in jeans and a hoodie. He looked more out of place than she did, wraparound reflective sunglasses hiding his eyes but doing nothing about his odd, relaxed grin. His hands were in the front pouch of his hoodie, and as Claire squinted, she could just make out the outline of something clutched in his right fist.

"Fuck," she muttered, realizing just how bad she'd screwed up by coming in here.

"Fuck is right," came a deep, lazy drawl from behind the register.

Claire opened her mouth, but before she could speak, a dark shape rushed her from the shadows, and everything went black.

...

Abby's gut dropped when the woman hit the floor face-first, her

nose exploding in a spray of blood. She tried to quash the wave of despair that threatened to steal her breath. Had she really thought some middle-aged Karen was going to save her? Apparently so, judging by the disappointment raging through her.

A low, grinding chuckle drew her gaze to the man behind the register. A third man stood at his ease, skinny shoulders hunched in a studded leather jacket, his dark hair thin in front, rodent-like teeth peeking from a smile that wasn't a smile. Everything about that face said he wanted to hurt her, and the shotgun clutched in both hands said he intended to follow through. The wretched twist of his nasty mouth told her he'd read her mind, watched the decimation of her hope. That pissed her off enough to dry her tears and she lowered her chin, refusing to look away. When he broke eye contact first, she counted it as a tiny victory and turned back to look at the woman on the floor, stirring now and groaning.

"Shane. Grab that bitch's purse, she looks like the type to carry pepper spray or some other cunty shit. Bobby, pull the grate down. We don't need any more concerned citizenry sticking their noses in."

Chet, the store's twenty-year-old night manager, spoke up in a cracking voice. "You don't gotta do that. I'll give you whatever's in the register, okay? Whatever you want from the merchandise, it's yours. This doesn't have to be hard."

The guy with spiked hair by the door, the one the rat-man called Shane, giggled. "Oh, bro," he said in a sinister little voice, gesturing to the body of the UPS guy slumped before the display dais. It was his blood that decorated the trees, and Abby felt sick when she thought of the way his head had exploded when rat-man pointed his shotgun at the would-be hero. Tim. His name had been Tim.

"Davey *likes* it hard, you get me?"

Chet whimpered and shrunk against the wall just as a wet, congested snort bubbled up from the blood-soaked floor.

Abby turned wide eyes towards the older woman in the bloody coat, who was pushing herself to her knees.

The grin dropped from Shane's face, and he rushed over with a speed that caused all three employees to cringe out of the way, but the woman on her knees showed bloody teeth and kept her ground.

"Something funny, *bitch*?"

The woman snorted again and Shane fell back, making sounds of disgust when blood and snot hit his face.

"Davey likes it hard, huh? I'm sure that's none of my business, but throwing it out there like that is funny as fuck, you gotta admit."

A current of shock froze the air inside the shop. Abby bit her bottom lip hard against the hysterical desire to laugh—she knew what happened when women laughed at men. Headlines of spite rape and murder told the tale every day of her life, and that was just in the crapshoot of run-of-the-mill interactions. The rat-man was something worse, and at the same time she fought laughter, Abby trembled for the older woman.

It didn't take long for Davey to lurch from behind the counter, his pock-marked face curled in an ugly smile, his dead eyes hard as he looked down at the still snickering woman. He pressed the muzzle of the shotgun to her chest and leaned in close.

"Wanna tell me what's so fucking funny, cunt?"

The woman ignored the gun and got to her feet, still a head and a half shorter than Davey, even fully erect. She looked up and grinned, her lips splitting, more blood pouring down her

chin. "I said," she began slowly. "That I think it's funny your buddy there is advertising the method in which you like to take it up the ass." Her grin widened. "Clear enough?"

Davey stared down at his middle-aged antagonist, hatred palpable in every inch of his body. His shoulders shook with restrained rage, his knuckles white on the shotgun. His lips trembled, then stretched around his protuberant teeth. "You're going to regret that," he said softly.

The woman shrugged. "Not likely."

His voice hardened further. "I guarantee it."

Abby turned her head, hot tears squeezing from the corners of her eyes. She didn't want to see another murder, but she had no doubt she was about to. She stole a longing glance at the door leading back to the employee break room. If only she could get to the paper-wrapped parcel propped under her purse.

Bobby and Shane also seemed certain of further bloodshed, but after a tense few seconds, Davey only gestured for one of them to put the woman against the wall with his other captives. She went easily enough, her arm over her nose to staunch the blood as she settled next to Abby.

"You okay, honey?" she asked in a nasal but warm under voice.

"No fucking talking," snarled Bobby, getting up in the woman's face.

Once again, the older woman only looked at him, her stillness unsettling to the big man. Nothing about her demeanor suggested subservience, and it seemed to make Bobby antsy.

"Manager-boy," drawled Davey. "What's your name?"

"Ch-Chet," he managed through chattering teeth. "I can help you. I have the codes for the register, keys for anything you want. There's no need to hurt anyone...else."

Davey grinned. "I appreciate that, *Chet*. Real helpful of you, but what I want isn't in this store."

His voice still shaking, Chet played along. Abby wanted to hug him—he was a dweeb, tried too hard to project authority around the store, but he always went to bat for them, and as it was turning out, he was braver than she'd given him credit for.

"Then what do you want? What do you need us for?"

While they'd been talking, Shane had drawn down the metal grate at the front of the store, blocking off any further help. Not that anyone short of armed guards could do them any good now, but the sound of the lock snapping into place dipped Abby's gut. She wanted to go home. She didn't give a shit about these guys or what they wanted—they could have the whole godforsaken lameass mall for all she cared. She thought again about the parcel under her purse, and wondered if she'd have the courage to use it.

Davey bent close to Chet, tapped the barrel of his gun on the manager's shoulders like some kind of fucked up knighting ceremony. "What I want is through that door back there, *Chet*." He gestured to the back of the store, where a door led from the stockroom to a shared hallway that ran between stores. "And I don't need *you* to get it."

The attack was so swift Abby missed it. One moment Davey was sneering down at Chet, the next her manager was releasing his last breath in a tortured whistle through lips pursed with pain. Blood pattered to the floor and Bobby backed away with a long, slim blade materialized in one sweaty hand, a superfluous set of brass knuckles on the other. He grinned behind his sunglasses as Chet flopped to the floor, clawing at his chest, at lungs that suddenly refused to fill. His eyes rolled toward Abby, and she wanted to go to him, at least hold his hand

so he didn't die alone, but Davey's dead gaze turned her to stone.

Another hand did reach for Chet's and clasped it tight, a soft voice murmuring in reassuring tones. Chet's eyes rolled away from Abby's, towards the woman in the wool coat, who looked down at him with the calmest expression. "Hey there, Chet, that's okay then. You did good, you hear me? It's okay now, you can rest. You did good."

Jace, who'd been the youngest employee until Abby came along, dropped his chin to his chest and sobbed.

When Chet was still, the woman kept her grip on his hand, even as she turned to look at Davey. Her eyes were cold and still, her face a mask of dried blood and curiously blank. Abby tensed, expecting remonstrance, an outburst. Something that would set the rat-man off again. But all the woman did was stare.

Davey finally broke the silence. "Probably think you did something good there, huh? Sniveling bitch. You're everything that's wrong with this shitty world. Probably done everything you were ever told, climbed a corporate ladder on your back. Think by dropping money in a Go-Fund-Me you're making a *difference*, right? We don't need soft-hearted cunts, you hear me? This world's out to fuck all of us, and the only way to get ahead is to fuck it first."

He straightened and grinned, but the woman kept staring in that cold way until he finally turned away, pointed his gun at the door in the back. "And my preferred way of fucking—right this moment, anyway," he said with a lascivious grin at Abby. "Is to take what I'm *owed*."

Shane and Bobby cawed and hooted, pumped their fists and peppered the air with sycophantic hell yeahs.

Abby's skin crawled and she wished she could slink out of sight. Whenever men worked each other up like that, it ended

poorly for the women in their path. What the hell did this guy think he was owed?

...

Claire held the dead boy's hand, thinking of young graves filled at the whims of cruel old men, and watched the girl hold herself together through sheer force of will. She wanted to tell her everything would be okay, use the same tone she had on the dead boy, the one she used for her kids when their own worlds came crashing down around them. But Claire fought her own battle as she knelt there, and it wasn't with fear.

It should have been. She knew that, knew something had gone haywire in her after she hit forty. It scared Evan to death—he wasn't afraid *of* her, as she'd always kept the same soft words and loving hands at home. Instead, he seemed terrified of what she'd do one day, biting off more than she could chew and pissing off the wrong person. When Claire got in situations that raised her ire, she kept his scruffy, impossibly dear face in mind, and those of her kids. She owed it to them to come home safe at night.

But as she knelt in a mixture of her own blood and that of a stranger, trapped in the darkness of what had been one of the first places she'd learned to be herself, Claire knew tonight was different. Whatever she owed her family didn't eclipse other debts that stared her in the face. To the boy who'd lost his life trying his best to protect his staff. To the girl who shook with the effort to contain her fear. And, maybe most of all, to the girl she herself had once been. She stared at the thinning hair on the back of Davey's head and thought deeply about debts owed, and the kind of person she didn't want to be anymore.

PUNK GOES HORROR II

Time passed without her knowing, and her thoughts weren't thoughts anymore. Pulsing lights of emotion; the bass thump of realization. *Be quiet. Be still. Do what he wants: don't make him mad. Appease the kingmaker; kiss the ring.* Each admonition a ricochet, a drum beat of reality. A throb of rage that turned her core molten. So angry it hurt—stole her breath, made her chest heavy. But so too did it melt her down, the rage sloughing off her comfortable middle age. No longer the woman in sweats and a messy bun, making lunches and doctor's appointments for the people she loved most. That Claire took a backseat, eased into the middle distance while fire-in-the-belly Claire drew a violent breath of becoming.

The men hadn't noticed, their focus instead on Davey and his bombastic claims. Something about a jewelry store which, when Claire considered it, made sense—there was a diamond place across the way, likely accessible through that service hallway. She didn't bother listening for any kind of plan—idiots like Davey always thought they'd come up with that one angle no one else ever had. And when that didn't work, because they'd vastly overestimated their own cleverness, they resorted to violence. It was all so tiresome, but Claire wasn't tired anymore. She was incandescent.

"...sick of following orders from cunts who ain't half as smart as me, thinking they're better just because they were born with a fuckin' silver spoon up their ass. And that fuckin' Black manager thinkin' he can tell me what to do, when you know his ass only got there 'cause of that DEI bullshit. Everyone's so fuckin' afraid to do what needs to be done, and men like us are left out in the cold, all 'cause of some woke shit. Not gonna know what hit 'em when the *real* savages pull up, are they, boys?"

More hooting from Bobby and Shane, whipping them into

excitement, until Bobby sidled up to Abby and brushed her dyed black hair away from her ear. "How about it? Wanna give us a little show while we wait?"

Abby pulled away, unable to mask the revulsion in her heart-shaped face, and Bobby immediately turned nasty.

"Think you're too hot for me, bitch? You ain't. And guess what? If we decide you're not useful anymore, you'll go the way of Chet over there, you feel me?"

"You want a show?"

Claire's voice was calm, measured, and strong, carrying throughout the store. All eyes were on her as she stood, unbuttoned her bloody coat and let it fall to the floor.

Bobby and Shane guffawed, bursting into derisive laughter. Davey stared at Claire with a cold sneer but made no move to stop her.

"You think you got something any of us want to see, you dried up cunt?" He grabbed at his crotch, thrust it in her direction while his buddies howled.

Claire's hands dropped to her waist, gracefully undoing the buttons of her jeans. Abby and Jace watched, mouths open. What the hell was she doing?

"What I think," Claire said in dulcet tones, shimmying jeans and a pair of black and white polka dot panties to the floor, kicking off her shoes while she did so. "Is that I've passed blood clots bigger than your dick. So the question really is, do you think any of you run-of-the-mill assclowns have anything that could interest *me*?"

Entranced in spite of themselves at the promise of a sight of flesh, it took the "alpha males" a few seconds to catch up to what Claire had said. When they did, it was Davey who reacted fastest. He dipped his head and ran at her, spitting the

same obscenities she'd heard her whole life, in different orders and inflections, but always the same. Their discomfort, their disappointment was her fault, and their disgust her problem. It was the disgust she counted on this time.

In a swift, practiced move that always drew an admiring breath from Evan, Claire stripped her shirt and bra off and flung them across the room. They hit Shane in the face and stopped him briefly, the catch on the bra whipping him good across one eye. He cursed and slapped the fabric away, but Bobby halted in hungry contemplation. Claire knew her breasts hung low, that cellulite jiggled her thighs and her belly rounded in a way that turned off men who wanted teenagers. But another fun part of turning forty had been ceasing to give a fuck what men thought of her body—the only purpose here was the element of surprise. Grateful for once that menopause hadn't yet stalled her heavy cycles, Claire reached between her legs, scooped out a handful of blood and clots, and lobbed the wad straight into Davey's face.

Much of it hit his eyes, but enough landed in his open mouth that he choked, gagged, and stumbled away from her. Spitting and cursing, he hit the ground at an awkward angle and Claire didn't lose a second of momentum. She landed with a knee in his gut which propelled a gout of vomit into the air. Davey choked and wheezed and Claire dropped her knee into his ballsack, grinding hard.

His screams nearly covered the sound of Bobby's scrambling approach, but Abby cried out a warning and Claire grabbed one of the wallet chains she'd meant to buy for Lilly and swung it full force. It was one of the long ones and whipped around the man's head, catching him hard in the eye. He screamed and dropped to his knees, blood pouring from between his thick fingers. Claire turned from him, wrapped the chain around the

rat-man's throat, and began to squeeze, her grin manic and wide. Choking would take time she didn't have, so keeping the chain tight, she maneuvered to kick his head, pulling in the other direction with the chain. There was a satisfying snap when his neck broke but still she held on, wondering how much force it would take to decapitate the piece of shit.

She turned her head at the sound of a scuffle, leaping to her bare feet as Bobby barreled toward her. She stood and bared her teeth, chest out, fingers curled into claws, not much giving a fuck if she lived as long as she took his ballsack with her. She kicked out at the big man's kneecap, hard enough to make it bend the wrong way and sent him to the floor screaming. Before Claire could move, an ear-piercing shriek filled the air, a gust of air, and a crunch of bone as a double-headed ax fell on Bobby's hand, severing the brass knuckles from the man's fat fucking fingers.

Claire grinned at Abby who stood panting, her teeth bared.

"Righteous," said the older woman, and Abby smiled back. The two women looked down at the big man floundering at their feet, snarling and making threats in his agony, his good hand grabbing for Abby's thigh. Their gazes met and Claire raised a brow. Abby nodded, then brought the ax blade down again with greater precision. The only move Bobby had left after that was a twitch of the foot, and piss darkening the leg of his jeans.

A quick glance around told Claire that Jace had Shane under control, the slim blade Bobby had used to murder his manager clutched tight in the young man's hands, jammed up close and personal in Shane's throat. When he swallowed, a bead of blood trickled down. Jace trembled, but held Claire's clear gaze. She was content to let him choose the older man's fate. A little disappointed when the kid went no further, but probably

best for his psyche.

Her movements stiff as the adrenaline leached from her aching bones, Claire bent to look at the wallet chain, still embedded deep in Davey's neck. She cocked her head and looked up at Abby. "You got this in purple?"

Abby took a minute to think, then nodded and stomped through puddles of blood and severed fingers to a swiveling display near the register. She thumbed through the offerings there and tossed one to Claire as the older woman pulled her clothes back on.

"No charge," Abby said.

Claire nodded, located her purse again, then put the chain inside. She nodded to the ax, still clutched in Abby's hand. "You get that at that kiosk across the way?"

Abby looked at the weapon. "For my brother. For Christmas. Been saving up."

Claire nodded slowly, easing into her coat. "Think I'll stop there after all. Like my daughter to have one."

Abby watched as the woman shuffled to the exit, bent and unlocked the metal grate, yanking it just high enough to duck out. Jace looked after her, eyes wide, mouth hanging open.

"Merry Christmas!" called Abby at the last second.

The woman raised one blood-soaked hand in return, then stepped out into the dying mall beyond.

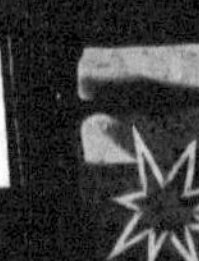
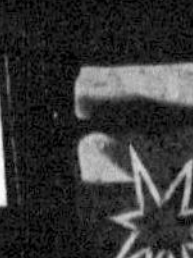

JOHNWAYNEISDEAD
i WAs boRN
oN A
SaTURdAY NiGhT
PUNK
goes
HORROR
II
2026 WORLD TOUR

I WAS BORN ON A SATURDAY NIGHT

-john wayne comunale-

THE PEOPLE OF WILES CREEK OREGON say Mean Billy Jean was born on a Saturday night. Billy's birth was part of a larger chaos the Universe unleashed upon Earth that day. That night was particularly dark in Wiles Creek, though *dark* didn't describe it adequately. Pitch-black came a bit closer but still failed to capture the severity of this darkness.

There wasn't a cloud in the sky, and yet the stars were strangely absent. The moon had also gone missing, having taken a cue from its fellow celestial bodies. Instead, whatever filled the space over Wiles Creek that Saturday night was the darkest shade of black anyone had ever seen. It sat, thick and heavy, just above their heads like a sagging soggy sponge. A looming dark which threatened to drop and suffocate the whole town at any second.

Then the power went out. All of it. This included emergency lights hooked to generators filled with gas, flashlights with fresh batteries, phones with full charges, and anything else capable of emitting light, regardless of the amount. Candles were out, since every lighter in town refused to work and matches politely declined to spark when struck. Any and every trace of light held hostage by the swollen inky bloat hijacking the night sky.

PUNK GOES HORROR II

A sudden shriek exploded from within the hospital, ripping through the paranoid silence. Inhuman screeches and squeals, heard throughout town, signaling Billy's birth. Billy's mother also screamed, but not because of contractions or labor pain. The child she carried actively ripped its way out of her body, pulling the poor women completely apart. The totality of gruesomeness was muted by shadows until the sun rose, hours later, revealing the full brutal and bloody scene.

A brave nurse named Dinah kept her wits about her despite the chaos. She scooped up the baby, fled to an examination room across the hall, and did her best to inspect the child in the dark while wiping slick cords of viscera from its soft flesh.

In the morning, as the rising sun attempted to smooth down the harsh edges left behind by one bitch of a night, Nurse Dinah was found in the parking lot behind the building. Her body was a ghoulishly twisted heap, most of her insides now on the outside. Police determined she'd jumped from the roof hours earlier, and the janitor helped scoop the piles of her nearly unrecognizable pulpy mush into a trashcan.

Dinah didn't leave any clue as to why she'd decided to abruptly end her own life, but there were theories. Other nurses who dealt with baby Billy experienced bouts of anger, depression, and thoughts of suicide. They *knew* something was wrong with the child.

Billy's mother was dead, and his father was a lazy alcoholic bastard with zero parenting skills and even less common sense; it was no wonder the boy was an instant holy terror. As he grew up, young Billy thrived on chaos, which he was perfectly happy to manufacture himself by starting fires, vandalizing homes and vehicles, and stealing. Lots of stealing. Billy would often steal items he deemed useless just to throw them away once he was

outside the store.

Old Man Jean was ornery, unliked, and far from perfect himself, but not even the general neglect and abuse he heaped upon the boy could be blamed for creating something as broken as Billy. Some claimed the boy's birth name, Billy Jean, was a catalyst for the way he developed. His father drunkenly named him thinking it was funny in a 'Boy Named Sue' kind of way. Billy didn't hate his name, he hated his father, but neither were to blame for poisoning Billy's soul with evil. Soon the boy's behavior earned him the prefix 'Mean', and it stuck like wet shit in the grooves of the soles of your shoes.

Billy grew up, and so did the town around him with ne—

...

"Come on, man." Leon interrupted his bandmate's story and snapped another beer from the tight plastic ring of the six-pack. "This is boring as hell. I don't need the life story of MBJ, so get to the good shit."

James exhaled a purposely over-exhaustive-sounding sigh, took a long drink from his own can, and spoke.

"First of all, *don't* refer to him as MBJ, okay? I hate the shit out of that. It makes me think of that poseur douche, MGK, whose full name I have no desire to say or hear."

"Only you would think that." Leon popped the beer open and slurped the quickly escaping foam. "You're so dramatic sometimes, dude."

"Look, just call him Mean Billy Jean, or at the very least, Billy," James snapped. "Just don't associate him with that asswipe! Okay?"

"Yeah, okay. Jeez, man," Leon muttered into his beer.

PUNK GOES HORROR II

"Calm the hell down."

Leon and James comprised one half of the punk band, *Eat Fat Pussy*, who were ten days into their current tour. The other two members, Spaz and Deek, played guitar and sang while James and Leon filled out the rhythm section. Their songs were fun and catchy with hooks about drinking beer, partying, and eating at their favorite restaurants. *Eat Fat Pussy* subscribed to the 'write what you know' philosophy. They knew about drinking *Coors Light* and eating at *Sizzler,* so that's what they sang about.

James and Leon's current discussion was happening in the back of the band's van, parked in front of a house where two longtime 'fans', Jennifer and Jennifer, lived. The girls had helped the band with food and extra gas money the first time they played in Wiles Creek, Oregon. After that, the Jennifers let *Eat Fat Pussy* stay with them every time the band came through town.

The reason James and Leon were in the van and not in the house was because of a strict rule the four always followed, regardless of where they stayed the night. One of them had to sleep in the van to guard the gear. No matter what. It was never a comfortable or coveted job, but braving extreme fluctuation in temperature, sleeping on a disaster zone of a lumpy bench seat and jumping up to check every little sound outside was totally worth not having their instruments stolen.

Eat Fat Pussy had heard too many horror stories from other bands about having everything they owned stolen while they slept, partied, or fucked, and they were determined not to make the same mistake.

This particular night, both James and Leon had elected to stay in the van together since Spaz and Deek declared they'd be 'balls-deep' in the Jennifers. Neither James nor Leon wanted to listen to the bedroom sounds of their bandmate's tag team fuck-

fest, so sleeping in the van was the lesser of two evils. Fall was a bit chillier in Oregon than the band was used to, but the frosty sting was easily dulled by alcohol. Plus, they'd take the cold over a steamy, humid, breezeless night ten out of ten times.

Aside from desiring to escape his bandmates' sexcapades, Leon wanted to get back the conversation he'd been having with James regarding the lore of The Dead Center, the venue they were playing that night. Leon wouldn't have given his bandmate's story a second thought save for one perplexing detail James had spouted as the van turned into the parking lot.

"This place has some major fucked up history. Can you believe we've never played here before?"

Leon could not believe it. Their venue for the night, *The Dead Center,* hadn't just been an old bar; it had been absolutely ancient. *Eat Fat Pussy* wasn't super-famous, but they weren't unknown either. They'd played through Wiles Creek eight or nine times prior. Leon did wonder why they hadn't played *The Dead Center* before now, and his interest piqued at the mention of a 'fucked up history'.

The guys had loaded in and began setting up the gear for soundcheck. Leon set his drums up in record time while his brain chewed on baseless theories of what was so 'fucked up' about the venue's past. Was *The Dead Center* haunted? Had a murder spree happened there? Was it cursed by a witch for not paying one of the bands? Did they find severed hands in the beer cooler? It was driving Leon nuts, so he fastened the last cymbal to its stand and made a b-line for his bandmate. There'd only been so much of the story James was able to tell in the greenroom before they went on, but it had been enough to get Leon hooked . . .

...

PUNK GOES HORROR II

The Dead Center had been around longer than most anyone knew, and the current building was not the original structure.

Some band called *Tony Fink and the Shit Kids* had been on stage when the original structure bit the dust, and were responsible for the inciting incident. Tony had been into some weird devil shit and purposely used lyrics and music from their songs to summon a demon. It worked, but the demon immediately set the place on fire, ripped everyone apart, and dragged the building down a hole, presumably to Hell. No one knew why Tony did it, or what the desired result had been, and they never would.

A few weeks later, after the dust settled, a small number of devoted fans began holding constant vigils day and night for Tony at the hole where the club had been. The group eventually morphed into a Tony Fink worshipping murder-cult that committed group suicide shortly after going on a bloody rampage.

Ten years later, the current proprietors of *The Dead Center* had rebuilt the place and kept the name. No one knows how they filled in the hole, or why they insisted on building in the exact spot of the venue's predecessor, but devilry was largely suspected. For the next five years *The Dead Center* ran successfully without a hitch. They had touring punk bands through weekly and were building a reputation for being one of the places to play on the west coast for indie up and comers.

Mean Billy Jean discovering *Tony Fink and the Shit Kids* was like fire finally finding gasoline. He learned everything he could about the history of the band and became scarily obsessed with their music. Billy went to great lengths to obtain bootleg recordings, videos of rehearsals, and even bought people's personal photographs of the band. Billy changed his look to mimic Tony Fink's. He already had the leather jacket. But then Billy took on Tony's vocal inflection and body language. It would've been

pathetic if the kid weren't so goddamn creepy and downright scary.

People in Wiles Creek were nervous Billy's extreme interest in Tony Fink could start a new cult, or worse. Nobody wanted that to happen.

…

This had been as far as James got with the story before *Eat Fat Pussy* had to play, and it was all Leon could think about until they were back in the van together hours later. He thought all the exposition was just okay, but Leon wanted to know what happened to Mean Billy Jean at *The Dead Center,* and what *Tony Fink and the Shit Kids* had to do with it?

"Shall I continue?" James asked tugging a fresh beer free for himself, still hours left to go on van duty. "Or do you have any other smartass remarks to make to your beer can before I start?"

"Okay, okay," Leon whined. "Sorry. I'm just . . . excited to hear the rest."

Leon wasn't excited, he was anxious. Nervous. But his mind was working hard to convince himself otherwise. James smiled, popped open his beer, and took a long drink.

"So," James recommenced. "Like I was saying . . .

…

As Billy grew up, the town grew up around him. Wiles Creek became modernized, chain restaurants popped up, and new businesses were built where beforehand there'd been fields or forest. Billy prowled the town, finding trouble to either start or get into. He smoked cigarettes and hung out around the lot

PUNK GOES HORROR II

where the new The Dead Center was being built. But this was way before Billy knew about Tony Fink, or that the same venue existed prior.

Billy was thirteen, but he already smoked cigarettes and drank the beers he stole off his old man. Like the beer and cigarettes, he stole a Walkman from his father when the old man was too liquored up to notice or care, and it came to be something Billy would never be without. Through one means or another, Mean Billy Jean began collecting tapes from *The Buzzcocks, Dead Kennedys, The Queers, The Misfits* and a handful of others, all punk bands.

Billy was too young to get into *The Dead Center* the first few years it was open. He tried to sneak in a handful of times when he was sixteen, but Billy was too easily recognized and thus forced to wait another year. Just before his seventeenth birthday, Billy's father up and died in his sleep. Instead of calling for help, Billy simply closed the old man's bedroom door. A few weeks later, on his actual birthday, Billy accidently came across his father's Tony Fink tape, having mistaken it for his Descendants album in the dark. He pushed play, and everything changed.

More than data stuck to magnetic tape playing through tiny, foam-covered, speakers; the music was a living entity that oozed from the headphones. It penetrated the spongy pores of his brain and filled all the holes in his soul. Each song spoke to Billy like it had been written for him, like Tony was speaking directly *to him* and no one else. The music of Tony Fink and the Shit Kids reshaped Billy's thoughts.

…

A hand slapped against the passenger side window of the van,

scaring the shit out of James and Leon. They both jumped, but relaxed when they saw their bandmate, Deek. He was completely naked, cupping his genitals with one hand while obnoxiously slapping the window with the other. James opened the sliding door.

"What . . . I mean, seriously Deek, what the hell is this?"

"Do we have any more condoms in the van somewhere?"

Deek peeked in the van through the open door as if expecting a condom to pop out and slide onto his dick.

"I honestly have no idea," Leon said.

"You're free to rummage around in here if you want," said James.

"Damn it!" Huffed Deek.

He glanced into the van, then back over his shoulder at the house.

"Ah, fuck it."

Deek reached between James and Leon and snatched a beer. He chugged it as he danced his way back to the house for some good-old, unprotected sex. They watched until Deek disappeared inside.

"Anyway." Leon turned to James. "The story is getting boring again. Can't you just skip to the good part? If there even is one."

"Alright you impatient bastard. Get ready to shit your pants."

...

He listened to Tony Fink's songs on repeat every morning on his walk into town until eventually choosing a bench where he'd sit, chain smoke, and listen into the afternoon. Billy was smart enough to make copies of the tape, so when he wore one out, he

could toss it and snap in another copy. He did the same with the few bootlegs he'd acqu—

...

"Dude, are you fucking serious?" Leon barked opening a fresh beer. "I thought we were getting to the *crazy fucking history* part. You're talking about Mean Billy Jean's best practices for preserving audio."

"You don't think any of this has been *fucking crazy* so far?"

"I mean, yeah I guess," Leon sighed. "I don't know. It's fine. I assume this is all building to what's so fucked up about *The Dead Center*'s past and what Billy had to do with it, but if you don't cut to the chase, I'm going inside to take my chances with the condomless compadres."

"While I'm tempted to have you do so," James said. "I'll cut to the chase as you put it . . ."

...

Through countless hours of listening to Tony Fink's songs, Billy was sure he'd figured out what went wrong all those years ago. The fatal flaw that made the entire place into a literal chaos zone. It was the people; the audience itself. Sure, Tony and his band summoned the demonic entity they were calling, but they gave no thought to taking the precautions necessary before doing so. Billy committed himself to learning how to do what the band attempted, but the right way. It was the only thing he'd ever studied for in his life.

Billy learned you couldn't just pluck an evil being from the Void, drop it in a crowd, and expect it to listen when you say *Hey, stop killing everyone please.* You needed an open, unpopulated space, a circle of salt on the ground to contain the entity, and candles

precisely arranged around the circle itself. Most importantly, you had to familiarize yourself with the demon you were summoning and to learn exactly what the thing will want, when it arrives, in order to make it *temporarily* obey you. Then a deal must be struck and signed in blood. It was a whole complex process which Tony Fink had taken no effort to investigate before pulling the ripcord on his plan. This was why the demon tore everyone to shreds before dragging *The Dead Center*, and everybody in it, back to the hell it came from.

There had simply been no one in control. Billy wouldn't make the same mistake.

When the big night came, Billy gathered his supplies, waited in the shadows for *The Dead Center* to close and clear out, then broke in easily through a rusty access panel on the roof. He dropped to the floor of the club, strapped on his Walkman, and blasted *Tony Fink and the Shit Kids'* music into his head before beginning to remove items from his bag.

He was in no rush and methodically set the scene for his summoning. The music had been the blueprint for everything Billy did. He was nervous he may not have interpreted it correctly, but there was no time for second-guesses.

Billy climbed into the sound booth at the back of the room, fired up the board, and connected his Walkman to one of the channels with an auxiliary cord. A moment later, *Tony Fink and the Shit Kids* were pumping through the house speakers, and Billy approached the circle to take his place. He'd made sure the scene was set correctly this time, but Tony Fink's music was the final crucial element. Fused within the riffs, rhythms, and lyrics was the key to opening the door.

Things happened quickly once the music was playing, but Billy was ready. A fiery red line burned a pentagram into the

PUNK GOES HORROR II

floor within the salt circle, and a blast of frosty air left Billy's face windburned. Spongy black smoke rose from the floor with glowing red orbs hovering at its center. Billy stared up at the very same creature Tony Fink had failed to control all those years ago.

The tremendous stink of sulfur rolled off the entity, stinging Billy's eyes and nose, but he shook off the distraction while furiously flipping through his notes. Billy needed to make sure the demon knew who was in charge, and to do so, he needed to recite the specific but simple phrase. He looked up from his notes into the floating red globes.

"I—"

Billy had barely opened his mouth when the billowy black smoke shot forward, defying the supposed power of the salt circle. Billy choked as the surprisingly dense smoke slid past his lips and burrowed down his throat and his body violently vibrated. Then, with no warning, and quite unceremoniously, Mean Billy Jean ceased to exist. He was still there physically, but everything else comprising Billy, his personality, memories, and sense of self were deleted; psychically shredded and cast into the void. Billy's body belonged to the demon he'd coaxed back from Hell.

Muscles flexed and bones cracked as the being familiarized itself with its new body. The demon knew it was in Wiles Creek, a small shit-town, but it was as good a place as any to begin th—

...

"Holy shit! Are you fucking kidding me?" Leon whined the question.

"What? What now?"

"So, this demon just possesses MBJ for what? To take over the world one Podunk town at a time? Wreak as much havoc as

possible while wearing Billy's skin, until the body's too damaged, then what? Jump into the next meatbag and keep going? This is so predictable, I can already see what's coming next."

James was quiet for a moment like he was thinking about something, like he was making a decision.

"Okay." James's tone was measured and free of annoyance. "If that's what you want to think happened."

"What I *want* to think happened? Seeing as you haven't said otherwise, I'm guessing I'm right. You know, you built this whole thing up, and I fell fo—"

Another slapping sound interrupted the two. Except the slap didn't come from the window this time. It was coming from the back of the van.

"Which one of the Wonder Twins do you think it is this time?" Leon asked, shaking his head.

The offender smacked the van a third time, and the force behind it rocked the vehicle on its chassis while James looked on silently.

"The fuck?" Leon steadied himself, then shouted at the person or persons outside as he moved toward the back doors. "Jesus Christ, hold the hell on. And why don't you come to the fron—"

Leon became stuck. Not stuck within the machinations of the van's interior, but stuck in general. He couldn't move any part of his body, and his voice refused commands to cry out for help. While Leon's limbs and body were frozen, he could still move his eyes. He didn't like what he saw. The blue-black smoke seeping through the poorly sealed back doors of the van was thick and buoyant. Helpless, Leon watched the undulating cloud, wondering what the hell James was doing. Was he in the same boat as Leon, unable to move or speak?

PUNK GOES HORROR II

Red spheres glowed inside the smoke, just like James had described in his story, and it dawned on Leon that his bandmate's story was true. All of it. Mean Billy Jean really had summoned a demon, and now *that* demon was in the van with James and Leon.

"Hey, Leon." James called.

Leon was elated James could speak. He strained his eyes to the side, trying to look back, but could only catch a sliver of his friends' profile peripherally. The cloud coalesced, swelling to fill the entire back of the van, and a beat later, James finished his thought.

"Bet you didn't see this coming."

The words entered Leon's ears, but before his brain received the message, smoke choked its way down his nose, mouth, and into his ears.

"I told you not to call him MBJ, you fucking twit."

Leon's body went slack, but the demon inside quickly took control to keep him from toppling over. James climbed up into the driver's seat and turned the key in the ignition.

"Sorry. It took way longer than I thought."

James looked over his shoulder to the thing that used to be Leon as it grunted a reply. Before pulling away from the curb, James fed a CD into the van's stock stereo, and the music of *Tony Fink and the Shit Kids* shot from the speakers. The demon moved to the front and sat shotgun.

The van sped away from the Jennifers's house, away from the suburbs, and away from Wiles Creek. The boys and the van were never seen or heard from again. Spaz and Deek were pissed about getting ditched for a while, until a phone call informed them both Jennifers were pregnant. After that, the two of them did their best to disappear as well.

The following morning, as the sun rose, *The Dead Center* fell back into the hole they'd built it over. No one thought to rebuild it again.

ReBEL YeLL
D. C. Phillips
PUNK goes HORROR II
2026 WORLD TOUR

REBEL YELL

D.C. PHILLIPS

CHRISTMAS EVE 1864

THE WAR HADN'T OFFICIALLY ENDED, but the writing was on the proverbial wall. And, much like the doomed King Nebuchadnezzar, Everett Hinton wasn't above consulting practitioners of the Dark Arts to plot his next blood-soaked steps. A stance which had led him here, to the ramshackle cabin behind his once-bustling family home.

Everett pounded on the door, desperate to be let in. Tears pooled in his eyes as he reflected on what he'd done.

The children had been easy. He'd tracked Jeb and Luisa out to the barn where they were taking turns reeling about fantastically on their hobby horse, a gift from their uncle. But as Everett stepped into the barn, his lithe boy and girl had frozen in place. Children were like animals in that way; they sensed shifts in energy.

Next came Harriet. His ultimate plan would require an abundant blood sacrifice to succeed. Or, so he'd been told.

The screen door squealed on its hinges as he slipped into the foyer that had received so many notable guests just a few winters prior. Merriment, and the tinkling of piano keys, had

PUNK GOES HORROR II

once seemed to echo for ages and acres across these grounds.

All that was gone now. Most of those people were gone now.

The piano music persisted, however, *Greensleeves* wafting from the parlor. Everett followed the musical trail until parquet floor gave way to threadbare rug. Harriet, arched on her bench, hardly glanced up from the sheet music in front of her. Eyes trained on the notes, she smiled dolefully and kept playing.

The day had been brisk, so she didn't question Everett's donning of his patched wool shell jacket, the color of dishwater, or the matching forge hat. Both enduring symbols of the failed war and his futile attempts to lead his wards to serve their beloved South.

Budding tears threatened to derail his resolve, blurring the candlelight that illuminated a sparse fir tree, decked in popcorn garland and propped in a shadowy corner.

"Blood must flow," he whispered without realizing.

The music stopped abruptly. "Darling, what—?"

In a flash, Everett turned and raised the musket-rifle he'd half concealed behind one shoulder. The bayonet affixed to its muzzle, though somewhat dull, penetrated the vulnerable skin of Harriet's throat with ease.

In and out, once, was all it took. Blood spurted and spilled, coating the front of Everett's jacket and faded denim pants, pooling between the piano's toothy keys. Harriet slumped, and the instrument protested discordantly.

…

Everett barged into the cramped shack, chest heaving, and locked eyes with Tess.

In a glance, she knew what he'd done. She'd helped him plan it, after all. Under duress, as if that mattered to her conscience. When the master of the house came knocking, armed with sword and scabbard, you answered his questions.

"What now?" He regarded her with unrequited mania, and when she didn't immediately answer him, he lunged for her, grabbed her by the shoulders. "Tell me what I do!"

"I need the book," she stated as calmly as possible.

He nodded. His hands dropped to fidget with the blood-spattered buttons of his coat.

Tess backed away slowly to a salvaged bureau by a roiling kettle. From its top drawer she removed a tome held together by linen scraps and generations of muttered incantations. Like its owners, it had survived untold abuses, exposure to the elements, to abrasive sand and briny sea. She opened the spellbook to a marked page and practically foisted it onto the eager Everett.

Their hands brushed for a fleeting moment—parched and pale against emolliated and ebony—causing Tess to recoil.

With the book in hand, Everett retreated to the porch. Dusk had begun to settle on the silent night—and with it, a chill.

Everett grabbed Tess' hands and, his breath visible, he began to read aloud with alarming voracity.

JUNE 1996

Thais Whittaker watched from her bedroom window as a Ford Explorer full of strangers cleared the brick mailbox and began the arduous ascent of her gravel driveway. She crossed herself, hoping she'd made the right decision by opening her family home—the plantation her ancestors had inherited, along with their emancipation, in an impossible turn of events—to the

public.

"Kumbayah, anka," she whispered into the atmosphere, invoking the protection of those who'd long since crossed over.

She'd have to accept that this nagging feeling–this certainty that her whole plan would backfire horrendously–wasn't going away for the time being. Was it her conscience?

Or was it a premonition?

…No…

It couldn't have been that; she didn't have The Gift. Not like Maamy or Grumma. She respected her ancestors' beliefs and practices, their deep connection to nature and the beyond, but she'd never allowed herself to go whole hog into testing her own proclivities. She refused to live her life throwing salt over her shoulder and burying roots after midnight. There was a compulsive, all-consuming aspect to it that her elders had refused to acknowledge… until it was too late.

In any event, the property tax on this place would be the end of her ownership if Thais didn't do *something*. This first crop of guests would be the perfect test run. For twenty-four hours she'd put on her hospitality face, answer questions with a smile, and make sure locked doors stayed that way. The same doors previous generations had sealed with charms and discussed reluctantly, and even then, only on a need-to-know basis.

She descended the stairs two at a time, bursting onto the freshly painted wraparound porch with its haint-blue ceiling just as the Ford slid haphazardly toward the end of the gravel drive. She flinched, bracing for the inevitable crunch of fender against rose trellis, but it never came. The Explorer stopped short, and its four doors popped open.

"Shit, man!" Four passengers—one couple in front and one in back—spilled out of the cab in a whirlwind of curse words

and squealing heavy-metal music. The backseat couple seemed more affected by their entrance than the driver or his presumed girlfriend.

"Chad, you coulda fuckin' killed us all!"

Chad, the driver, simply shrugged. "But I didn't," he said, yanking the keys from the ignition and cutting short a gnarly guitar solo.

Thais tamped down her immediate visceral disdain for Chad, whose ruddy cheeks and swaggering gait strongly suggested drunk driving. If she wanted to pull this off, she'd need to reserve judgment for at least a couple of hours.

Thais opened her mouth to properly greet the group just as a fifth passenger stepped from the SUV's back seat. Although the girl's facial features were obscured by thick sunglasses and a baseball cap, she exuded confidence. Her beaming smile was narrowly outshone by her golden-brown skin, only a shade lighter than Thais' own.

The token friend, Thais thought, although not unkindly. She'd been that friend; at least she'd tried to be. Growing up, her circumstances hadn't allowed for much of a social life beyond her studies. More often than not, she'd been here, tending the land. Watching those locked doors. It felt more like guarding a house rather than living in a home. During the time she'd spent at school, she'd always felt eyes on her, assessing her. Making assumptions about her and her kin.

They're witches, you know. Every last one-of-em.

Thais had been mortified back then. To kids who lived in town, something as innocuous as reading from an almanac could be interpreted as conjuring from a spellbook.

Now, Thais laughed.

"Welcome to the Hinton-Whittaker Home," she said with

as much cheer as she could muster, feeling grossly overdressed in her pleated skirt and crisp blouse, in contrast to her guests' t-shirts and cutoff shorts.

Chad's girlfriend ran French-tipped, press-on nails through her crimped hair and stepped forward. "I'm Shelby. We talked on the phone. You've got a beautiful place here." She seemed slightly less intoxicated than her boyfriend. "We've toured some real dumps looking for somewhere to have this reunion. The crew's gonna be impressed with this one."

"Class of '86! Hell yeah, baby!" the girl behind her (Darla, Thais would later learn), trilled.

Thais' teeth ground involuntarily. This was going to be a long night. She was sure it couldn't get any worse until…

"Goddamnit." Her facade shattered like fine china on concrete. The recent arrivals turned to follow her gaze. A second vehicle—a kelly green minivan with CHANNEL 8 NEWS emblazoned on the side—ambled up the path. A cloud of gravel-dust billowed in its wake.

"What the hell's the news doing here?" The second male passenger (Brandt, as Thais would also later learn), asked of no one in particular.

"I wanna be on TV like those *Girls Gone Wild,*" Darla teased, tickling his ribs through his shirt mesh jersey.

"Is that the same van that was parked outside the diner?" the fifth-wheel friend (Bethany) added. Only Shelby seemed to notice.

"I think Bethany's right. Were they *following* us?"

A month ago, when a local news producer had reached out requesting an interview about the new B&B, Thais had jumped at the chance. The reporter had seemed genuinely excited for Thais, wanting to know all about her plans for the former plantation and

gushing over how lovingly everything had been restored–with the exception of the outbuildings that had been demolished to make room for the pool. As the questions turned to the darker aspects of the property's history, Thais had become wary. She'd rushed to wrap up the chat without committing to a set date or time for the formal interview. It figured they'd arrive unannounced now, at the least opportune time, tailing her first guests like private detectives.

The incoming van rumbled into place next to the Explorer and a petite young woman hopped down from its passenger side. With a sharp bob cut, a smart red skirt-suit, and alabaster skin, she led with presence before even opening her mouth to speak. She paused to receive a microphone from her chauffeur-cum-cameraman, who seemed to appear by her side out of thin air.

"Who's she, some kinda Connie Chung wannabe?" Chad chuckled, disproportionately amused by his own wit.

A red light flicked on over the cameraman's shoulder and the woman, unabashed by the sleight, launched into her spiel. "This is Andrea Lim, reporting live from the former Hinton Plantation, now the controversial site of a new event venue and bed and breakfast."

"Oh no, no, no." Thais swooped down the front steps to intercept the intruders. She snatched the mic, eliciting a disapproving look from Andrea, whose cameraman's lens dropped toward the ground.

"What the hell's going on here?" Shelby demanded.

"That's what I'd like to know." Thais smiled tersely. Addressing the quintuplet of guests, she said, "Why don't you all go on in and leave your things in the foyer? I'll be right in to show you around." Then, returning her attention to Andrea, "I didn't expect this type of *ambush*."

PUNK GOES HORROR II

The tourists took their time ascending the stairs, too intrigued by the drama outside to eavesdrop discreetly.

...

As soon as they crossed the threshold and stepped out of earshot, the reunion coordinators launched into a recap of the scene from the front lawn.

"Did you see the way that news lady waltzed right up?"

"She looks shorter than she does on TV."

"Is this some kind of *Candid Camera* prank?"

Chad shifted the boombox he carried from his side to his shoulder. "I don't even care. We drove all this way, we're in a mansion, and I'm ready to get plastered!"

Shelby tittered, as she did at almost everything Chad said. Suppressing a belch, she said, "Be serious. This is official Class of '86 business. We're here for a reason."

"And on the committee dime," Chad gloated, reaching out to engage Brandt in their top-secret handshake, which involved the slapping, bumping, and intertwining of digits.

Shelby rolled her eyes. "Whatever, the lady told us to come inside, so let's do this. We've got to drop our stuff somewhere." Taking the lead, she took the path of least resistance, which led to the grand staircase. Darla and Bethany followed, while the guys lingered in the foyer, reveling in the residual effects of their respective alcohol-and-pot-induced hazes.

"It's a cute house, but the hallways are kinda tight for our group," Shelby observed, winded as she climbed.

"Yeah, well, these old houses aren't built for the bodies of the 90s. Not the 1990s, anyway."

Shelby paused momentarily on the landing. "Are you

calling me fat?"

"Get real" Darla teased with a shove.

At the top of the stairs, the girls found the open door of a modest bedroom featuring a twin bed, canopied in floral lace.

"This is cute. Feels more like a dollhouse than a mansion," Bethany mused.

Darla simply grunted in reply. Her attention was drawn elsewhere–to a bare window opposite the door. "Creeeepy," she breathed, tapping against its warped glass.

Shelby joined her. "What is that, a chapel?"

A blazing sunset bisected the dusk sky, illuminating a squat stone building beyond the pool, whose darkening surface rippled under a summer breeze. Its ornate columns and curlicue cornices seemed out of place in the back yard of what had once been a family home. They seemed better suited for a...

A cemetery. Darla took a step back, bumping into Shelby. "It's a mausoleum. There's...dead people out there."

"Why's Chad walking toward it?" Bethany asked. The trio huddled together.

Below, Chad stopped mid-stride, as if he'd heard. He lowered his boombox to the pool's concrete perimeter and cranked the dial, Van Halen blasting through its speakers with shocking potency. The sound waves reached the girls on the second floor, vibrating the window's peeling panes like a swarm of agitated bees.

"We're not even here ten minutes and he's gonna get us kicked out! What does he think he's *doing?*"

...

From her vantage point on the porch, Thais asked the same

question. Her conversation with Andrea had escalated into argument territory, and a small part of her welcomed the interruption.

Without excusing herself, Thais bolted. By the time she rounded the back corner of the home, Andrea and cameraman in tow, Chad had ascended the mausoleum's crumbling front steps. He stood on tip toes, palms flush against its oxidized double doors. Squint as he might, he'd never be able to peer through the layers of grime that obscured the stained-glass mosaic.

He could, however, make out shadows. Shadows that do-si-do'd under the penetrating rays of the setting sun.

"Yo, somethin's movin' in here!"

Thais, momentarily overwhelmed into inaction, sprinted for the boombox Chad had left behind.

"No. No! You don't get to do this!" she raged, fumbling with the clunky buttons, which only heightened her frustration. "How do I turn this goddamned noise off?!"

"It's not noise! It's metal!" Chad extended fingers in a poser's attempt at a rock-and-roll gesture.

Hissing silence ensued as one song transitioned to the next, offering Thais false hope. Within seconds, guitars thrummed and drums thumped–even louder than before.

Darla squealed. "This was my jam! Oh my God, he was so sexy."

Thais pressed more buttons, depressing fast forward, then play in rapid succession. Billy Idol's voice jumped from come-hither murmur to full-on caterwaul.

Thais kicked the sound system in imponent rage, which somehow increased the volume. She let out an exasperated growl and began to make a beeline for Chad instead.

Glass exploded in a kaleidoscope of colors from panels

that flanked the mausoleum's front doors. A single, crepey hand emerged, reaching deftly for Chad's throat, beating Thais in her attempt to intervene.

Thais knew there was nothing she could do. To insert herself into the fray would constitute suicide. Her wildest fears were coming to fruition while she watched, helpless, and 80s pop-punk synth continued to seethe in the background.

Chad slammed his fists against the cool, unforgiving limestone until blood began to spatter. Tendons bulged along the corridors of his neck, vessels popped all around his glazed eyes, and foam churned from his gaping mouth. He'd bitten his tongue, and blood streamed freely, sluicing onto the knuckles of the mummified hand that wouldn't let go.

Thais covered her mouth and nose with both hands. She told herself this couldn't be happening, but guilt needled away at her stomach, threatening to turn her inside out. She stepped back, sinking into the mass of impotent onlookers, which had grown to include Darla and Bethany.

"Bruce, look alive!" Andrea demanded, gesturing at her cameraman to get with the program. The pair stepped forward hesitantly, forming a loose chain with Brandt and Darla. No one rushed to render aid.

No one except Shelby. She lunged for the twitching mass that, moments ago, had been Chad; whose head now clanged again and again against wrought iron, collecting additional shards of glass with each impact like a human pin cushion. Her fingers struggled to find purchase, desperate to wrench her boyfriend free from the clutches of the thing that had awakened inside the mausoleum.

Shelby's screams mimicked the boombox's vocals as the thing from the mausoleum took a chunk out of her cheek. She

reeled backward and sprawled prostrate onto the springy grass, sending summer spiders scattering, and gore quickly painted her neck and shoulder in ghoulish watercolor strokes. She babbled inaudibly, grasping at the flap of skin along her exposed jaw.

Without warning, Chad's feet lifted off the ground. His sneakers *thunk-thunked* to the concrete below as his torso disappeared through the jagged remnants of the narrow, breached window.

Brandt stumbled forward to kneel by Shelby's side, chivalrous duty overcoming instinct. Darla hung back–and shrieked.

The doors to the monument undulated up and down their shared seam, the sound of iron on iron akin to nails on a chalkboard until they burst outward in a cloud of dust and decay.

Two adult forms lurched forward, bookended by a pair of children. Dressed in tattered layers of faded muslin and worn leather, they looked as if they'd stepped out of a time machine. The father figure was coated in fresh blood, which glistened against his parchment-like skin and pilled gray suit.

The boombox blared on. Wailing lyrics and throbbing bass ramped up the ominous ambiance as the long-dead family descended on Shelby and Brandt. They moved as a pack, in a way that was disjointed yet somehow agile.

Thais looked from Andrea on her left, whose cameraman had presumably fled for the refuge of their van, to Bethany and Darla on her right. Bethany turned to meet her gaze. Her expression conveyed pure terror, and…something else. Was that blame?

Thais interpreted it as such and sprang into action accordingly. "Come on," she hissed, motioning for the other women to take advantage of their attackers' fleeting fixation

on Shelby and Brandt's innards.. The quartet reached the front porch in record time and spilled into the foyer, gasping for breath in the throes of utter shock. The storm door clacked shut behind Andrea, who turned to fiddle with the lock.

"Don't bother," Thais commanded without looking back. She'd need all hands on deck if there was any hope to pull off this incantation–if the stories her mother and grandmother had told her were true. At this point, she had all the evidence she needed to believe they were. If only she'd paid more attention, heeded their instructions and leant more credence to their warnings... But no, her hubris had gotten the better of her.

Crossing the threshold of the parlor, she shook her head. The damage was done, and there was no time for regret or doubt. She lifted the lid of the ancient piano, toppling its bench in the process.

"I hardly think now's the time to tune that piece of junk," Darla quipped, her breath hot on Thais' shoulder.

Thais shrugged her off and reached deep into the guts of the instrument with both hands. She crooked her right elbow just so, jangling chords until her hands reemerged, now burdened by a thick leatherbound tome.

"Andrea, the van's running!" a voice called from over the muffled cacophony outside. "Where are y-?" The question dissolved into pained gurgling, causing them all to tense.

"Oh my God, Bruce!" Andrea squealed, hands cupped over her face. Bethany grabbed her by the forearm, as much to console as to stay her.

"The men are a lost cause," Thais stated, all business now. "Gather with me around the coffee table. I need an unbroken circle. Immediately."

The other women obeyed, even Darla despite her protests.

PUNK GOES HORROR II

"Did you know those…*zombies* were out there?"

Thais shook her head. They weren't *technically zombies,* but she couldn't afford to split hairs. She dropped the book on the antique table and grime puffed from its disintegrating interior. "They were under control. Supposed to be…dormant," she explained, even as her fingers riffled to find the right page. "It was an agreement my ancestors made, a caveat that gave us ownership of this home and determined our future. My present," she added, looking to Bethany for subconscious reasons. "We all make our compromises. Sometimes those compromises screw us over."

They all had questions, which no one bothered to ask.

"Now, link hands and close your eyes." So far as Thais knew, the latter wasn't necessary, but she threw it in for good measure. As a general rule, she struggled to perform for an audience.

With Thais anchored at the head of the low, clawfoot table, they each did as they were told; too desperate to argue.

Thais' eyes scanned the dog-eared page with manic fervor, and her lips uttered the words found there. An electric energy practically leapt from the page, jolting her into an altered state. The other women felt it, too. They were bound together in a current that passed through clammy palms.

As Thais read aloud, shadow figures danced in a carousel all around the room. The other women seemed oblivious to these entities, but the entranced Thais acknowledged them, welcomed them into the fold. As she reached the last line of the page, her body shuddered and the room came to rest. The women, each tingling with pins and needles, dropped their hands. A dizzy Thais blinked, and they all looked around.

The screaming had ceased, as had the boombox. Not even

the churring of a summer cicada could be heard.

A single twig snapped outside the front door. The women looked to each other and, wordlessly, filed out into the hallway, which seemed to have doubled in length. Through the screen, they watched as four shadows, darker than the black woods, came into focus.

Andrea gasped–and was shushed posthaste.

"You no longer have authority here," Thais said, projecting all the confidence she could muster.

Although no one could be sure, the tallest figure appeared to nod. Then, in the stilted voice of the grave, it rasped, *Tess says she's real proud…"*

Thais reached for Bethany's hand and squeezed. They waited for a second that stretched along immeasurably, much like the foyer in which they stood. She'd read the incantation. *What more?*

And then, without further fanfare, the four figures shuffled off the porch and disappeared into the dense blanket of black woods.

Thais' breath came out like a laugh. She had no idea how she'd explain any of this–the family's convoluted history, or the death on her lawn, much less the power of the book–but at least it was over, and she wasn't alone.

She turned to face her compatriots, who continued to sniffle and moan as they clung to each other. "So," she said, hands on hips, "we've got to get our story straight."

doN'T ReAch
FoR ME
PUNK goes HORROR II
2026 WORLD TOUR
24ч

DON'T REACH FOR ME

JUSTIN MONTGOMERY

GRAY WAVES CRASH AGAINST A COAST strewn with detritus from the sea. Ash falls in a rain of soot, burying sun-bleached fragments of seashells, shards of Poseidon's own skull. I inhale the breeze, shuddering at the scent of charred flesh and embers cast adrift from the monstrous husk on the horizon. Whatever majesty it once held has bled away, reduced to divine carrion on the wind. My stomach pangs, wretched with hunger.

A breach of the water. Close. I hurry back to the cave to ponder the failure of my hunt. To linger is to die, as the scent of carrion brings but one thing with it.

Vultures.

...

Burning salt air on the breeze. Twilight casts the coast into writhing shadow, full of teeth and claws and hunger. I cough phlegm into the grime of the floor, into the blood which pools from my groin. My feet, half submerged in filth, itch, but I cannot resolve the irritation. Already, my fingernails have begun to peel, my teeth have begun to soften. The falling ash has done something to my body, and I fear that which I will become. Less

twisted than the vultures, I hope.

The vultures came from the sea. Warped, depraved things. Bastardizations of nature's logic. What had been mammal now scuttled on legs of chitin, bodies honed to purpose by millennia of survival now ravaged with illogical cruelty. What had been internal now drags through sand. Useless, oozing chaff.

A fistful of pale grass was all I could manage to find for my evening meal. I gnash the coarse stalks with what remains of my teeth, choke against the roughage I am unfit to consume. How I long for bread warmed by the fire and smeared with hot oil as Mother used to make, before she lost her vision. I look at the back of the cave, feel pinpricks of tears on my cheeks.

There would be no more bread. When the old cave flooded, we lost everything. The tools. The yeast. The books.

How I lament the books.

Only one remains; a notebook, written by my mother, filled with as much information as she could remember, what had been passed down from her mother and the mother before her.

Secrets from the olden days.

Before God rose from the sea.

Without the knowledge so painstakingly scribbled within, I would be dead already. One with the soil, buried and forgotten beneath the singed bits of corpse that cover the land. I remember her skeletal hands, wounds weeping pus over calcified bones as she handed the notebook to me.

I fetch it from her resting place at the back of the cave, open the spine—gently, now—and trace her scrawl with my finger. I scratch mold from the bloated pages and inhale their scent. I trace the letters, speak them aloud so that I do not forget.

I feel the weight of her gaze from the abyss of her empty

sockets. But not completely empty, no. There's a pinprick of *something* in them, some glint which catches the light now and again, and I know that, at this moment, she is *here*. Watching over me.

Wind gusts from the back of the cave. The pages flip, settle. I mouth the words, hold the notebook to my chest.

A recipe.

"Thank you, mother."

...

I don't understand.

I trace Mother's scrawl beneath some tree that's not-yet turned completely to ash. I'd followed her instructions completely. I fed the yeast. Moistened it with my own drinking water. What should be bubbling and alive is arid chalk. The wind kicks, casting the product of my labor adrift.

What is the point? Of stumbling through the wreckage of this decayed Eden, when I hold the ghost of what was before me? The stories, the sketches, the recipes...I am stricken with insurmountable grief at what has been lost—never will I taste vegetables cultivated by my own hand. Never will I taste sweet fruit. The trees have become skeletal, maimed things, perpetually barren, unrecognizable against the sketches within the notebook. Never will I see the sunset over the ocean, feel lush grass beneath my feet. Even the weak cicada song of my youth has ceased, replaced with an intolerable silence, broken only by the weak waves on the coast and the scurry of vultures in the dark.

I cast the notebook into the dirt and scream, stomp the damned thing. That which is supposed to be my guide, my birthright, my *lifeline* taunts me, teasing knowledge but with no

means to execute its teachings. How much has been lost, spoken aloud, and stolen by the wind? How much had my mother left unsaid for me to glean?

I spit onto the notebook, fall to my knees.

I never asked for this.

This wasn't my doing. Yet here I am, on my knees in penance for the sins of those who came before. To hear mother talk of fruit, of how the sweet juice would run down your chin like sugar water, the way she'd drool and cry in the summer, moaning for a taste of sweet melon…how could we have squandered such a gift?

The gurgle of vultures. Revenants from the sea.

I continue to wail. Let them come. Evisceration would be more merciful than languishing in the dark, lamenting that which has been forever lost.

…

Blood smears the notebook page. It's happening again.

The sallow light of embers dance on the cave walls. My eyelids have fallen slack, my face numb. My eye hangs on my cheek, dangles by the nerve there, the warped perspective nauseating. I wait to regain feeling in my face and, once it returns, I suck the grime from my fingers and gently put my eye back into its socket.

I scream. The tears burn against the debris in my eye sockets from repeated adjustment. My body shudders with hunger. There's no food. There's no water.

I itch my arm with my palm, as my nails flaked from my fingertips long ago. The skin moves too much. A loose sleeve.

Maybe dead would be better.

After all, there's nothing left.

Nothing but the grand dead God on the horizon and its bastard children.

...

Smoldering slabs of corpse slough into the ocean. Whatever majesty the creature had once commanded, whatever divine mechanism had shaped such a colossal being has forsaken it in death, as its precious flesh now serves as naught but lowly kindling.

I stand with my feet in the sand, watching the pale waves lick the gnarled remains of a boat left, overturned, to decay in the shallows. Nausea floods my core. Starvation looms.

A vulture has scuttled beneath the curved hull of the boat, hiding from the weak light. Its shell knocks against the wood as it moves. I look to the horizon; great, jagged peaks of bone cup the heavens. Not much flesh left to burn, now. What will become of the world when all goes dark?

What will become of me?

A splash draws my attention back to the boat. To my prey. I grip Mother's femur in my hands, her bones fashioned into a crude spear and reinforced by the calcification of salt and ash alike. I stroke the bits of petrified flesh and sinew still clinging to mother's skeletal hand to steady the tremor in my own legs. Use me to live, she had said, bile coursing through her ragged lips. *Use my body to survive.*

Enough cowering. Enough hiding. I must use my own hands to see the sun rise again.

I charge, crashing into the boat and pushing it over. The vulture writhes, temporarily blinded by the light. What had been a large fish now scuttles about on shelled legs which jut from its vivisected belly. Its mandibles snap at the air as its cataract

eyes roll. I stand still, watching the creature flail with panic and blindness, looking for an opportunity to strike before it retreats into the sea. A pause in its movements, antennae twitching in the air, and I strike into the carapace that has grown over once-sleek scales. Mother's femur pierces its shell easily and I descend upon the thing, tearing its legs from its body and suckling the sweet, raw meat from within. Its juices flood my gullet, warm and alive, my mind glazing as I feast with increasing fervor. It has been so long since I've had such meat, and I plunge my hands into the thing's belly, greedily shoving its rancid entrails into my toothless mouth, giddy at how the slop of slimy tissue slides around my gums, itches the sores there.

The mirror-like surface of the water begins to ripple.

I vomit into the sand, having eaten too much too quickly after such a prolonged fast. I scoop the regurgitated meal back into my mouth, ignoring the grit of sand, and flee to the cave. Mere moments after I clear the knee-high water, a mammoth creature crests the waves and extends a claw of impossible size to seize the remains of my kill. Its frilled sails pulse color and undulate in the air as the creature vocalizes, a deep moan that vibrates my bones. I stare into its milky eyes, eerily familiar, and a spark of recognition ignites the brush of fear in my mind.

Enough of the original animal remains for me to identify what it once was. I have seen such creatures sketched inside mother's notebook.

A whale, she had called it.

For a moment, I fear that the creature will scuttle alien-like out of the water and rend me in its colossal jaws. But it stares into my eyes, and I notice bloody tears run down its hide.

Perhaps I'm not the only one suffering.

...

Hushed voices, in the dark. I roll to my feet with practiced stealth, control my breathing. I feel around for Mother, but my fingers run through only hard-packed waste. The cave should not be this dark. Before drifting to sleep, God's soft glow had warmed the walls. There should be light, and the sound of the waves…

Footsteps, at the mouth of the cave. Something dragged across sand, a hollow cacophony of shells clicking as something scuttles through the black.

Vultures.

Defenseless and naked, I backpedal on all fours until I feel the cool bone of mother's skull on my heel. This isn't how I imagined the end. Whimpering in the dark, shaking with fear. A blind coward. I press myself between the wall and Mother, beg her to rise from the dust and protect me. The vulture scampers in my direction, no doubt catching my scent on the air with its antennae.

Footsteps descend upon me and the cave sparks into a blinding crimson light. A silhouette stands before me, the twisted shape of a man.

My prey from the afternoon flashes in my mind. How I've become the vulture, wretched and cowering beneath my boat.

No.

I grab a sharpened length of Mother. Despite the red light, I cannot see into the deep shadow from my place at the back of the cave. I scream, thrusting into the black until the spear finds purchase, sinks into flesh with too-little resistance. Fluid squelches to the floor and there is a high-pitched shriek as the thing I've planted my weapon into sputters and dies, chitinous legs twitching.

"Blasphemer," the silhouette at the mouth of the cave

spits in a grating, guttural voice, deeper and rougher than any human throat should be capable of making. Callous hands force my face to the floor and bind my hands behind my back. The jagged edges of Mother's ribs cut into my face. I thrash, kick at the too-many hands restraining my arms, but I'm weak. They force my face into the bubbling carcass which I felled. I recognize this beast from the sketches in Mother's notebook, as its eight tentacles remain intact despite its gruesome transformation. Acrid ooze fills my nostrils. I gag, and slime runs down my face as I sputter. My eye has come free from its socket again, dangling, the warped perspective making me sick as my eye swings about.

I am forced to my knees in the sand outside the cave. Mother's spear is brought before me and broken over the knee of a tall man, clad in flowing garments. Something moves beneath them, an inhuman movement that sends a chill down my spine. "Please," I plead, still coughing slime and blood and who knows what else. "Don't, not…not her."

The man throws Mother's broken bones into the water. I cannot see them land in the dark. Then I am hit from behind, hard, and the world begins to slip away. I turn my head, but the impact has done something inside me. I can do nothing but stare upward at the flickering sky, at my captor.

A man without a face.

…

Blanched wood, bright as bone and covered in pale, fossilized starfish. I am bound to a pillar beneath some forsaken pier. Tattered crimson banners whip in the harsh wind, any eyes drawn there blinking from the dying light on the horizon. Six figures stand before me in purple robes.

They have no faces.

One strides toward me, robes trimmed in gold lace. "Blasphemer," he spits, voice guttural and wet. "To kill God's child, it is unforgiveable."

"Please, don't." I cough, mouth dry. "I needed to eat."

The figure scoops ash from the ground, places his hand beneath his robe. "The mana," he says, and I realize that when he speaks, the shells on his chest bounce. "You are provided with the endless bounty of His flesh on the wind, and yet you are not sated?"

"Please, I-I didn't know—" I stammer, but the man strikes me with the back of his hand. Chitin has grown over the skin there, and the world reels before me as if I am out at sea. The urge to resist bubbles up my throat, hot and furious, but then I remember that Mother has been destroyed. The anger is snuffed by grief, and I collapse against my binds.

"I will not hear your heresy." The man limps to the edge of the water, to where a boat is moored. "Onto the boat with you. You may shun the gift of His flesh, but He will not shun the gift of yours." The back of the robes flutter. An insect, adjusting its wings.

"What do you mean?"

"You are...a shame," the man says, then steps onto the boat.

I fight my bindings as robed figures move toward me. My feet slip on the dead fish, and I fall, the ropes peeling the skin from my hands. I am thrown into the boat. The skin of my hands lay atop the landscape of petrified marine life, nothing but discarded, blood-soiled gloves.

The man in gold lace stands at the helm, one foot on the bow, the other on my neck.

PUNK GOES HORROR II

"Onward. To God."

...

The sea is still, the waves of the past silent. Embers glisten on the horizon, the remnants of what flesh still clings to such colossal bones. My eye hangs, moves with the rowing motion of the boat as it traverses the silent sea. Nausea strikes, and my mouth fills with vomit, thick clumps of undigested meat choking me. The robed man has taken his foot from my neck, and I purge the contents of my stomach onto the floor. The regurgitation glistens, slick with oil. A singe of agony as it trickles over my eyeball on the deck.

None of the figures acknowledge me, their faceless forms set in their movement of rowing. The man in gold lace sits at the end of the boat, stares at me. Through me. Behind him, the ruined pillar of a lighthouse on a cliff, high above the sea. I know this from the notebook. It was used to guide those lost in the dark, its great eye of light a beacon of hope amidst the endless expanse of the sea, a signal to weary travelers that relief was near. The eye, for me, however, remains shut. Indifferent.

Dead.

I lay in the puddle of my own sick and sob. The movements of the boat begin to slow, then cease. The figures kneel and bow, prostrate, in the direction of the horizon, deifying the corpse of their god. The smell of vomit hits the back of my throat and I wretch, try to stand, to get away from the putrid smell. I cannot. I am held down. Not by force, but my own weariness.

The boat sits still on the ocean. The virile waves of mere weeks past have died away. Silence weighs heavy in the air, suffocating in its absolution.

I am unsure how much time passes before I hear it.

Subtle, even in the silence.

Something has left the water.

Pale white fingers curl over the lip of the boat.

I fight to rise. I've seen what crawls from the sea.

I must rise.

Be still, Beatriceeee…

I freeze. Mother's drowned voice.

Black hair, shimmering with wet and tangled with seaweed floats into view.

Beatriceeeee…

I look around at the robed men.

Steadfast they kneel, unmoving.

I look back at the figure and see Mother's pallid, pale face, sunken and slick. Her eyes bulge from their sockets, bloodshot. She crawls onto the boat, bending…*wrong*, bones popping as she contorts with impossible movement.

"M-Mother, you're frightening me," I breathe, but she does not relent. And then she is upon me, massive eyes inches from my own.

I dream of a cleansing wave, Beatrice.

"I don't understand. How…what are…"

Mother's head rolls back, her jaw unhinging. Lodged in her throat is a white, solid mass. The flesh around it writhes and the thing moves toward her mouth. Mother gags, tears streaming down her face.

"You're choking!" I scream, but still I am held to my place on the floor.

You must use my body to survive, Beatrice. Use me to live.

Knobbed bone hangs from her bloody, pale face. But Mother's eyes never leave mine, despite the tearing of her face. Her eyes bulge, unblinking.

PUNK GOES HORROR II

Take me, Beatriceeeee

And I understand. I grab the bone lodged in her throat and pull. The jagged edge of the spear cuts her cheek as I remove it from her body, and her jawbone hangs limp in a swaddle of flayed skin.

May they never praise their God again.

...

Something hits my stomach hard, and I wake. Mother is gone. So is her spear. Before me is a pale blob of flesh where I believe a human face had once been.

"Get up. The hour of your doom is nigh."

I am lifted and thrown overboard. I brace for the icy sting of the water, but land on something hard. A rope has been tied around my neck as I slept. It burns as it grates against my skin.

"Walk or be dragged," the gold-trimmed Priest spits. He looks to the horizon.

I follow his gaze. Bones claw the sky, stretch to the heavens until they disappear into the dark. The stench of charred flesh is overwhelming. Ash and water and meat have congealed into a thick paste, only able to be crossed on foot, despite still being miles from shore. There's a weakness in my legs as I behold the sheer enormity of the creature towering above. My captors are silent, solemn, the only sound the lazy dripping of blood from my raw hands. Despite my circumstance, I want to speak, to ask what this place is, how it came to be. But to do so would break whatever enchantment has befallen us, and we push on in silence, huddled together.

Carcasses litter the area, skeletal icebergs. The remains of some colossal serpent's vertebrae and ribs act as an arched tunnel past the bleached jaws of its gaping maw, forever open in

death. Torches flicker inside, lead underground.

Into the corpse of God.

…

I am forced to my knees before the pit.

The fire has gone; only a dull glow remains. The robed men shift from foot to foot as the man in golden lace speaks. His voice is distant, swallowed by the cavern before us. They're hesitant to approach the edge of the chasm. I can hear the click of their chitin as they cower.

"With this, oh holy one, we have brought you a blasphemer, one who would inflict pain unto your children." A shaking breath. "Not only has she killed your children, but she has desecrated thy covenant by *consuming* your flesh, rather than the mana you so generously provide."

Silence, his words lost.

The man in gold lace strides away from the precipice and cups my face in his rough hand, bringing my eyes to where his should have been.

"If it were up to me, I would feast upon the flesh from your bones."

I realize that this is my last chance.

I slam my forehead into the middle of his chest. There is a softness there, and the priest reels backward, falls into the chasm screaming. The other priests are stunned long enough that I am able to stand. They had undone my bonds as part of their ritual, and in the flickering light I see a hilt of bone protruding from the grin of a nearby skull.

I lunge for it as one of the priests lunges toward me. He slams into my side, but fails to find purchase. His momentum carries him past, and he slips over the edge. The others correct

PUNK GOES HORROR II

course and are upon me—but not before my skinned hand grabs the knob of bone from the skull's mouth.

I pull Mother free, brandish her against the remaining priests. They charge, and I skewer one in the chest. The bone breaks, and we are toppled screaming over the precipice.

Into the black.

...

I've been falling for longer than I can comprehend. My memory, blurred vignettes. My voice will no longer sound. The corpses of the priests I feasted upon as they fell have disappeared into the abyss. I haven't torn meat with my mandibles or claws in forever. Oh, how my own beating heart teases me, taunting me with fresh blood. The air, thick with ash, with mana, has kept me alive. Pain as my body warps. Reshapes into His image.

I fall into the infinite, in complete darkness, nothing more than an animal kept alive against its will. A mad god's plaything.

...

How I yearn for death.

I had timed my descent from my menstruation, but even that stopped long ago. The stories have left me. I remember the taste of Mother's sweet water, of the sugar bread which flowed over my tongue as it warmed by the fire, slathered in cold sand. Of the lush grass in the trees and the sunset in the sand. Of how the water washed overhead and the sky crashed against the beach, swimming with birds.

It's been so long.

So very long.

The smear my mind has become, losing the brief flashes

of clarity in a mess of confusion. I yearn to touch something, anything, even the cold of bone. Something to remind me that I'm not alone. I sense what remains of the priests falling near. They don't reach for me.

I look for a light in the distance, something to signal the end of my fall. As I have for decades, now.

But there is nothing, only infinite darkness, eternally savoring its meal before it swallows me up.

OUR BLACK
HEARTS BEAT
AS ONE
BRIAN ASMAN
GOOD DOGS
BRIAN ASMAN
MAN, F*CK
THIS HOUSE
BRIAN ASMAN
WRoNG
WAY KiD
A dEX
cRAVEN
stoRY
ASMAN
PUNK
goes
HORROR
II
2026 WORLD TOUR
RESEARCH STUDY
Are you 21-25 years old?
Interested in participating in research
on alcohol & attention?
Willing to come to our lab at UW?
Earn up to $385 for participating!
Learn more at
react-study.com
WE WANT
YOU
DO YOU HAVE DIABETES?
ARE YOU LATINO/A/E?
Join Our
HEYTEA
Family

WRONG WAY KIDS
A DEX CRAVEN STORY

BRIAN ASMAN

EAST OF THE 5 FEELS LIKE A DIFFERENT WORLD. I usually don't stray far from downtown Long Beach unless I'm on a job. That's why I'm out here, in the rundown, industrial east/ass-end of the OC, sitting in the parking lot of a mall that was abandoned way back in 1996.

Weird to think, when the Romano Mall closed its doors for good I was a little kid. My parents were still alive. Brett Gurewitz still played live shows with Bad Religion.

A different world.

Dex Craven's the name. I'm a PI. Most of my cases involve insurance fraud or infidelity, but I've also garnered a rep as the go-to guy in SoCal for weird shit. Anything that doesn't make sense, smells the teensiest bit occult? I'm your man. Some people even call me the Horror Detective, which is kind of corny and not something I'd ever put on my business cards, even though it's true.

As a kid, I survived a home invasion where both my parents were murdered. I was raised by my great aunt Lana, who played the Mummy Queen Amunet back in the '50s and 60s. She's who taught me how on-screen horror can help you process real-life trauma. I followed in her footsteps, slashing up horny

PUNK GOES HORROR II

teens in two *Campgrind* flicks.

And now I hunt down philanderers, worker's comp cheats, and, occasionally, things that go bump in the night.

This case is more on the mundane side. I'm out here looking for two teen runaways who've gone missing from a halfway house. Part of me's loathe to find them, since I know not every parentless kid hits the extended family lottery like I did, but their case worker seems nice enough and genuinely worried.

"I'm scared they're going to hurt themselves," the case worker, a matronly woman named Mona who favors cat-themed cardigans, told me over a diet soda at the 4th Horseman, the pizza place that serves as my de facto office.

The joint is horror-themed, and they blast metal, so I felt a little guilty for not meeting her at Starbucks, but she seemed unbothered by the raucous atmosphere.

"Why do you say that?" I asked.

She showed me the one kid's Momentous account. Milo Grigson.

I scrolled through. Lots of photos of him and another kid, Rodney Zisker, both crust punks with patch-covered battle vests and spiked neon mohawks, hanging out in drainage culverts and rundown houses to a backdrop of equally colorful graffiti, all tagged with stuff like #urbex. There's even one place I recognize, an abandoned Chuck E. Cheese up the street. Both kids are holding an animatronic Chuck E. head, cramming balls into a derelict Ski-Ball machine in another, and tagging the walls with the names of bands I'm mostly still cool enough to recognize, thank god.

"Got a thing for shitholes," I said, then winced. Old habits.

The case worker didn't seem to notice. "They're obsessed

with urban exploring." She threw finger quotes around the phrase. "You know what that is, right? I tell them to be careful, but—"

"They're kids." And punks, to boot.

"They're good kids," the case worker said. "Smart, creative. Sure, maybe they sneak into places they aren't supposed to go, but they always come home. Last night, they didn't."

"Have you called the police?"

"They took a report." Her voice dripped with venom.

"Couple of wrong way kids," I said.

"What?"

"Just something my friends and I used to call ourselves growing up. My friend Peter? He had one of those *Wrong Way* signs in his garage. We used to hang out there. Watch horror movies, stuff like that."

"Oh."

I leaned across the table. "All I'm saying is, I get it. There was a time in my life I could've gone any which way. I'll do my damnedest to bring them back."

She dabbed her eyes with a napkin. "Thank you."

"Now, any idea where they've been exploring lately?"

...

Which brings me to the Romano Mall. The last place they tagged themselves online.

The building is an immense, multi-story red brick structure. Built in 1979, the mall was the site of several mysterious disappearances. It was abandoned on February 27th, 1996, after a gas leak killed several shoppers, store employees, and a security guard.

PUNK GOES HORROR II

That's odd. Gas leaks happen, but it seems weird the mall never reopened, or at a minimum was bulldozed. A few articles about various liability lawsuits sort of explain it, but I'm skeptical.

This much acreage? Even in, let's face it, one of the least desirable zip codes in Orange County?

This should all be condos a million times over.

Instead, it sits empty, the Anaheim Hills looming disapprovingly in the background. I start to think this might be a little more unusual than just a missing kid case.

Which is why I grab my tools from the trunk.

Two items I only use on certain jobs:

A crowbar, which has mucho sentimental value because the same Aunt Lana I mentioned earlier used it to pry open a stuck soundstage door back in the '50s, saving the lives of the cast and crew of *Scream of the Mummy Queen* after a curtain caught fire. It's made of cold iron.

And my mask.

The mask is a fucked up patchwork thing, made from my mom's spiked leather jacket and one of my dad's flannels. It looks scary AF.

That's intentional.

The men—or people, I guess—who killed my parents wore masks.

In the aftermath, I made one of my own.

If I ever encounter them again, we'll be on an even playing field. I'm not a frail eight-year-old huddled in the closest anymore. I'm not fucking *scared*.

I'm scary.

I stretch my legs and check Momentous for updates. There's nothing new. But the kids' last post was from inside a shoe

store called Foot Feetish. Milo's filming while Rodney messes with single shoes off the wall display. He finds a pump-style sneaker, an insane '90s artifact, and jams out on the basketball shaped button on the tongue.

"Whoa! What does this do, anyway?"

"Makes the shoes cost an extra twenty bucks a pair."

This kid's funny. I like him. I like both of them, really. It's cliché but they remind me of me. Or maybe they just remind me of being younger. Nobody wants to get old, right?

Shut the fuck up, brain. You're not here for validation.

I shove the mask and crowbar back in a cross-body satchel and throw it over my chest. No need to scare anyone unless I have to. I cross the parking lot quickly, the relentless OC sun pounding the pavement, and I approach the western entrance. The smoked glass windows are streaked with filth. A thick-but-rusted chain wraps around the door handles.

Kids must've found another entrance. I debate whether to break in. I can't imagine there's any security to speak of, considering the mall's sat empty for three decades. Why would anyone pay to keep this place alarmed?

My phone chirps. Not a text, but a Momentous alert. I pull up the app. There's a notification from @bentgreg, who I followed earlier. Don't worry, my account's actually cool, not some Steve Buscemi *hello fellow kids garbage.*

I click the link.

Oh shit, they're live.

"—one help!" Milo screams, the camera close on his face, which is pallid and dripping with sweat, the meager light casting a sickly glow over his features. "They're trying to get in!"

There's a scratching sound in the background, like an angry cat murdering a sofa leg. The doorframe judders. Milo

PUNK GOES HORROR II

frantically glances over his shoulder.

Behind him, there's stacked boxes emblazoned with a logo: *Create-A-Cat Lounge.*

"They're coming," Milo says, breathlessly, then turns to brace the door.

The video cuts off. There's no sign of his friend.

Crap.

I pull the crowbar from my satchel.

Smashy, smashy!

...

The inside of the mall is quiet, dark, and smells like ass.

Actually, that's imprecise. This smells worse than ass. More like death. That stomach-churning, sickly-sweet stench that feels so goddamn wrong and makes you want to run for the hills.

That's this.

I've still got my crowbar in hand, flashlight in the other, although I've not donned my mask yet. I want the kids to come with me, not run from me. I'm walking down the concourse, head on a swivel, wondering just what the hell I've gotten myself into.

Part of me knows I should call the cops. There's two reasons I don't.

First, the boys: they're trespassing. *I'm* trespassing, but I'm also a semi-productive member of society with ties to law enforcement who can afford a lawyer. I'm not a scruffy punk kid who's a couple strikes in and looking at spending the rest of his youth in juvie.

Second, the hair on the back of my neck's standing up and I'm starting to get the feeling that this is turning into one of

those cases. The weird ones.

The cops would just get in the way.

I find a dust-covered directory and wipe enough gunk away with my elbow to look for Create-A-Cat, which I'm assuming is like Build-a-Bear, but knowing this mall, probably shittier. Just my luck, it's upstairs on concourse B. Whole other side of the building.

Milo's desperate words come back to me: *they're* coming.

Whatever *they* are.

I rush down the concourse like a mall walker who's traded in her butterscotches for crystal meth. As I beat feet past empty benches and refuse, I get a whirlwind flashback tour of everybody's favorite retro shopping destinations, drenched in eerie shadows courtesy of the sunrays fighting gamely through the dingy skylights above.

Grape Brutus. Dulcez and Glitziana. Gladiator Sporting Goods. Playtime Toys.

Hey, there's Foot Feetish!

And finally, Rekkii's of Bollywood. I spent many an adolescent moment manufacturing ways to stroll past those windows, ogling the lingerie-clad mannequins. The sight I catch in the window now is decidedly less than erotic. Someone's disassembled a half-dozen mannequins and put their limbs back together with duct tape and glue in the most fucked up way imaginable. You ever see one of those "biblically-accurate" angels? These ladies are just a shifting arrangement of limbs, looking like a human game of Tetris gone awry.

I'm about to continue on my way when the angel-fuck moves.

"Oh, shit—"

Is all I manage before the window shatters, spraying me

with broken glass. I drop the crowbar and cover my face. The angel-fuck crashes into me.

I land on my back, hard, punching and kicking plastic and trying to roll away while my mind's screaming all kinds of fucked up shit, because I'm being attacked by a goddamn mannequin—

It's not moving.

Of course it's not moving. It isn't alive.

I shift my weight, lifting the thing up and scrambling out from underneath. The angel-fuck lies there motionless on the moldy tile, looking like one of those found art pieces.

Which, I guess, is exactly what it is.

A hissing sound comes from within the store. I spin around, flashlight scanning for the source. Yellow eyes burn in the darkness.

It's biggest fucking rat I've ever seen.

The thing's the size of a raccoon, squatting on its haunches in broken glass, foaming green saliva dripping from its mouth. Guess that's what knocked over the angel-fuck.

I really wish I hadn't dropped my crowbar.

The rat hisses at me one last time, then turns and retreats into the darkness of the store, presumably to chew through more thirty-year-old bra and panty sets. Its tail looks like a bullwhip.

Think I figured out what Milo's hiding from.

I look around for my crowbar, find it under the angel-fuck. Feels good to have that iron bar back in my hand. There isn't a single goddamn thing to feel good about here otherwise.

"Screw this," I say, tucking the crowbar between my knees and reaching for my mask.

If you can't beat 'em, join 'em.

...

My mask is just a mask. No special properties, no magical powers. Its effect is purely psychological.

When I tug that thing over my face, I feel like I could go ten rounds with the devil himself.

Which, given my track record, isn't outside the realm of possibility.

No more detours. I sprint through the mall, hell-bent on reaching the Create-a-Cat lounge before those rats can break through and treat themselves to a crust punk buffet. My pulse is racing, and not just from the exercise.

I'm no rodent expert, but there's no way in hell rats can get that big naturally. If I had time, I'd like to see what the Guiness World Record is for largest rat, although there's a nonzero chance it'd just say *Whitey Bulger*.

I reach the food court and jog up a long-dead escalator. I can't hear anything yet, which worries me. Hopefully they haven't gotten in already. Hopefully Milo's okay.

Because his friend sure isn't.

I find Rodney sprawled at the top of the escalator. Or rather, I find what's left of him. His face has been eaten clean off, is just a mess of blood and gristle and shattered cheekbones now. Bite marks cover his body. I can only tell it's him because of the vest.

Unless this is Milo, and I'm too late, and his buddy's some other mutilated corpse lying somewhere else in this godforsaken mall.

Then I hear it.

Scratching.

Rather, clawing.

Fast, furtive. They're still at the door.

I'm hoping I can scare them off with my tac-light. Twenty

thousand lumens tend to do the trick against most creatures of the night.

Cautious, gripping my crowbar so hard my knuckles go white, I cut the light and ease inside the Create-a-Cat Lounge, my eyes straining in the ambient light from the skylights on the concourse.

The rats clearly had their way in here, destroying effigies of their mortal enemies with abandon. All the shelves are knocked over. Explosions of yellowing stuffing mark the spots where children's toys fell and were eviscerated. A small, shining glass eye stares up at me from the floor, begging me to avenge it.

I can't think of anything reassuring to tell the dead stuffed animal because now I can hear the scrabbling at the storage room door in earnest. But it's too dark this far in. Time to go lights-on and announce my presence.

I aim my flashlight at the sounds, offer up a quick prayer to Barker and Hooper, Carpenter and Craven—no relation—and hit the beam.

HOLY FUCK THAT'S A LOT OF RATS!

It's like a pack. Maybe ten of them, all at least as big as the one downstairs.

They instantly stop scratching at the door—which is deeply gouged, damn near see through in places—and turn to look at me.

Their eyes glisten, their jaws slaver, tongues lolling between jagged teeth in anticipation of a meal that's not protected by a locked door.

Maybe that's why they've grown so big. No apex predators.

Until now.

"Ratatouille time, assholes."

God, I'm so fucking cool when I'm not talking to women.

The rats let out a screeching battle cry and charge.

So do I.

There's almost a flicker of surprise, or maybe hesitation, in their eyes when they realize their meal's running right at them instead of turning tail. I raise my crowbar, preparing to swing--

And bang my fucking shin on a now-horizontal metal shelf.

The flashlight flies from my hands, the beam tumbling wildly end-over-end like a lightsaber duel. It comes to rest somewhere near the storage room, shining directly in my eyes and blinding me, because remember what I told you about 20,000 lumens?

Blast someone's eyes with that, they can't see shit.

I yelp and shut my eyes, which is very bad, because now I can't see and the rats can, but I've still got my crowbar because I'm a goddamn professional.

Time to Daredevil these fucks.

Sorry, time to *Don't Breathe* these fucks. That's more on brand. Except dude was a rapist and that's kind of counter to the whole "good guy" vibe I'm going for—

—Rats snap at me. I swing the crowbar wildly, feeling each impact crush skulls and pulp bones. The stink of hot rat blood fills the air. I pivot quickly, my eyes and shin still throbbing until I'm pretty sure I'm facing away from my flashlight beam and open my eyes again.

Just in time to see a hulking rat jumping at my face.

I swing my crowbar. It connects solidly, sending the rat flying towards the far wall, splatting against the Create-a-Cat logo and creating a snail trail of blood as it slides down the wall.

Breathing hard, I spin around, assiduously avoiding

PUNK GOES HORROR II

blinding myself again. There's more rat corpses than I thought. It's practically a mouse-acre.

Fuck you, not sorry.

"Who else wants some?" I snarl, spinning my bloody crowbar.

In answer, two surviving rats go scampering out the door.

I can't believe I didn't get bitten, which means I didn't contract rabies in the last thirty seconds, which is about all I can ask from any day ending in "Y" at this point in my life.

I retrieve my flashlight, double-check the corners to make sure there's no more hungry mouths lurking anywhere, then knock on the storage room door.

"Milo? You in there?"

There's a long silence, then a scared, shaky voices asks, "Who is it?"

"My name's Dex. Mona sent me."

"Mona?"

"Yeah, she was worried about you. I'm a private investigator." Remembering my own well-spent youth, I add, "I'm not a cop. I'm just here to help."

"How do I know you're real?"

Weirdly, this is not the first—or likely the last—time someone has asked me that.

I should really have a stock answer.

"I can't prove that to you. All I can tell you is who I am."

Then, with one eye watching out for more rats, or anything else that might be creeping around this goddamn mall, I tell him everything. Or, not everything, but enough. Who my parents were, and what happened to them. Being raised by Aunt Lana ("I remember those movies," he says). My old friend group and how we called ourselves the Wrong Way Kids, after that sign

in my friend's garage.

"I'm sure you think nobody over thirty gets what it's like," I finish. "I sure couldn't when I was your age." I wince, feeling like a boomer.

"I doubt I'll live that long."

I almost say you will, but then I think about his faceless homie out on the concourse, then say, "maybe you won't. But you're not dying today if I've got anything to say about it."

He's still hesitating. "I don't know. Everything you're saying sounds good, but you could...it could just be the mall again."

No idea what he means by that. And while I'd like to get to the bottom of what's going on here, I need to get him out and then figure out what to do about the dead kid, which is never the highlight of my day.

So I tap the door. "You realize I'm holding a crowbar, right? I can just pry this thing off its hinges at anytime. But I'm talking to you because I don't want you to be scared. Because ultimately, I'm on your side. Even if it doesn't feel like it."

There's another long silence, then finally he says, "Okay. I'm opening the door now."

I step back, giving him room. The door swings open.

Milo sees me, his eyes go wide, and he screams.

Whoops.

Forgot I'm covered in rat blood and wearing a fucked-up mask.

My bad.

...

I find some sheets in a department store and cover Rodney's body. Maybe I shouldn't, but I don't care if CSI gets mad at me. I'm also

not sure we're going to report this. Milo told me Rodney's only family is a very racist uncle out in Fontana. Maybe it's better to let him live on in the minds of people like Mona. Tell her he beat town. I don't like lying to clients, but sometimes I've found it's better to give them comfort over truth.

I'm not worried about anyone finding the body. The mall's been empty this long. And I know there are more rats hiding in the shadows.

There's always more rats.

Maybe it's fucked up, if you think bodies mean anything, but I've seen enough to know that they don't.

We're passing the angel-fuck in front of the lingerie store—Milo averts his eyes, while I scan the shadows for that chonky boy I nearly tangled with earlier—when something occurs to me.

"What did you mean, back there in Create-a-Cat? When you said *it could be the mall again?*"

Milo looks at me, eyes wild. "It talked to us. Said things."

I blink at him. "The mall…talked to you? How do you mean? What did it say?"

"It's not what it said, it's how it sounded."

We pause, a respectable distance from the angel-fuck. "How did it sound?"

"Like—" Milo opens his mouth, wider than a human mouth should open, and a squelch of static comes out, then, "—attention shoppers, we're so glad you could attend the grand re-opening of the Romero Mall. Pardon our dust, but we're still the fun, family-friendly shopping destination you remember."

I'm backing away, slowly, crowbar held low at my side.

What the fuck is this?

"Check out half-price TVs at Transistor Terry's. Score an

amazing deal on new living room sets at Lazy Boyd's. Get a skull piercing at Christa's. That's right, a metal rod right through your fucking skull. All the cool kids are doing—"

I gently touch my crowbar to Milo's arm. He instantly collapses into a sweaty pile of punk rock patches. He'll be okay, I hope.

Cold iron: the Swiss Army knife of the occult. Maybe it can't do everything, but it sure as hell does most things. From what I can gather, iron is the ultimate representation of reason. Nothing unreasonable can survive contact.

Killed a whole universe like that, once.

I'm not feeling particularly reasonable now, myself. I turn in a slow, protective circle, keeping an eye out for whatever this goddamn mall's got planned next.

"Well?" I shout, shaking my crowbar at the ceiling.

Nails click on tile. I whirl around to see three figures emerging from the darkness: two mastiff-sized rats on leashes with spiked collars and a ghoulish guy in a security uniform. He looks like a Grandpa Munster impersonator who got fired for getting too handsy with the convention-goers. Ice-pale skin, hollowed eyes, slicked-back hair, a mouthful of mossy, rotting teeth. A tumorous goiter's growing around his neck. His belly strains his half-tucked uniform shirt at the seams, the buttons like bombs about to explode. He's covered in disgusting stains, including some fresh ones that might've come from the dead punk kid at the top of the escalator. His yellow nails curl menacingly around the rat's leashes.

Kind of makes sense. I'm sure there are absolutely fine people in this line of work, but when I was growing up, mall security guards and punk kids were mortal enemies. Of course this shitty mall would manifest a ghostly rent-a-cop.

Plus those rats.

"I'm going to have to ask you to leave," the rent-a-cop says, then cackles like Vincent Price. "The hard way."

"That's fine," I say, pulling my mask back over my face. "I'm on my way out. And so are you."

The rent-a-cop lets the leashes go and the rats charge.

So do I.

Yeah. There's a reason I don't spend much time east of the 5. But as I crush two more rodent skulls and zero in on the rent-a-cop, I try not to laugh, because you know what?

Things like this fucking mall don't want me spending time east of the 5, either.

hiddEN tRacK
PUNK goes HORROR II
2026 WORLD TOUR

HIDDEN TRACK

CLAY MCLEOD CHAPMAN

THE MIXTAPE IS A LOST ART FORM. As archaic as a Dead Sea Scroll medley by today's streaming playlist standards, the handpicked assemblage of songs and crudely crafted cover art speak to a bygone era, where the mere possession of one of these antiquated artifacts—the cassette and its homemade cover, complete with handwritten liner notes—suggested the desire to possess the very music itself. To claim ownership over its innate power.

To the recipient of such a mix, usually a significant other, the tape may have been a gift. Alms for the ears. The heart. The architect of this musical song-list seems to say, in their own wistful way—*These songs are just for you, my love. Only you…*

Most modern listeners wouldn't know what to do with a mixtape. They wouldn't even have the proper equipment to listen to one. The technology is lost on them, practically antediluvian. Physical media itself no longer holds value in our contemporary culture. No longer do young lovers pass hand-crafted cassettes with photocopied covers and doodled track lists as a means of expressing their affection, this adolescent mating ritual gone along with the dodo.

A positive, all in all, given this particular mix.

PUNK GOES HORROR II

The tape in question—TAPE #237—should never, under any circumstances, be played again. *Ever.* The end of our world as we know it is on this particular mix.

As program manager here at the archives, it has been up to me to oversee the analysis, cataloguing, containment and—dare I say it—proper demolition of TAPE #237. The level of trust our hallowed institution has bestowed upon me for such a heavy task is certainly something I don't take lightly. To the contrary, I am quite thrilled by the challenge.

The destruction of something so destructive.

So beautiful.

I come to work every day and I find myself in the company of a god.

Its songs, at least.

A total of twenty-three lives have been lost by listening to this particular mix. Outside of these fatalities, we can also tally fifty-six hospitalizations stemming from injuries incurred listening to—or being within proximity to someone else listening to—the tape. Fifty-six that we know about. It is difficult to say with any certainty if that number is exact, given the sonic seepage of the music itself.

There is so much we do not know about TAPE #237. Even now I find myself at a loss to quantify its carnage. We just don't know. *Yet.* That is the task at hand, is it not? *Hand.* If it can't be my own ears, well, then it will be these very hands that decide the fate of this tape.

I only pray I have the fortitude my predecessors did not.

Would you like to hear of its origins?

TAPE #237 was first found at a flea market in Copiah County, Tennessee, tucked into a moldering shoebox full of various obsolete bits and bobs from a bygone era. The asking

price for the cassette was twenty-five cents, along with everything else in the box.

A quarter, that is all. The price of our own apocalypse.

Our best forensics analysis suggests it was created somewhere between 1987 and 1992, well before the tide shift to compact discs as a means of listening to music.

There is no paper trail, no chain of ownership, no receipt that maps out the trajectory of TAPE #237. It resurfaced at some point at an estate sale, purchased as part of a cornucopia of miscellaneous cassette tapes. Self-help audiobooks and workout tapes.

How long before the purchaser listened to this mix remains a mystery. It could have been in their home without the owner knowing the true tonnage of their frivolous purchase for quite some time. Months, if not years, spent collecting dust.

The apocalypse is patient.

How TAPE #237 finally came into our possession is another mystery. I have asked—countless times—correctly speculating that such knowledge might help in dismantling it. My higher-ups have deemed this information *privileged*. Above my pay-grade, as it were.

My peers and I serve as components to a larger whole. The right hand never knows for certain what the left is up to. Or the rest of our body, for that matter. We all work independently from one another here, blissfully ignorant to whatever threat might be just next door, in the lab right down the hall. That is how we survive. How we alleviate TAPE #237's gravitational pull. Its unnatural allure.

I am at peace with this. I have a wife and children. Two of them. Daughters. Gemma and Ally. Such tender sprites. Gap-toothed girls. I do this work for them. Their safety.

PUNK GOES HORROR II

May my darling girls never listen to this mix. May they never know of its existence.

Ignorance. Bliss. This is all I have.

What helps me sleep at night.

Without any further ado, here are the forensic details of the cassette itself:

- Maxwell UR 90 Normal Bias Blank Audio Recording Cassette Tape.

- A 90-minute recording time, 45-minutes per side.

- 10.6 ounces.

The Maxwell brand's low noise surface makes it a suitable cassette for recording music, a preferred choice amongst mix-makers of the day.

The cassette's clear plastic protective case has remained mostly intact, though it shows visible signs of duress. The plastic is scuffed, so the casing is no longer as transparent as it no doubt once was. The front pane is cracked in the lower left corner, a fissure spreading across its surface, a lightning bolt branching throughout the night's sky.

The sleeve is a standard cardboard stock, shellacked in Wite-Out and Scotch tape. The artwork is a collage of corresponding images, presumably cut from teen magazines: Glossy eyes without faces, lips without mouths, an ascending trail of hand-drawn hearts, much like bubbles of air escaping some subaqueous fissure.

If I may take a moment to admire the adolescent craftsmanship. It's quite striking in its primitive simplicity. I

would have made something quite like it, back in my day.

Perhaps I had.

It's hard not to be enamored with the memory of mixtape making. To reminisce. It's been so long since I've made a mix, but back in high school, I put together song-lists much like the mix in question. I can't even tell you the number of hours I spent, toiling away, getting the final track list just right, painstakingly considering the sequence of songs.

Did I ever give my wife a mix? I can't remember… Isn't that awful? I should know.

There are a total of thirteen listed tracks to be found on TAPE #237.

Six songs on Side A, seven on Side B.

The songs themselves are safe to listen to via other mediums. Streaming services, vinyl records, etc., etc.… Just not on this *particular* mix. Never *this* mixtape.

The songs represent your standard blend of hard rock and pop fodder. Music we may not be personally familiar with, given the generational gaps between our specialists and the architect of this insidious mix. We wish not to show our age, for fear we will be castigated for "being out of touch" with this particular era's music. Our intent here is to merely be observational and not to make any judgement on the quality of the song selections.

I wouldn't have picked these particular songs. This simply isn't my type of music. Then again, the mix wasn't made for me— was it? Of course not. I'm not its intended target.

The Mystery Recipient.

Who made this mix? Again, it is impossible to tell. We may never know its creator. Suffice to say, the attention to detail— the photocopied clip art, the magic markered illustrations, the organic font covering the flap, along with the handwritten track-

PUNK GOES HORROR II

listing—all suggest this mix was made with a loving hand. A *caring* creator.

The best mixes are.

Was it from a girlfriend? The bubbly, bewitching penmanship certainly suggests so. The hearts replacing the dots above every lower case 'i', along with the flowery font, leads us to believe it, though forensic fingerprint analysis has turned up no discernable patterns.

All we have… is the music. The songs themselves.

The evil within.

Our top analysists have spent countless hours attempting to unlock the secrets found within this particular mix, in hopes of discovering the true source of its powers.

Are we any closer to knowing its origins? Its inception? The tonnage within?

Sadly, no…

Countless questions abound, including, but not limited, to: *Is there any observable quality in the recording itself? Can one avoid the effects by fast forwarding? What if one were to tape over the original recording? Would playing it backward have the same effect as playing it forward?* And, perhaps, more pertinently—Who in the hell made this mix?

Sadly, we may never know.

I have dedicated myself, my time here within the institute, perhaps even the entirety of my professional career, if not my own personal life, to answering these questions.

I stare at the dual tape reels and I find myself drifting deeper into that pair of vortexes, losing myself for hours. Hours upon hours. Desperate for answers.

For truth.

But truth is reserved for the listener, isn't it? *If a tree falls*

in the woods and no one is around to hear it, does it make a sound?

What about a mixtape? Does its music exist if no one listens? How does one lose themselves to its music? Succumb to its sound? Simply slip the headphones on your Walkman strapped onto the belt loop of your blue jeans and press play? *How can I hear?*

We are getting ahead of ourselves again, apologies…

Without further ado, we present to you a selected cross-section of TAPE #237's songs—highlights, if you will—along with their sonic consequences to the best of our knowledge. There is still so much that we do not know, cannot comprehend, of this mix.

I'm not certain we will ever truly know.

Unless we listen.

TRACK ONE: "Can't Stop Thinking of U," Pantheon (1984)

Beginning a mix with a rock ballad is certainly a bold choice, so applause seems necessary. Give our mix-maker a hand! We commend our aural-architect for their—her?—decision to start off soft and methodical. And what a lengthy track, at that!

The song clocks in at a hefty seven minutes, primarily due to the two minute and thirty-four second synth solo at the heart of the ballad, with all of its early-80s schmaltz. It establishes a rather playful, if not completely puckish, tone straight out of the gates for our mixtape, as if to say (with the faintest hint of wink) directly to the listener—

I can't stop thinking of you… I just can't stop thinking of yooooou… I just can't stop!

The effect of this song, however, is most unpleasant for

PUNK GOES HORROR II

our poor listener.

It is, in fact, an earworm.

A little over halfway through the track, around the four minute mark, when the synthesizers get arpeggioing, it becomes clear that something has crawled out from the headphones and into the recipient's ear canal. This grub-like parasite seems intent on making its methodical sojourn toward the tympanic cavity. It isn't long before our audio-symbiote worms its way across the curving cochlea, where it hitches a ride along the 7th or 8th cranial nerve, well on its way to setting up shop within the host's brain.

It roosts. Home, at last, amongst the soft cerebral matter.

Our parasite promptly goes about laying its eggs—somewhere up to two or three hundred roe, all told. After quickly gestating within the listener's mind during the duration of the song, these eggs quickly begin to hatch. Why waste time? Their incubation stage seems to match that of the synth solo, whereupon once the keys finish their fiery finale, the tender offspring of our song feast on what remains of the host's brain. It won't be long before these worms emerge from whichever orifice is most convenient for their egress.

I think it was Kylie Minogue who said it best—*I just can't get you out of my head.*

Pardon the pun.

I was fortunate enough to conduct an interview with our particular listener—Subject AGA742—during this gestation process. He was cognizant enough to offer myself a step-by-step playback of his listening experience. Here is a small sample of the transcripts:

XXXXXX: How are you feeling? Can you tell us what sensations you may

be—

AGA742: I… I can hear them. All of them. Like whispers. Like—like my mmmm… mmmm…

XXXXXX: I'm sorry, can you repeat that?

AGA742: Mmmmmaaaaaaw…

XXXXXX: Your… mother?

AGA742: Mmmmaaammmaaaaaammmmy…

AGA742: Mmmmmammeeeemmmaaaaaaammmeeeeeemaaaaaaaaaaaaw…

This was around the time during our interview when the first worm emerged from our AGA742's oropharynx, charting its expulsion across the soft palate by devouring his tongue.

Forgive me this slight digression, but I just had a memory of my eldest daughter:

Gemma loved to dig earthworms out from her mother's kale garden in our backyard. Particularly after it rained. They would rise up to the soil's surface, blind to my child. How proud she was of her writhing prizes. *Look, daddy!* She would exclaim to me, holding one up.

I guess I just remembered that.

TRACK THREE: "Feel You Inside + Out," White Tiger (1989)

Our mix picks up its pace with subsequent song selections, kicking into higher gear by the third track. The mix-maker seems

PUNK GOES HORROR II

ready to get playful, selecting a song that values sex appeal over decorum with its bawdy lyrics and propulsive beat. It is a funky track, thick with a slapping bass line seemingly designed to resonate within the listener's loins.

The decibels of this particular song are so low in frequency, though, that it is enough to disrupt one's own most basic bodily functions. At around 150 db, nausea settles in. Difficulty breathing. Disturbances in equilibrium.

The song's subterranean frequencies reverberate throughout the listener's body, inflicting a sonic sickness that inevitably ruptures nearly every last physiological structure.

This song, quite literally, melts you from the inside out.

First visible signs usually include a bloody nose, followed by bleeding from the eyes and ears. Before long, the listener is spitting out gouts of blood, vomiting the contents of their intestines, hollowing themselves out by ejecting the soup of their own internal organs.

"Hair" metal was never a personal favorite of mine. Again, there is a particular cheekiness to its inclusion. The music is cueing the listener in to the notion of having fun. Not taking ourselves so seriously. Letting our hair down, as it were, and letting nature take its course.

Letting the libido loose.

To say my wife and I have hit a dry patch in our relationship is a bit of an understatement. We've always valued our professional lives over the personal, holding each other's work in the highest regards. The toll to this, however, is somewhat *chilling* at home. There's a gulf in our bed and we sleep on opposite sides. Just the other night, when I reached my hand over that mattressed chasm, my fingers finding her warm hip, caressing the skin just underneath her nightdress, I found myself rebuked.

HIDDEN TRACK | CLAY MCLEOD CHAPMAN

She pushed my hand away. *Not tonight,* she mumbled. *I'm tired.*

What if she were to hear White Tiger's cry? The high-pitched croon of lead singer Lane Coverdale as he wails—*I need to feel you, every inch of you, caress you, lick you, inside and out?* Would she still force my fingers away from her thigh? Would she still resist?

We'll never know, will we?

This mix is not for her.

Only *I* answered White Tiger's battle cry that night. I pleasured myself. It definitely helped that I could remember—and conjure up—the corresponding video for the song, where Coverdale's wife and mega model Tawny Kitara thrust and gyrated across the hood of a Lamborghini, all while wearing some see-through negligee.

Whether my wife was aware of the self-abuse underway mere inches from her side of the bed, miles by my standards, is yet another mystery to add to a litany of mysteries.

My wife has never been much of a music fan. I learned this too late into our relationship to do much about it. It wasn't a dealbreaker back then. Now… I'm not so sure.

I want to give her these songs. The music from my heart.

But she's unwilling to listen.

What happens when you have a mix, but no one listens to it? To hear the songs your soul has to offer? What happens to the mixtape itself? Does it still thrive with life?

What happens to its maker?

I have a gift to give. To offer someone's ears. Who's willing to listen?

There is music inside me.

I hear it, even now.

PUNK GOES HORROR II

TRACK FIVE: "Do That Thing You Do 2 Me (Uh Huh)," Britney Whitmore (1992)

A surprise turn from our witchy mix-maker, including such a poppier track.

This song may stick out like a sore thumb from its rock 'n roll mix-mates, but there's something quite beguiling about its inclusion, a knowing wink to whomever dons the headphones, seeming to say yet again—*Look at what you do to me, my love (uh huh)*.

This track certainly has a hypnotic effect on the listener. The proverbial mermaid's siren song. Once the song's initial bubbly strains take hold, it becomes increasingly difficult, if not entirely impossible, to stop the song's audience from listening to it. They remain, in essence, caught in a self-imposed loop, choosing to rewind the track and to listen over and over again until personal care or self-maintenance no longer matter. Hygiene or basic bodily functions become secondary to the song. Defecation, urination, lack of appetite, dehydration, and loss of sleep are all common once the music takes over.

One of our own institute's observers was caught in such a loop for an estimated two thousand and thirty-five cycles before his body gave out, collapsing under the weight of his own wasting form, dead before what remained of his emaciated frame even hit the floor.

How I wish to make a mix. I miss it. The joy of creating a tape.

I wonder if I could capture it again.

The *magic*.

I spent the previous evening at home, after work, unable to fall asleep, just noodling on the computer, wandering across

Spotify to piece together a playlist. I wanted to see if I still had it in me. That magic touch. When you're young, a teen, the song possibilities are absolutely endless. The conversation between songs. The sequence. It's an exploration like no other, manifesting a mix, a track list of songs never heard before. But this… this just wasn't the same. The songs didn't sound the same. Not the way they used to, back in the day. Now, they're too digitally crisp. Too clean. There wasn't that hiss in my headphones.

I want that sound back. I miss making mixes. Giving mixes. Getting mixes.

Listening to mixes.

Mixes.

Mix.

Mm…

TRACK SEVEN: "Don't Give Me That (Just Gimme Your Love)," The Howitzers (1972)

As the oldest known track on the mix, this song offers a rather brisk vintage of power chord pop, reminiscent of the early Kinks, even predating Elvis Costello.

The song is something of an antique. It makes us feel quite sentimental. Strange, then, that the song itself seems to manifest murderous impulses within its listener.

It's not long into the song, say, somewhere around thirty or thirty-five seconds in, where the subject gets driven stark raving mad, reduced to some rabid animal donning headphones—including, but not limited to:

- foaming at the mouth
- bloodshot eyes

- loss of basic language skills
- a reduction in vocal capabilities, indecipherable grunts

All of these symptoms seem to culminate in the listener's determination to destroy every living thing in eyesight by their bare hands.

Tragically, this track has led to the largest loss of life within our laboratory, including our team leader, XXXX XXXXXXXXX, whose skull was crushed against her desk by Test Subject #7, leading to a tightening in our overall security protocols throughout our lab.

What if you don't listen to this mix? What if this mix listens to you? Your soul?

What music is inside you? What is your internal track list?

TRACK TEN: "Ascension," Nemesis (1987)

This song mutates you into something quite monstrous. An amphibious gestation awaits those who listen to the guttural utterances of this speed metal ditty. A genetic unrelenting, as it were, as if there very sequences of our DNA unravel at the bewildering rhythms hidden within this breakneck litany.

Test subjects were shot before reaching the apotheosis of their transformation, their bodies incinerated after an autopsy proved inconclusive as to the root cause of their evolutionary sidestep, retreating into that primordial ooze our genetic forebears first sprung from, millennia ago, as if the listener desired to crawl back into the muck and swim away, landbound no longer. Free from humanity.

I feel as if my own insides are all mixed up now. The

sequence of intestines has switched up into some new order I can't quite explain. Organs aren't where they are supposed to be. Not anymore… and I haven't even listened to this mix. I've just been around it, in proximity to it, on the other side of thick plexiglass, behind concrete barriers, three feet thick.

Is it wrong to take a song off its original album and re-sequence it? Insert it into another hand-crafted album alongside other strains of music? Are we playing God? Blending the genetics of bards, bending the dimensions of their own craft? Are we making monsters out of these mixtapes, some unholy Frankensteining of funk, soul and punk?

These are the thoughts that keep me up at night.

If a band made these albums to be played in a specific way, assembling the songs so that they are heard in a certain order, what happens when we extract the DNA of an album and inject it with another, mixing the strands of songs into some ungodly thing…

What songs hath us gods wrought?

TRACK THIRTEEN: HIDDEN TRACK

Interestingly enough, the final track is unlisted. A "hidden track," as it were. There is no title or band name. I wish I could tell you what it was, but everyone who has listened to it is no longer with us. The song itself remains unquantified, but its impact is unmistakable.

This song opens a portal.

The exact nature of this threshold is up for debate, particularly considering no one who has come into direct contact with said portal has survived.

Through various video feeds placed within the testing

area, we have estimated the diameter of the doorway to be no larger than a quarter. The rift never dilates, never expands, keeping its diminutive radius, but the effect of this opening is catastrophic.

Inevitably, every listener to this hidden track chooses to step up to the portal, as if seduced by its sonic tide. They quietly lean forward and peer through the opening.

What they see on the other side is a mystery to us—to me—as we observe from a safe distance, behind soundproof glass. From our gathered data, however, we have ascertained that what lies beyond is "beautiful," "wondrous," "so black," "endless," "breathtaking," even "God."

Regardless of their verbal description, the next step is always the same: Each listener leans forward even further, bringing their eye directly up to the portal, wherever it may be, either in the wall or suspended mid-air. The subject then presses their face against the opening, whereupon their eye is subsequently summoned out of its socket, sucked from the safety of their skull and sent rocketing into the cosmos that awaits on the other side.

The rest of their body soon follows, folding in on themselves, cracking and flexing into abstract shapes, winnowing and bending and breaking until the entirety of their shattered frames make their way through to the other side, the last wet sliver spinning in a dizzying motion until it's all sucked up with a sickening hiccup. Then the portal closes.

It is easy to see why it is the final song on the mix, a fitting grand finale for a collection of cosmic canticles. No other song could follow it. No listener could survive.

I have dreamt of vertebrae.

A mixtape made of bone.

A never-ending track list, winding like a sprawling spinal column, where every song is yet another vertebra stacked on top, notch for notch, miles upon miles. Endless. Eternal.

I feel young again. *Alive.* A teen once more. All of this music is here at my fingertips, just waiting for me to sequence them. Cue them up. Press record.
It is a litany. An incantation.

A ritual.

I have so many songs to share.

...

The identity of our mysterious mixtape maker will never be known, regrettably. We can only imagine what sordid mix of alchemy went into its construction.

Was this some teenage witch, wishing to assemble a sonic grimoire, gathering all the apocalyptic songs of our world or beyond, much like an ancient book of spells? Isn't that all a mixtape is, after all? An aural spell book, filled with incantations and curses?

Half the joy, one may recall, in receiving a mixtape was discovering new music. Class is in session when it comes to mixes. Can you expose your listener to an entirely new batch of music? Unlock songs by bands your intended audience has never heard before?

Can you open their minds to fresh melodies?

The other half is the sequencing. The conversation the mix-maker has with the listener. The songs themselves become a discussion. Each listing must *mean something*. Whether it's a lyric or the song title itself, there's always something binding this music together, and it's up to the intuitive listener to discover its

hidden meaning.

You imbue these songs with love. With a shard of your own soul.

I am talking to you, communicating with you, through these songs…

Hear me. Listen to me.

Sing for me…

Even now we feel TAPE #237's gravitational pull, plucking at our ears from the endless corridors of our underground laboratory. Even beyond its proximity, sealed behind impenetrable walls of concrete and iron, we hear it calling to us.

To me. I yearn to listen.

My plan is to play the tape in its entirety.

All thirteen tracks.

Let it all unravel, 90 minutes of this infernal mix, without cessation, without breath, to see what darkness awaits us all on the other side.

Fortunately, our stereo cassette deck has an "autoplay" feature, permitting a continual loop of music that doesn't require manual intervention.

Even without me at the controls, once I'm gone, it will continue to play all on its own.

And play.

And play and play and play and play and play and…

WANT MORE PUNK?

Go check out PUNK goes HORROR Mixtape (2025)!
It is the first anthology to kick out this series and it's available
where all books are sold.

15 Authors. 15 Songs. 15 Nightmares.

PUNK goes HORROR is a mixtape anthology, full of terrifying tales inspired by some of your favorite authors' favorite punk, or punk adjacent, songs. Get ready for hymns of rebellion and stories of musical mayhem which connect body horrors to bass drums, rhythm guitars to psychological terrors, and microphones to human monsters.

Contributing Authors:

William Sterling	Liz Kerin
Eric J. Guignard	Carson Winter
Glenn Rolfe	Shannon Riley
Max Booth III	Kayli Scholz
S.A. Bradley	Ian A. Bain
Wendy Dalrymple	JR Billingsley
Christoph Paul	Brian McAuley
Brennan LaFaro	Rachel Harrison

NOTE FROM THE PUBLISHER

We want to thank our readers for their support and enthusiasm. Your passion for stories fuels our commitment to bring you the horror that is strange and horrifying in the best of ways.

We appreciate any and all reviews, so help us out by leaving your thoughts online.

Thank you again for spending your time with us and remember to…

Follow us everywhere: @trubornpress

www.trubornpress.com

ABOUT THE EDITOR

William Sterling is an author, editor, podcaster, screenwriter, and apparently an actor now (?). Despite his inability to focus on any one trade, he is proudly, always and forever, keeping his lens trained on the spooky things.

William has published multiple novels with mid-sized presses, including STRING THEM UP with Crystal Lake Entertainment in 2023 and DEAD MENS CHESTS through Hedone Press in 2024. He has had works included in multiple anthologies, including the Stokercon-aligned Charity Anthology SHADOWS IN THE STACKS. He hosts the Killer Mediums podcast, is a reoccurring member of the Redwall read-along Books and Badgers podcast, and his first short film, CANDY, is currently in post-production. Lastly, but certainly not leastly, he has put out *PUNK goes HORROR: Mixtape Anthology (2025)* and *PUNK goes HORROR II: Hardcore for the Encore (2026)*, both through Truborn Press.

https://thewilliamsterling.wixsite.com/main